May I see here before me

The throat of my enemy

May my hand hold the dagger

That severs his life

May the hated be cut off

All his sins unforgiven

May he lie in his coffin

His hands round my knife.

—Corsican curse, or *voceru*, eighteenth century

THE RUNESTONE
BOOK II SAGA

VENDETTA

CHRIS HUMPHREYS

ALFRED A. KNOPF
NEW YORK

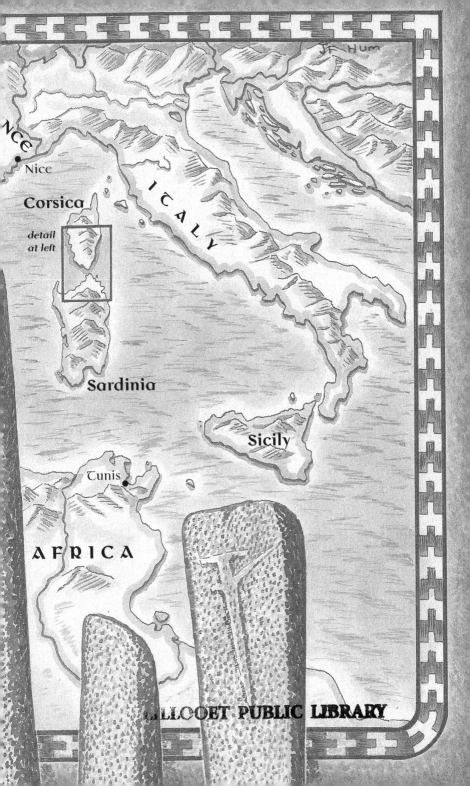

NCe

Nice

Corsica

detail at left

ICALY

Mt. Hum

Sardinia

Sicily

Tunis

AFRICA

Other Secrets
Different Blood

THE SQUADRON OF DEATH

He'd been dreaming of hands. Of his own hands. The right one with the four slashes across its back, still livid, purple, barely scabbed over. His left, the very tip of the forefinger gone, sliced off. Sacrificed. Both of them stretched out before him, reaching, reaching . . .

For what? Mist obscured it, terrifying him as he continued to push into the gray, into whatever was within.

His fingertips slipped into softness. It felt like . . . fur. Then something growled.

A hand grabbed him. Sound came, but not from an animal. A man was shouting, unintelligible things.

Sky woke gasping, his hands instinctively grappling with the one that held him. His eyes shot open, and at first he thought he *did* see fur, a thick pelt of it right above him. Then he focused, realized that the fur was a beard, that the hand he clutched belonged to a man, and that both stank of cigarettes.

The bus driver jerked his hand free. *"Descendez! Descendez! Nous sommes arrivés!"*

"Sartène?"

"Oui. Oui. Sartène. 'Ow you say? 'Zee end of zee line.' " The driver grunted this last in English, then jerked his thumb. *"Allez-y!"*

Sky's backpack was already on the ground beside the bus. The driver followed him out, began slamming the luggage holds shut.

"Uh, monsieur, s'il vous plait? Ou est le . . . 'ostel?" Sky's French, which he'd been trying to improve all summer with language tapes at the library, seemed to fail him at two-thirty a.m. But he'd found that as long as you dropped the "h" and looked like you were sulking when you spoke, you could get by.

"Pour l'auberge? Là-bas! Mais a cette heure, c'est fermé, je crois." He pointed with his nicotine-stained beard and then was gone. The bus, sputtering into life, lurched off.

Yeah, I bet it's closed *now,* thought Sky. And whose fault is that? A breakdown on the road, a lot of shrugging and pointing into the engine. Finally, three hours later, a replacement bus arrived, dropping him in a strange town in the middle of the night. Sky looked around him, at the narrow stone houses of the square. No lights showed in the grayness, their windows shuttered like closed eyes.

WITHAIN, he thought, shivering. It was a shorthand he'd come up with at various points on the journey from England. WITHAIN, or Where-in-the-hell-am-I-now? He'd thought it often in the small hotel in Toulon where he'd had to hole up for over a week with a raging flu before he could catch the ferry. He thought it now. He knew the name of the town—Sartène. He knew that town was in southern Corsica. But at two-thirty in the morning, having slept for maybe two hours in two days, he struggled to remember why he was there.

"Sleep," he grunted. But where? There was a bench beside the bus stop, and he nearly collapsed onto it. But it looked hard and likely offered only a couple of hours of sleep, followed by some policeman moving him on. . . .

He shook his head. He'd try to wake someone at the hostel. They'd be pissed off. But he didn't really care as long as he got a bunk for the night—and all the next day. Shouldering his pack, he began to stagger in the direction the bus driver had indicated.

The streets were steep, as the town was built on hills, and the night air was still warm. Within a few hundred yards he was sweating. He paused to catch his breath, look around. There was not a soul about, no one to ask for better directions.

Then, glancing up, he saw it—a metal arrow mounted just below the first-story window. It pointed to the right, and written on it was *L'Auberge de Jeunesse*. Two stick figures with backpacks leaned into a slope. Great, Sky thought, hoisting his own pack again. He took a few steps, stopped. There weren't many lights in the town, but the street he was being directed down—more an alley, really—seemed to have none. Then suddenly he saw the faintest glimmer. It came and went, as if someone had opened a shutter, closed it again. This sign of life was, strangely, the opposite of comforting. He glanced back down the hill to the square where he'd arrived. There was the bench, beneath a lamppost. It was starting to look more comfortable.

Bollocks, he thought. After all the things he'd seen and done in England, in Norway, in the past as well as the present, how scary could a dark alley be?

He stepped into that dark—and instantly it felt like he'd crossed some threshold. It wasn't just the lack of light; it was colder and he shivered for the first time since he'd got to Corsica. There was noise too—a scraping? Or was that a whisper behind him?

"Hullo?" He turned back. To nothing.

With a grunt, he pushed on. The alley curved and he passed from the little light to none at all. Then, slowing almost to a stop, he noticed a glow slipping from what had to be doorways, throwing faint patches out onto the cobbles. He moved from one to the next, pausing briefly, moving on. This stuttering progress took him to another bend, round it . . .

And then there was light. Just a single bulb above a doorway but it seemed like the midday sun to Sky. He squinted, stepped forward eagerly. There was a brass plate to the side of the door, but the lightbulb wasn't

4

bright enough to let him read what was written on it. Reaching back into the side pocket of his pack, he pulled out his lighter. He needed to know if the brass plate said *Youth Hostel* so he could begin hammering upon the wooden door.

But the words disappointed. " 'Lucien Bellagi,' " he read. " '*Avocat.*' "

Well, I don't need a lawyer. I need a bed, he thought. He looked down into the burning yellow, its blue core, savoring even such a little light. Then he flicked the lighter's arm down, took another step forward.

He heard a whisper . . . no, not one, *whisperings*, several voices, some in answer and response, some joined in a chant. It was as if, from an empty sky, a flock of starlings had descended on him. He turned full circle, looking all around. But neither feather nor flesh appeared. Nothing moved.

Sky stepped out of the pool of light, backing fast into shadow, his new friend. His backpack collided hard with another curve in the walls, stuck him there for just a moment, that one when he still could have pulled away, fled the voices, run back to the square. But the moment passed, because he couldn't move. Not when he'd have to pass through a space suddenly crowded, every inch of it filled with flickering figures.

Shapes and voices came, went. There, gone again, then back—human shapes in and out of his vision, of his hearing, disappearing, reappearing in a slightly different pose, like dancers under a strobe light. Sky saw a sleeve vanish; a moment later, a hand appeared from it.

5

There was a glimpse of skin within a dark shroud. There. Gone. Then it was like one of those magic pictures, random dots gelling into a photographic image. Latching on to the smallest part—a hooded head—he suddenly saw the whole.

Women, at least a dozen of them, spun in a circle between him and the doorway. Each was dressed identically in a long black skirt and dark blouse, their heads hooded. Nuns, he thought, until he realized there was nothing holy in their twittering. Their birdsong was crow, not robin, malevolent, cruel. It was unintelligible . . . and then it wasn't, not entirely, his ears attuning just as his eyes had done. Not to it all—but two words came clear. A name repeated over and over. A name Sky had just read on a brass plate.

"Bellagi!" the voices shrieked out. "Lucien Bellagi!"

Something stirred within the house. Light etched the shutters above the door. A woman—a real woman, not these shades—cried out; a man bellowed. And instantly the twittering doubled in volume, rising to a keening pitch that hurt Sky's ears. He raised his hands to block them but could not drag his eyes from the flickering crowd—for in its center, a deeper darkness began to form. From cavernous sleeves hands appeared and latched on to this shape now hovering at shoulder height, grasped and bore it forward, just as a light came on in the hallway, just as a bolt was thrown. A key turned in a lock, and the shape—the length of a man, as deep as a man—was lowered to the ground.

6

Sky could now see into it, see instantly what it was, what it contained.

It was a coffin. It was open, and a corpse lay in it.

He wore a black suit, white shirt, black tie, polished black shoes. His graying hair was slicked down, his eyelids closed to bear the weight of the coin that sat on each of them. His hands were across his chest. In them he clutched a framed photograph.

The door was opening slowly; light was flooding out. Sky couldn't help himself. The alley was narrow; he only needed one step until he could bend and read the name scrawled at the bottom of the photograph, beneath the face.

Sky knew it. He'd just read it on a doorplate. And it was the name still being chanted.

Lucien Bellagi.

Beneath the name were dates.

20.1.55 à 19.9.07

He recognized the second one. It was tomorrow. No, he realized. Since it was three in the morning now, the second date was today.

He stepped back into the shadows, one hand shading his eyes. A man stood silhouetted in the doorway, and Sky could not see him properly at first because the light was so bright behind him. Then the man turned to shout something into the house, and Sky saw his profile. It was enough to recognize him. Sky was looking over the coffin, over the corpse of Lucien Bellagi . . .

. . . at Lucien Bellagi.

7

CHAPTER TWO

OLD ENEMIES

The shadows hid him, and perhaps the man's eyesight wasn't so good. Because Lucien Bellagi didn't react to Sky being there, just turned and shouted back into the house, up the stairs. And Sky, fully awake now, understood the French words.

"Cease your weeping, woman. I told you there'd be no one there."

As he spoke, the flickering, black-clad women, whose cries had turned again to whispers as soon as the door was opened, now redoubled their shrieking. Sky reeled back, both hands again over his ears. But the man did not hear. With a glance up and down the street, he shrugged and turned back into his house. The door closed, bolts were thrown, a key turned.

The shrieking stopped in an instant. For a moment the black shapes solidified, all facing the door, their backs to Sky, the coffin in their midst. And then, as one, the shrouds turned. Within each was the bone-white face of a woman with eyes that were pools of total blackness—and entirely focused on Sky.

"Oh, crap!" he muttered. He'd been able to move before, had found this place against the wall. Why couldn't he move now?

They began to flicker again, in and out of his vision. And the whisperings returned, high-pitched, unintelligible. Then, as one, the shapes began to move toward him. As one, hands as white as the faces emerged from the dark sleeves, reaching for him.

His shoulder was gripped . . . but not from the front, from the side. He jerked it away, turned from the approaching nightmare . . . to another! There was an alcove beside him, an old bricked-up doorway; in it stood two people. The first thing he saw was that, even if they didn't flicker, these two women were also dressed entirely in black. The second was that each woman held a knife in her mouth.

9

He would have run, if his legs were not frozen; would have screamed, if his throat worked. As it was, he let out a grunt of terror. Then one of the women, the younger one, raised another knife and held it, handle first, toward him. With her other hand she removed her own dagger just long enough to say, *"Faites comme ça."*

Perhaps it was the calm way she said it. Perhaps it was because, without turning back to look, he could sense the shrouded horde within a foot of him now, could feel their phantom hands reaching. So he did as the young woman said, took the knife and held it in his mouth, his teeth gripping the wooden handle, its cutting edge facing outward.

Whisper became shriek became wail. He half turned now, enough to see the phantoms withdrawing their hands as if burned. Then, on a rising shriek, the horde bent, picked up the coffin, and ran down the alley. They vanished before they turned the corner.

In the sudden silence, Sky could clearly hear his heart, thumping against his rib cage. He became aware that he could move again, and he staggered away, just as far as the light under the lawyer's door. His feet hit the front step, his legs crumpled, and he was sitting, staring up at the two dark figures opposite, still half hidden in the shadows.

Each woman reached up now and took the knife from her mouth. Something was whispered; the younger one stepped toward Sky. She spoke and he did not have a clue what she said.

"Ungh," he replied before realizing that he still had a weapon in his mouth. Removing it, he said, "Are you . . . one . . . of them?"

"How could I be?" The voice was low, heavily accented. But to his great relief, the words were English. "For they are dead. And I—" Her hands lifted the veil down from her head. "I am alive."

A girl stood before him, around his own age, maybe a little younger. She was . . . *petite,* the word came to him, perhaps a foot shorter than him, yet the right shape for her height, not too thin; the dark dress was tight on her. Her hair formed a second veil, shadowing her face in two black waves that fell to the shoulders. But the darkest thing about her were the eyes.

She studied him as closely as he did her, unblinking. The silence held for a moment and then was broken by a shuffling and a cough. The girl reached back to the alcove. A hand emerged, as old as the girl's was young, with skin that looked like stained parchment, blue veins a map of rivers upon it. It gripped, like talons, and Sky saw the girl wince, forced to bend and take the weight as she led the second figure from the shadows.

He saw immediately that they were related, even though the old woman was so thin, the dark dress hanging off her, while the hair beneath her veil was white and bound in a severe knot. But the similarity showed in their faces, despite the age difference. The old woman's white skin was drawn tight against prominent bones, her lips a shocking gash of red, the makeup emphasizing her pallor. But the eyes were also twin pools of infinite dark, even if hers were filmed over, like the surface of a pond too long without rain.

After a moment, Sky reversed the knife, held the handle out toward the girl. "Thank you. I don't know what it did but . . ."

Slipping her hand from the older woman's, she

11

took the weapon. "I always carry two when I stalk the Dead. They do not like an open blade."

Sky took another deep breath. His heart was just beginning to slow. "The Dead?"

"You see them, here, before this door. We watch you see them, these ghosts. Il Squadra d'Arrozza."

"The . . . what?"

"*Squadra* is . . . like in army."

"Squad? Squadron?"

"So. And *Arrozza* is our name for . . ." She frowned. " 'Erodda? The king who kills the babies. Looking for Jesus?"

"Oh . . . Herod!"

" 'Erodda. Yes!"

Sky shuddered. To anyone else, he supposed this conversation would be absurd. But he had already had dealings with the Dead. "What were they doing here?"

"What is the word? 'Gathering'? Perhaps, yes? Gathering their own." The girl turned to her grandmother, spoke rapidly. After a moment, the grandmother nodded. The girl turned back. "But what do *you* do here?"

"Here?" It was a multiple-choice question for which he really didn't have a good answer. So he just said, "I was looking for the youth hostel."

"Youth hostel? It is closed."

"Yeah, I know. But . . ." He shrugged. "Maybe I'll wait till dawn."

Another whisper from the older woman. The girl turned. "We have a room you could stay."

He was shocked again—and delighted. "Well," he said, suddenly very English, "if it's not too much trouble . . ."

"No trouble. You come!" She held an arm out again to the old lady, who latched on; then they began to walk, quite rapidly, back toward the main town— away, Sky noted thankfully, from the direction the phantoms had taken.

He caught up. "This . . . Squadron of the Dead?"

"Yes?"

There were a million questions he could ask. He chose one. "Well, I . . . I was there—by chance but . . ."

The dark eyes shot up, searching his. "Chance? You think so?"

"Well . . ."

She shook her head. "We were not there by chance. My grandmother knew the Squadra would gather tonight."

"There? At that house?"

"Certainly. Only there. Because . . . how do I say this?" She stopped, looked straight into Sky's eyes. "Because it was my grandmother who killed Lucien Bellagi."

They had reached the main street. Sky spotted the bench he now wished he'd stayed on. "Killed? What do you mean? He's not dead. I saw him in his doorway."

Instead of answering, she walked on, to the entrance of an alley opposite. "Come," she called back.

Reluctantly, he crossed to her. "Do you mean she's . . . cursed him?"

13

"No curse . . . ," the girl began, but was then distracted by the old woman talking rapidly. She listened, looked up. "Grandmother is right. We do not know your name. How can we welcome you into our house?"

They'd stopped again, before a large oaken door. The old woman was reaching beneath folds of cloth. A key emerged. Sky was a little bemused by the sudden switch of conversation, but he replied, "Uh, my name's Sky. Sky March."

"Sky? It is strange. Like the . . ." She pointed up.

"Exactly. And you?"

"Jacqueline Farcese." She offered her hand, Sky took it, and she gave him a brief, formal shake. Turning, she said, "And this is my grandmother, Madame Farcese. *Grandmaman, je te présente Monsieur March.*"

The old woman pulled up her veil, stepped forward, and the hand that he'd seen fasten on Jacqueline's now descended on his, not taking it in a handshake but resting on top. As bony as it looked, the grip was fierce. He found it hard to look into her eyes. But when he finally did, he gasped. "She's . . . blind, isn't she?"

"Yes. You did not notice this before?"

"No." Now he was looking so closely into the old woman's eyes, he could see that what he'd mistaken for light was actually its reflection. They were more mirror than lens, and the darkness behind them was lifeless. She asked a question.

"I am afraid my French isn't good enough to . . ."

"She does not speak French but the older tongue of our island, Corsican," Jacqueline said. "She asks if she can touch your face."

"My face?" Sky swallowed. "Um, why?"

"To see you."

At last he nodded, bent so she could reach him. Jacqueline said something, and the claw-hand left his, rose up. He flinched when it first touched him, again when the other joined it. But the journey they took was light, skimming the contours of nose, cheekbones, mouth, tracing the line of the two eyebrows he'd let grow into one. The only discomfort came when the hands sank from his brow. He felt the slight pressure of finger pads on each closed eye, and it made him think of the body in the coffin, silver coins weighing down the lids. The hands pressed there a moment, then both dropped away, one hand taking his once more.

She was talking again, and the girl translated. "She see how you see the Squadra. She says you have the sight, the gift. Gift that can also be a curse. So she is happy for you . . . and sad for you also. She says she knows your sight has brought you pain."

Perhaps it was the recent pressure on them, but his eyes began to smart. It had been a night of such strangeness at the end of a long journey from even more. And here was a woman who touched upon all he'd been through—and whose pretty granddaughter

15

had offered him a place to sleep! But before he could put any of his gratitude into stumbling words, the old woman spoke again, gripping him harder as Jacqueline translated.

"But she wonders how it is that you have this sight. Few do, even in Corsica. And she has heard of none from outside our land who can see the Squadra."

Sky wanted to remove his hand, so fiercely was it now being squeezed; he'd have liked to look away, so intense was the old woman's sightless regard. But he found he could do neither. He had to answer her . . . and he didn't know how to begin. He looked down to his own hand, saw, beneath her skeletal fingers, the four purple, puckered scars—still healing, still scabbed—and they reminded him of all that had brought him there. How could he even begin to explain it, to two strangers, in a strange town, in the middle of the night?

16

But the dull black orbs demanded an answer. And looking directly into them, he found the beginnings of one. "I have talked to my own dead," he said softly. "I know where they can be found."

He said it in English, and the old woman didn't even seem to speak French; but she cut off her grand-daughter when she began to translate, and Sky knew she'd understood well enough. She released him, reached again for Jacqueline, who guided her to the door. When she opened it, a wave of warmth, a scent of baking emerged, making Sky realize just how hungry and tired he was. Then, as the women beckoned him in, he remembered the other reason he could have been attuned to this land. It was definitely something he could share.

"I'm also half Corsican," he said, stepping forward, then halting because they'd halted, though they did not turn.

A whisper came from one mouth, words from the other. "From where?"

"From? Near here, I think. I'm not sure."

Another whisper, quieter, yet harsher too. "Your name?"

"I told you, March."

"Your Corsican name?"

"Oh." He had to think a moment. He'd only learned it himself a few months before. "It's Marcaggi," he said. "That was my grandfather's name." Both women turned now to face him. He coughed. "I'm probably not pronouncing it right, am I? Mar*caggi*?"

"Mar . . ." It was the old woman who spoke, said just half the name. Only half because the rest was lost in the shriek she gave. Suddenly she was rushing at him, throwing herself off the step with a speed Sky could not believe she possessed. It was only because he moved back fast that her hands, their sharp nails leading, missed his eyes. She slashed at his face again, and he was forced to grab her wrists. She twisted and struggled in his grip, and he didn't know what to do except push her back toward her granddaughter. It was

17

only a little shove, but she tottered and the girl caught her, sank with her onto the step.

For a moment the only sound was the fast breathing of all three of them. "What . . . ," Sky blurted at last. "What was *that* about?"

The old woman was weeping now, a low moan like a growl building in her throat. Jacqueline had pulled her close, was rocking her in her arms. "Go," she said fiercely. "Go away."

"But what have I . . . I've done nothing."

The grandmother's sobs grew louder, taking on a note at once sad, lost, and furious.

"You have said your name," the girl hissed. "It is enough. Now . . . go!"

18

Sky backed away, staring, disbelieving. Then he turned and ran back toward the main street, toward light, away from the voice now wailing his father's family name like a curse into the night.

"*Marcaggi!*"

CHAPTER THREE

THE LAMENT

It was almost possible, sitting in the shade of the chestnut tree, for Sky to forget it all. To imagine that he was
on vacation, that his parents had just popped off to
sightsee and left him to doze in the late-morning
Mediterranean sunshine. They'd return; the three of
them would go for a meal at some outdoor café. That
night he'd sleep in a comfortable bed, with clean white
sheets, untroubled by dreams.

He sighed, shifted, slid down till his head rested on
the top of the bench back. People passed by; he heard
several leave the hostel behind him, excited chatter in a
variety of languages. But he resisted opening his eyes.

Don't think about it, he said to himself. So, of
course, he immediately did, and opened his eyes.
Everyone before him was in the lightest, brightest
summer clothes. No one was shrouded in black. Yet
that's what he imagined he saw, flickering in and out of

the shadows. Death's Squadron, come to claim another body.

What the hell had that been about? And that blind old bat, shrieking his family name? Excellent! Just what he needed. More weirdness in his life!

He shook his head but it didn't clear. Too many thoughts crowding in, too little sleep. He'd managed three hours, from when the hostel doors were opened, at six, till they insisted everyone leave the dormitories, at nine.

What am I doing here? The question kept buzzing in his brain, and he still had no answer. Yet it had all seemed so clear that day two weeks before, back in England.

20   His grandfather Sigurd had betrayed him . . . twice! First, by pretending he was dead, a kindly ghost teaching Sky about the power of the runestones, how to use them to journey back in time to his Viking ancestors, there to learn the secrets that whispered in his blood. When, in fact, Sigurd was alive and the "secrets" he needed Sky to learn were designed to turn him into a killer. He *had* helped to kill a man, helped to unleash the awesome power of death that had allowed Sigurd to transfer his Fetch into Sky's beloved cousin Kristin.

And that was the second betrayal. For now Sigurd possessed her, feeding on her life like some . . . parasite! Using her so that he could live on.

Sky sighed, remembering the vow he'd made that day: to get Sigurd out of her, to give her back her free will. But he could never hope to fight Sigurd through the runestones. Not yet, not when his Norwegian grandfather had spent a lifetime studying them. So Sky had vowed to seek other secrets, in different blood. Find the weapons he would need to return and free his cousin.

But brave words back home sure sounded like dumb bravado here. Sigurd had mocked his vow, his hopes.

Just what was he basing all those hopes on?

Almost reluctantly, Sky reached into his pocket and pulled out the brass cigarette lighter. It had belonged to his other grandfather. The visions he'd had when he'd first held it had led him to tell Sigurd that he would go to this other ancestor's homeland.

Corsica.

He flicked the lighter now, stared into the flame, beyond the yellow, into the blue core. Nothing new came, but his original vision was burned into his memory, and he tried now, as he had tried a hundred times before, to decipher its meaning.

First, there was a wolf howling at a standing stone. His guidebook showed pictures of such stones not far from Sartène. So it had seemed like a good place to start. But his second vision, of a bald old woman singing a sad song? Did she exist? How would he find her if she did? And as for the third vision . . . a lynx, dying, with Sky's own scarred hands turning it, seeking its eyes . . .

21

Sky flicked down the lighter's arm, snuffing the flame. He stared at the ground, his gaze unfocused. The last time he'd seen Sigurd, his grandfather had come in the form of a lynx. "Borrowed" was his disgusting term, for it was Kristin's Fetch, and Sigurd used it while Kristin slept. Sky had read that objects in dreams were symbols of something else. So if his cousin *was* the lynx, was Sky going to witness her death?

Was Kristin dying the only way to eject their grandfather from her soul?

There were too many questions crowding him now to sit still and enjoy the sunshine . . . and no answers to help him decide what to do. And yet . . . the night before, he'd only been in town ten minutes and he was witnessing Sartène's dead in action. That had to tell him something, surely? That he was on the right track?

He stood up, looked behind him. The bench was marked with graffiti, scored with hearts and the names of lovers. And something else . . .

Sky sighed. The trouble with seeking the wisdom of the runes was that they were everywhere, formed by the random acts of man or nature—an oil stain on the ground, a hair on a bar of soap, a slug's trail of slime up a rock. Here, even the casual slashes of bored travelers could have meaning for him. If he chose to interpret them.

There was the inverted "U," *Uruz.* Bjørn the

Berserker's rune, the one he'd carved on his axhead, rune of sacrifice. And there was an "R," *Raidho*, the journey. And there was another, the most deceptive, the simplest to carve—"I," the straight line of the rune *Isa*.

He ran his finger down it and shivered. Unsurprisingly, as the rune meant "ice." Thus it also meant things frozen, blocked, on hold. The opposite of progress. Runes usually reflected the state of mind of the person asking the question. And hadn't he just been musing on questions without answers?

"Thank you so very much," he muttered, turning away. Then something made him turn back. *"Isa,"* he said again, intoning it like a prayer. The sound of it stirred something in his memory, a different book he'd read on the runes, a different Web site he'd visited. *Isa* could also mean . . . what was it?

Then it came. "A spear," he said aloud. Odin's weapon, and Tir's, a symbol of power. A weapon to use in a struggle, to overcome great odds.

Sky pressed his fingers into the straight line again. Taken another way, *Isa*—not ice, but *Isa* the spear— well, it could mean the challenge facing him.

"Okay," he said. "Bring it on."

His declaration made him feel a little better. And it was so tempting to just stay there, pulling these random slashes into a story, into the answers he craved.

Shuddering with the effort, Sky forced himself to turn and walk away. The runes were Sigurd's, the very source of his power. He'd used them to transfer his soul into another. And no matter how much Sky had studied them, he knew he couldn't fight Sigurd with his own weapons. Not yet. If he wanted to free Kristin, he was going to have to forge weapons of his own.

He came to the entrance of an alley. People, single, in pairs, and in groups, passed him, going in, coming out. It was clearly a busy shortcut during the day. He wouldn't be alone. Still, he hesitated—because it was the other end of the one he'd been in last night. Just ahead was where he'd seen the Dead.

He nearly turned back. But the thought of Kristin came again. Whatever had happened to him last night was connected to his Marcaggi blood. And that was what he'd come to this land to explore.

"Other secrets, different blood," he muttered, and moved swiftly on before he could change his mind.

Even in daylight, the alley was far darker than the square, the houses tall, made of dark granite, looming over the cobbles, all their shutters closed. And it was distinctly cooler between the stone walls. Not cold exactly—a party of schoolkids passed him in shirt-sleeves and seemed not at all bothered—but different. As soon as they came toward the sunlight, they burst out chattering, as if something had held their voices till then. Other people passed him, not talking, their heads bowed.

He rounded a bend—and saw why people had gone silent, and stayed so, when they passed this spot.

Death had come to call at the house of Lucien Bellagi.

His senses told him so, one after the other. A smell—not the whiff of rotting flesh; it was too soon for that. But there was a taint in the air that overrode the sweet herbs being burned to disguise it. It smelled of what it was—the *absence* of life. Cooling skin, slackened muscles, pooling blood.

Sight came next; the wreath on the door, made up of woven flowers and branches, threaded through with a black silk scarf.

Sound confirmed death's presence. Not the low moaning that, he realized now, had accompanied every step down the alley. This was a new sound.

The smell of death had slowed him, the sight of death had halted him. But it was the song of death that froze him.

He had heard it before, submerged within a lighter's flame. It was still not a song in any sense he knew, sung in words he could not understand and did not need to. A groan rising to a shriek, descending again to a near inaudible mutter of despair, only to rise again. This was not just about one death. It was about them all. The grief of those left behind by someone who should not be lost, not yet, not this soon.

The door the wreath hung on was ajar. The alley was deserted. Swiftly Sky stepped up to the entrance and slipped inside.

He stood there blinking, waiting for his eyes to adjust. Shapes gradually formed—a chair, a coat stand, a table. Stairs led up and down. To his left, a door stood half open. The song was coming from in there, so, taking a deep breath, he put his head into the gap.

If the hall was dark, this room was darker, despite the single candle that burned at its center. Its tiny pool of light came and went, and it took him a while to realize that it wasn't caused by flickering but by shapes passing between him and it.

Gradually his eyes adjusted, enough for the shapes to become three women. One was older, two were middle-aged, all dressed entirely in black. Holding hands, they circled around something in the very center of the room and its one source of light. Black veils blended them into darkness; only their faces stood out, creased in sadness, traced in tear tracks glittering faintly in the flame light. All three moaned as they danced.

But the lament came from the far end of the room, opposite him at the door. As his eyes grew more accustomed, another shape grew, as if shadows were coming into form. He watched it come clear, saw a veiled head, an edge of scarf, the bone whiteness of skin.

He knew the song. So he'd guessed who the singer must be. But he still gasped when he saw the bald head and the face from his visions.

He couldn't look at her, tore his gaze away. It settled, inevitably, on the only light. On the flame at the center of the deepest darkness in the room.

He was drawn to it. He couldn't help himself, took one step, one more. Until he could see the dead man lying there and the wax that had flowed down and fused Lucien Bellagi's fingers to the candle.

Sky yelled, staggered back. The women broke apart, three separate shapes now, shrieking first in fear, then in fury. He saw himself as they did—a young man in jeans and a T-shirt, an intruder gate-crashing their grief. They shouted unintelligible things, raised their hands to strike him, and he backed away fast. But the worst, by far the worst, was the face of the woman whose voice had lured him in. Her shroud had slipped off, and candlelight glimmered on her bald head, on lips parted in anguish.

"You are dead!" she whispered. "Dead. Dead! Why have you strayed?"

The others were nearly on him. He banged into the door, slipped round it, and ran.

27

CHAPTER FOUR

VILLAGE OF THE DEAD

He didn't run far. Couldn't, though he wanted to. He had seen the first of the visions that had brought him to the island—the bald-headed woman singing for the Dead. He had to know who she was.

People passed the alcove where he hid himself, a doorway long since bricked over. It was around a bend from the house of the late Lucien Bellagi, but the alley funneled the sounds of renewed mourning to him. When at last they stopped, Sky crept from his concealment, peeked around the curving wall . . . just in time to see a tall, black-clad figure disappear around the next bend. He gave it a few seconds, then followed.

She moved fast for an old woman. Head down, arms wrapped round herself as if braced against a chill wind. It wasn't cold out of the alley; it was a hot September day, and Sky began to sweat as he followed her along the streets that crisscrossed the steep hills on which the town clung. Up, ever up, she led him, until the houses started to become less crowded together, the spaces between filled with chestnut and arbutus trees. He had hoped to stay concealed within the bustle of the town, but people began to thin out, until there was just him and the figure he pursued, tirelessly marching on. Since she never looked back, he could only hope she didn't know he was behind her until he was ready . . . for what, he did not know.

The figure disappeared over a crest. When Sky reached it, he saw that it was a plateau, that the road he was on petered out to a dry mud path, that another went to the left, but only as far as a gate in a high whitewashed wall. "She's gone through the gate," he muttered, heading toward it, "unless she's bloody disappeared. Which somehow wouldn't surprise me at all."

He paused as he went through. He was standing at the entrance of a graveyard. He'd had some recent experience with those. In Lom, in Norway, he had gone to the grave of his grandfather—only to discover later that he wasn't in it. And in Shropshire two weeks before—*bloody hell, two weeks, how can it be just two weeks?*—in the cemetery of Eaton-under-Heywood, he had helped the draug of his ancestor to his rest.

This one was nothing like those. Lom's cemetery had small tombstones in ordered circles round a wooden stave church. The English one had ramshackle headstones in a variety of sizes scattered about the grass, the square Norman tower of an old stone church rising in the center. There was no church here. It was more like a village of the Dead. Small plots lay between mausoleums big and small, which lined lanes of cracked white paving stones, weed-rich. As Sky walked down the central path, he saw that a few had a more modern look, with black lettering on marble plinths and posies placed in urns before photos like the one that Lucien Bellagi had clutched the night before. Most, though, were ancient, untended, whitewash flaking off granite lined in moss, their iron gates rusted shut, the names obliterated by weather and the years.

He came to a crossroads and hesitated. The cemetery was vast; it rose over the hill beyond, spread across the slopes. More crossroad choices lay ahead, each one perhaps taking him farther and farther from his quarry. He could not even go back and wait at the gate, for it was probably not the only one. Then, as he swayed, indecisive, he heard the sound of an old hinge squealing open. It came from his left, and he immediately set off along that path.

He saw it, the one gate standing open, heard the faintest of scraping sounds from within. It was not the biggest tomb there, but neither was it small, and it looked like it had received at least one coat of whitewash in the last decade. Painted perhaps by the same person who had carefully redone the letters in gold above the entrance.

Marcaggi.

A black lizard, studded with yellow spots, appeared

on the triangular pediment above the door, slid down, paused for a moment on the painted word, its long tongue flicking, then vanished into darkness. Sky wiped the back of his hand across his forehead, felt more sweat immediately start onto it, knew it was not solely caused by the chase up the hill. Then, taking a deep breath, he descended into the tomb of his ancestors.

A wedge of light came from the doorway, filled with dust motes. In it, he could see the heel and sole of a boot. He took his time, let his eyes adjust; gradually the rest of the body came into focus. The old woman was kneeling before what looked like a series of shelves. They were on the other side as well, four ranks of them, each level holding three boxes. No, not boxes. Coffins. Twenty-four dead Marcaggi faced each other through the dancing dust.

"Go. Leave now—this place. This island. There is nothing for you here." She did not turn around. Her voice came out in a hiss, completely different from the one that had sung the dead man's lament. But the words spoken were English.

"You . . . know me?"

"I know who you must be. When I saw you, I thought that you had somehow crossed back to guide Lucien Bellagi to his rest. But the grave here lies quiet." A slight nod of the shrouded head. "So I knew you were not him."

Sky had not moved from the door. Now he took a step farther in. "Who did you think I was?"

31

The woman didn't answer; instead, a hand emerged from the black cloth and a finger pointed toward a coffin. Screwed onto the front of it was a framed photograph. A photo he had seen before, on the night he was given the lighter, in his father's den back home. A man sat at a table, a shotgun across his lap, a pipe in his mouth, a half smile on his face.

"My grandfather."

Again, she didn't answer, didn't move, and Sky peered closer. There were dates written in ink just above the bottom of the tarnished frame. The second one was a year after his own father's birth.

"How did he die?" he whispered.

"What is that to you?" She had risen from her knees, turned, stepped close. Her face was in the sun now, and it was twisted in rage. The head scarf had dropped onto her shoulders, and her bald head shone. "What do you seek here? To find out who you are? A cozy family story? Isn't that what everyone seeks today?" Her voice was harsh, sarcastic. "Well, I tell you there is nothing like that here. This story is cruel and cold, and it will gain you nothing to learn it. Nothing! And if you learn it, you may have to give . . . everything!" A hand came forward, pushed him in the shoulder. "So, I say to you again, and for the second time of asking, go!"

He took a step back, surprised at the strength in the old woman's shove, frightened by her fury. The motion tempted him into the beginning of a retreat.

He took another step back before he remembered. Saw a flash of Kristin's face. His only hope of helping her lay in the visions he'd had. Beginning with the woman who stood snarling before him now.

"I won't go," he said quietly, "until you tell me why I have to."

Her voice lost none of its harshness. "But if I do, you will not be able to go. For you have his blood, boy. And that blood will force you . . . to vengeance!"

"I am English," he replied, trying to make a joke. "We don't do vengeance."

"You are also Corsican," she whispered, "and we do."

It was hard to tell how old she was, the baldness making her look both old and strangely young. Her face was lined but not too much. Her eyes were not the dark he'd seen in most people on the island but a blue that could almost have been Norwegian.

"How did he die?"

"He was murdered."

"Was his murderer called . . . Farcese?"

Her face colored, only to drain again. She staggered slightly toward him, snatching her hand away from the one he reached out in support. "How do you know that name?" she hissed.

"I met them, last night—a girl and her grandmother. They . . ." He swallowed. "We saw something together. Outside the house where I found you today. They called it the . . . Squadra, uh, something. . . ."

She stepped away from him, out of the sunlight,

sinking back into the shadows of the vault. "You saw the Squadra d'Arrozza?"

He nodded.

"Then you have the blood of the Marcaggi, true. And if Emilia Farcese has gazed upon you with her sightless eyes . . . if you have let her hands dance upon your face . . ." She shuddered. "This third time I say to you—leave. Leave today! This very hour."

He shook his head. "I can't."

There was a long silence. Then he saw a light come into her eyes, a smile to those bloodless lips. "Good," she said. She straightened. "And may God have mercy upon us . . . and not them!" She made the gesture of the cross before her. "For what all thought was over is begun anew."

It was such a strange switch. Before, she'd been re-garding him as if he were some horror. Now she was grinning, as if he were her dearest wish fulfilled. He swallowed. "What? What's begun?"

Instead of answering, she took his arm, pushed him backward. "I will tell you everything. But not here. Not with them." She jerked her head back, to the coffins in their stacks. "They would gather close to lis-ten. They would confuse you as they whisper their own stories. For of the twenty-four Marcaggi who lie here, only three did not die by bullet, by blade, by rope. And they would scream out to you the word they died by." Her voice rose again. "Vendetta!"

She had walked him back as they spoke, and now

they stood in the sunlight before the tomb. She turned a key in the lock, then tucked it within her clothes.

Before he could ask the first of a gazillion questions, she took his arm again and began to walk rapidly down the path, asking one of her own.

"How did you find me?"

"I came back to that house because of what I saw last night. Then I heard you singing. I'd . . . I'd heard it before."

She didn't seem too surprised. "How?"

Instead of answering, he pulled the lighter from his pocket. She stopped when she saw it, took it from him, flicked the arm up, struck the wheel, gazed for a moment into the flame. Then, snapping the arm down, she handed the lighter back, set off again. "I knew I should not have parted with it. But your father seemed to need it. He wanted to know something of *his* father, and I could see he did not have . . . the vision. He saw no Squadra here, felt nothing stir in his blood. And he was gentle too, in a way that you are not." She glanced to see if he was insulted. "He was not the chosen one."

Sky didn't feel insulted. If he'd ever been gentle, that had gone once he'd entered his Viking ancestor. But he was curious. "Chosen for what?"

They were passing people in the avenues, visitors to other tombs. She glanced at them, pulled the shawl tighter around her, muttered, "Not here."

Sky saw he had to change the subject. "You have the key to the Marcaggi tomb. So that means you are one?"

35

"Sister of your grandfather, Luca Marcaggi." She stopped, extended a hand in a formal gesture. "Pascaline Druet. I am your great-aunt."

Sky took the hand, shook it. "I am Sky March."

"I know." She looked at him for a moment, started walking again. "And now tell me how Luca's lighter brought you here?"

They had passed through the cemetery gate, and she was leading him along the crest above the town. He explained as they walked, about what he'd seen when he'd first held the lighter. She listened in a silence that continued so long after he had finished, he spoke again to break it. "What was that singing you were doing in the house?"

They took a path down toward the town. "I am a *voceratrice*. There are few of us left, few wanted—for the old ways are mostly forgotten. But a few remember them and still call me to sing a *voceru*, a lament for the Dead."

Sky shivered as he remembered the wailing. "Is it a cry for revenge?"

"No. Well, not usually. If the man died in his bed, as Lucien did, then no. Revenge is something else that has been nearly forgotten."

She said it in a way that made Sky think, Not quite, obviously. But he said, "How is it you speak such good English?"

She smiled fully for the first time. It changed her face. "Is it still good? I think I forget everything. But

Monsieur Druet—my late husband—and I, we were both teachers of English. In Paris, other places."

They had entered the town proper. She guided him right, then left, stopped before the door of a quite modern apartment block. When she opened the door to a small, neat apartment, with modern art on the wall and a good stereo in the corner, she must have seen his surprise. "What? Did you think I should live in a cave with my bats?"

She whistled, and a small dog, of no one type that Sky could recognize, trotted out from the kitchen. He nuzzled Pascaline's knees delightedly as she stroked his ears. The dog moved stiffly, and there was a lot of gray in his muzzle and wiry coat. Bending, Sky held out a fist, and the dog came, sniffed it, and began pushing against it.

"He likes you. It is good. For Amlet is a very fine judge of people."

Sky rubbed the animal's side, and it curled in on itself with pleasure. " 'Amlet'?"

"Like the Prince of Denmark. In the play?"

The dog had dropped onto its back, and Sky scratched the exposed belly. "Why *H*amlet?"

She looked at him strangely. "Because my Amlet is also a seeker after ghosts."

With that, she disappeared briefly into another room, then came out in a colorful blouse and skirt, a patterned scarf now wound about her head. Next she went into the small kitchen, reappeared some minutes

37

later carrying a tray with a coffeepot on it and some pastries. "Amlet! *Au lit!*" Reluctantly, the dog left Sky's scratching and slunk off to a bed beside the fireplace. "Sit there," she said to Sky, gesturing to a sofa, pouring a cup, offering a cake. As he bit into it, she got up and reached out of her windows, bringing in each shutter by turn until the room was nearly dark. She closed the windows, reducing the noise from the street to a distant hum. Then she picked up a matchbook from her mantelpiece, tried to strike matches. Three sparked, did not catch.

"Shall I?" Sky held out the lighter.

She studied it a moment, then nodded. "Why not?"

He crossed to her, lit two candles and, at her gesture, a stick of incense beside them. Then he saw what he'd missed before—the same photograph that he'd just seen in the tomb, that he'd first seen in his father's den in England.

When he was done, she reached forward, took the lighter from him. He sat; she stood before the candles. "Now," she said, turning the brass over and over in her hand, "I will tell you how Emilia Farcese murdered your grandfather"—she smiled that terrible smile—"and why we have been waiting for you."

CHAPTER FIVE

BLOOD FEUD

She flicked the lighter, and the blue-yellow flame made a fourth point of light, along with the two candles and the glowing end of the incense stick. Its smoke filled the room with a scent both herbal and cloying. It made his eyes droop for a moment, then shoot wide, as if he wanted to sleep and, simultaneously, leap up.

She was studying him closely. "You recognize this?"

"I'm not sure, I . . ."

"It has been in your nostrils from your first moment on the island. For it is the scent of the wilderness that is called, in Corsica, 'the maquis.' It is made up of rosemary, lavender, thyme, and a hundred other plants. It covers Corsica, is the essence of our island, the air in our lungs, as important to us as the blood in our veins." She stood for a moment, breathing deeply, then continued, "And just as this scent is unique to our land, so we are not like the other races of Europe. The

Romans, the Goths, the Arabs, Spanish, and Italians, all have come, all have believed they ruled us. But we took to the maquis and fought them all. We spilled their blood onto our earth, absorbed what we could not spill, and watched one conqueror after another pass on. They are gone. We are still here."

Sky didn't want to appear completely ignorant. "But the French came in the . . . eighteenth century, didn't they? And they—"

She interrupted him. "The French? Oh, yes, they are still here. But you must know that the man they claim as their greatest leader was Corsican?"

"Napoleon . . ."

". . . Buonaparte. *Oui.* One of *us* ruled *them.* They have never truly ruled here."

There was a flame in her eyes, not just reflected. He was impressed with her passion for her history. His history, he supposed. He suddenly had a flash of his schoolmates back home, probably sitting at that very moment in a classroom, studying the Industrial Revolution or the Battle of the Somme. While here he was, with a bald Corsican patriot ranting at him about Napoleon. He leaned forward. "So what does this have to do with my grandfather?"

She looked down at him and a slight smile came. "Everything. For it tells you where he is from. What he is from. For a people who will not obey a conqueror's laws must make their own. And the first law we made for ourselves was the law of vendetta."

40

"An eye for an eye."

"More than an eye." A gleam came into hers. "A life for a life. A family for a family until one family is destroyed."

"That's . . . barbaric!"

"Oh, my little English nephew! You have no idea."

He stared at her, shocked by the pride he heard in her voice, the aching sadness at its core. "So, if someone killed someone, the victim's family took revenge?"

"*Must* take revenge. Their Dead cry out for it, would never rest until vengeance was had." She shook her head sadly. "But in the old days, it did not need a death to provoke it. I have heard of a vendetta begun because one man's dog urinated on another man's wall. Of fruit dropping over a wall into a garden and being claimed by the gardener."

Sky was horrified. "And people killed for this?"

"Oh, yes. Because it was not about the crime itself as much as the insult—the violation of one's honor." She nodded. "We have a saying: 'Honor is like ink. Once it has been spilled, the stain will never be washed clean.' "

"Never? Surely when a death answers a death?"

"No. Because each side believed that their own was the one wrongfully killed. No death ends it. Every death has to be avenged. And so it goes on."

Sky stared ahead, thinking again of his school, of how one boy would punch another's arm, the victim would retaliate, each blow getting harder until someone

41

backed down or a teacher intervened. That was re-venge, he supposed. He'd done it himself, lots of times. But you ended up with a sore arm. You didn't end up dead . . . along with all your family!

He looked up at her. "Sometimes you say 'is,' sometimes 'was.' But it's over now, isn't it? In the twenty-first century? Vendetta must be finished!"

"Not for everyone."

He saw the hatred in her eyes, the same he'd seen in the blind ones the night before. He swallowed. "So why do the Farcese hate us so much? How did this vendetta begin?"

Up to then, his aunt had been looming above him, standing at the mantel, staring down fiercely. But the question seemed to take something from her, for she sank into a chair. "No one knows."

"No one . . ."

"The origin is lost to memory. My father told me it began hundreds of years ago. His father had told him that. And there are other rumors, old tales. Of love turned to hate. Of murder during a time of war. But no one truly knows."

"That is insane." It was Sky who was fired up now. "Surely, Aunt, you must think it insane."

She touched her head. "I know it here, nephew. The English teacher who taught poetry and grammar and Shakespeare knows it. But she knows something different here"—she tapped over her heart—"and here." She clenched a fist over her guts.

Sky frowned. "Yet you are alive. So is Emilia Farcese."

"Women and boys are not usually . . . *usually* killed."

"So I might get away with it?"

He'd tried to smile. She did not respond. "You are not a boy. Not anymore."

Sky grunted. "And my grandfather . . . he was the last of the Marcaggi men to die in this vendetta?"

"And the last to kill. For he killed the last two Farcese men before he died."

Sky shook his head. He thought of his own father, with his home-brewed beer and his cricket. Yet one generation before . . . "What happened?"

She got up stiffly, went to lean on the mantelpiece. He could see her face in the mirror there, framed by reflected flame. "Over the years, every vendetta waxed and waned. Families died out naturally, many emigrated. And sometimes whoever occupied Corsica at the time enforced their laws against it with the noose or the guillotine. Also, we of the island lost more in the First World War than any other *département* of France. For a while, there were no men left to kill."

She turned back. "But vengeance is a fire. It lies banked down, smolders underground, never quite extinguished. Just waiting for the right combination of tinder and spark to set it flaming again." She closed her eyes. "Your grandfather was the tinder. Emilia Farcese was the spark."

43

"That old blind woman?"

"She was not always old. Nor blind. She was as pretty as her granddaughter, prettier. Yet there was something dark in her beauty, something cruel. Her family was rich, and they looked down on us Marcaggi, honest farmers, happy enough, struggling to get by."

She sat again, continued, "Luca came back, a few years after the Second War. And he was handsome, a fighter pilot for the Free French, and she felt a huge passion for him. This was not like today, where a girl only has to say 'I like you' to a boy and he will kneel at her feet. . . ."

Sky smiled. He'd never knelt at any girl's feet.

"Then, a girl could not even walk alone with a boy, would barely get a chance to speak to him. But there were ways. A look across the aisle of a church, a veil dropped in the street. Emilia looked, dropped. It was like Shakespeare, like *Romeo and Juliet*. For her . . . but not for Luca. He had only ever loved one girl—your grandmother, Maria. And when Emilia saw this, all her love became hate. She remembered the blood feud, the fire that still burned, and fed the embers into her soul. Then she roused her two brothers against their old enemy."

"But why didn't my grandfather just . . . just leave?"

"He could have. But he was proud, Luca. And he'd been away, seen the world. He thought he'd help to make a new society, and he trusted the laws of France,

44

laws that were now being strictly enforced. The authorities heard—maybe he told them himself—and the police swore that, should anyone in either family be touched, both families would be stripped of everything. The Farcese had far more to lose than the poor Marcaggi. Her family reined her in. Or so they thought."

Her voice had grown hoarse. She leaned forward, picked up her coffee, grimacing at its coldness, swallowing anyway, then continued, though her voice was so low now, he had to lean forward to catch everything. "Luca married Maria. They prospered. Some years passed. They had your father, Henri. All seemed well. But Emilia's hatred was a deep well. She waited patiently till it was filled to the brim, waited for one special night when she could lure Luca to a place where laws and civilization do not apply. It is a tradition older even than the vendetta, a place open only to a very few, to those given sight beyond sight. She has it, as did Luca. As do I."

She stared at him then, and there was something awful in her look, something made up of both pity and horror.

"What is it?" he said softly.

"It is the Way of the Mazzeri. The Dream Hunters. Those chosen—the blessed, the cursed—they go out of their bodies at night to hunt. And their quarry is Death itself."

She's talking about the Fetch, he thought excitedly.

45

A different kind of Fetch! And as he saw it, he also saw what her look meant. "I have it too, don't I? This . . . blessing? This curse?"

"You do." She made the sign of the cross in the air before her. "God help you, but you do!"

He tried to keep his voice casual, despite the stirring her words caused in his stomach. 'These Mazzeri . . . is it hard for them . . . for us . . . to go out of the body?"

"Hard? Once you have learned the way of it, it is as easy as breathing out."

Yes! This was it, the reason why he'd been drawn to Corsica. Sigurd could become his Fetch at will. That was part of what gave him his power, his ability to double, to come and go as he pleased, to take any form he chose. But for Sky it was hard; he'd always needed ritual, sacrifice, pain . . . and Sigurd there, controlling everything. If Sky could master it himself, make it as easy as . . . as breathing out . . .

But there was something else here. "You said that Emilia used this . . . place—for vengeance?"

"She did. And it violated all that the Mazzeri are meant to be. But she did it anyway, such was her hatred."

He couldn't sit anymore. Jumping up, he shouted, "Tell me more. Everything. Now!"

"I cannot."

"You must!" He was almost shouting at her. "This is what I came here to learn." He looked at his shaking hands. "I need it."

She rose, came and took his hands. He almost growled, but there was something in her touch, in her eyes, that held him. Softly, she said, "I cannot tell you because it cannot be 'told.' To try and explain it will only confuse you. The only way to see it is by doing it. The only way to become a Mazzeri is to hunt with them."

In her words, Sky heard an echo—Sigurd, at their first meeting, telling him he had to go back to his ancestor, Bjørn, to learn something "by doing it." What he'd learned then was how to be a killer. Memories— of Viking slayings, of helping to murder Olav in the mountains of Norway—all came back in a rush. He shuddered. "You said the quarry was Death?"

She reached up, fingers grazing his cheek, as if gauging the turmoil within him. "Not in the way you think. It . . ." She shook her head. "No! I tell you, this cannot be explained. You must come with me. Tonight. There you will have your answer. Or, at least, perhaps your question will become clearer." She studied him, the struggle clear on his face. "Trust me, Sky. If you say you are here to learn something, the first lesson will come tonight. When you go hunting as an apprentice of the Mazzeri."

47

CHAPTER SIX

THE APPRENTICE

It was agreed that he would return at sunset and bring his bags; his great-aunt had a spare room, and he could save even the little the hostel charged. He didn't tell her that he could have afforded the best hotel in Sartène, that he had ten thousand pounds in a bank account in London, proceeds of the sale of one of Sigurd's diamonds. But a sixteen-year-old spending big would draw attention. He imagined his parents would try to find him, though the note he'd left had not said where he was going, obviously. Just that he was fine, needed some space, usual teen rebellion crap. They might buy it, and his plan was to get tourists to post cards from him from their hometowns in Italy, Sweden, other places. But Sigurd knew he was bound for Corsica, if not to Sartène exactly. That was more worrying. He definitely didn't want to see him again. Not until he was ready for him.

He took the longer route back to the hostel, not wanting to walk again past the home of the dead lawyer—twice he had and both times had been . . . weird, to say the least. He arrived at his lodgings a little tired and sweaty from the climb, distracted by his thoughts . . . and unprepared for the person sitting on the bench beneath the chestnut tree.

He'd thought she was pretty the night before—but she was prettier in daylight. Gone were the black clothes; she wore white jeans and a pale blue blouse that emphasized the deepness of her tan. Her feet were bare, dangling above sandals that lay beneath them. Tan lines made V's on the top of each foot, and it made him think of the rune *Kenaz*, the torch. "Initiation," it meant. Or the apprenticeship Pascaline had just talked about? The thought came—how he'd much rather learn from this girl than from a bald old woman, blood or no blood. A feeling that only increased when he saw something glint above one foot—a gold anklet.

He looked up, closed his mouth, met her eyes. She'd been reading when he'd first spotted her. Now she was looking at him. Their gazes held for a long moment before he walked toward her.

"*Bonjour*," he said.

She had raised a hand to shelter her eyes because the sun was right behind him. "*Bonjour,*" she replied.

"*C'est Jacqueline, n'est-ce pas?*"

She nodded. "*Jacqui. Et vous?*" She lifted a thumb to the sky.

49

"Oui." He pointed at the bench. *"Puis-je . . . ?"*

"Je vous en prie."

He sat at the invitation. She laid down her book, looked up at him—even sitting, he was about a foot taller. If her eyes weren't the black he remembered from last night, they were still a very deep brown, under thick lashes, lashes like veils, like the one she'd worn last night, like the one her hair now formed around her face, each side falling as she tipped her head, now one way, now the other.

The previous night had taught him that her English was much better than his French. And he didn't want to be at a disadvantage. "Were you waiting for me?"

"Waiting? Why? This is a nice place, no?"

He smiled. "Sure. But there must be plenty of nice places that aren't outside where I said I was going."

She shrugged, but not in denial. The questions that first came all seemed too direct. Hard to just chat when your only shared experience was the Squadron of the Dead! So instead, he said, "You speak good English."

"Not so good. But I went to a school in . . . Bourne-Mouth." She pronounced it as if it were two places. "There I learned. And your French?"

"I learned a little at school. And, this summer, with CDs. *Pas bien.*"

"So perhaps you stay a little here and you will speak it better."

She looked directly at him as she spoke, and he

wanted to reply, "With you as a teacher, I could." But he wanted to try it in French, and in the time he took to think of the words, a noise had intruded. A scooter rolled into the square, all gleaming polished steel and mirrors. The muffler was poor or had been tampered with, because the engine gave out a loud, throaty roar, louder when the rider pulled up before the bench and revved it.

He was dark, as dark as the girl, though his hair was gelled. It stood up like the comb of a cockerel above a tanned face and green eyes, which darted between the two of them in unconcealed anger.

"Brother?" asked Sky uneasily.

"*Cousin,*" she said, in the French way. "His name is Giancarlo." She didn't introduce them, just gabbled something fast that Sky could not follow. The youth—Sky guessed he was maybe eighteen—glowered, leaned forward, spat close to Sky's feet, then gunned his engine. On the rear tire, he exited the square, the engine noise fading fast, then cutting off.

"Cousin, eh?" Sky realized he'd been holding his breath, and let it go on the words. "That's good."

"Why good?"

It was Sky's turn to shrug. "Well, can't be your boyfriend, then, can he?"

"Why not?"

The directness of her gaze made Sky shift on the bench. "Well, you can't . . . I mean, at least in England, you can't . . . you know . . . date your cousin." His squirming grew slightly as his own cousin's face flashed into his mind. He had never thought of Kristin in that way . . . well, not much. Not very often . . .

She seemed to be enjoying his discomfort. "But this is not England. In Corsica people marry their cousins sometimes."

"Keep it in the family, eh?"

"What?"

"It's an expression." He smiled. "But doesn't it mean the children can be a bit . . ." He let his jaw go slack, stuck a tongue out, crossed his eyes. When he uncrossed them, he saw that she was unamused.

"Like me, you mean? My parents were cousins."

"Were?"

"They died when I was young. Car accident."

"I'm sorry." Sky cleared his throat, desperately wanting to change the subject. But family was on his mind. "Your grandmother? Is she okay? I mean, last night, she seemed a little . . . upset."

"Upset? This is not the word. I remember in Bourne-Mouth how the English always say less than what they mean." She finally took her gaze from him, looked ahead. "She was . . . *désolée*." She looked at him again. "How is this in English?"

"*Désolée?*" He thought. "Like, 'desolated'? Um, very sad?"

She shook her head. "Again, not enough. Too small. For years she thought there were no more Marcaggi. Only the Hairless One. And then . . . you are there."

"But I'm not . . . not really . . ." He looked up into the branches. "I'm English, half Norwegian. My name's March, not—"

"To her you are Corsican. As if you were born here, lived here all your life." She leaned forward, her gaze intense. "You understand? You are a Marcaggi and you remind her of all she has lost."

He decided to play dumb. "Lost?" he echoed. "But I've taken nothing from her."

She frowned. "You do not know?"

"Know what?"

She stared at him. "About the vendetta."

"What's that?"

It was too much. Or he was not a good enough actor.

She shook her head. "No. I think you *do* know . . . Marcaggi! You would not be here if you did not. And you would not have found us last night." She stood up. "So this is what I come to tell you—whatever it is you seek here, you forget it. Go. Leave Corsica. Never return."

"But that's crazy," said Sky, infuriated, dropping the act. "I mean, you must think so."

"I must?"

"Yes! This vendetta, its beginning so ancient no one can even remember what it's about? This is the twenty-first century, for God's sake."

Softly, she replied, "Not here, it isn't." Then she put her fingers to her lips, gave a loud whistle. Instantly there was the sound of an engine firing up. Within

53

seconds the scooter careered into the square, stopping violently before the bench. Jacqui climbed on the back.

"Shouldn't you both be wearing helmets?" Sky said.

The young man scowled, then spat out a stream of words that Sky could not understand, though the meaning was pretty clear.

Sky stood. "Why don't you climb off, mate," he said quietly, "so we can talk about it?"

Giancarlo looked as if he were about to oblige. With another curse, he lifted the bike onto its stand. But a word and blow to the head from his passenger stopped him. Furious, he dropped the wheels onto the ground, gunned the engine. "*À bientôt,*" Jacqui said, and then they were gone.

Sky knew the phrase. It was just a standard, casual farewell. "See you later." Except she hadn't said it casually. And Sky had a feeling he knew exactly what she meant.

Pascaline had told him to return at sunset. But it was a little after when he finally turned the corner into her street. He had set out from the hostel in good time, but his pack had seemed to get heavier with each step; his feet dragged past the cafés and their occupants, all out enjoying the last of the late-summer weather. He found he was slowing to stare at people having a good time, laughing, drinking, couples holding hands, whole families, from babies to grandparents, celebrating some event. They all appeared to be so carefree, with nothing to do but enjoy themselves, while he . . . He wondered if anyone looked up to see him trudge by and knew that he was off to hunt Death.

"You are late," Pascaline reprimanded as she opened the door. She was dressed as he'd first seen her, entirely in black, though a dark scarf was bound around her head, not a veil.

"I'm sorry, I . . ."

"Never mind." She drew him in. "Do you have black clothes?"

"Uh, I do. Jeans and a—"

"Good. Put them on. And bring a sweater; it may get colder later."

She gestured to her bedroom, and he carried his pack in there, dug out what he needed. As he changed, he called to her, "Are we going somewhere?"

"The Mazzeri hunt near the villages of their ancestors. That of the Marcaggi is not far."

When he was ready, he came out of the bedroom. "This okay?"

She barely glanced at him. "Fine. Now, come! And bring this."

She pointed to a wooden crate. It had some wrapped items in it, a loaf of French bread, a bottle of wine with a foil top and no label. "Picnic?" he asked.

She ignored him. Amlet was looking quite lively for an older dog, turning circles at her feet. "Yes! We go now." She held the door, and the animal shot through. "Come," she said.

Her car was an ancient yellow Citroën 2CV, held

55

together by dust and rust. The gear stick came out of the dashboard and squealed as she shifted to crawl up the steep hills above Sartène. Sky had the impression that the car was not powered by gasoline at all but had a giant rubber band instead that she wound up and released with her shiftings. Amlet sat on her lap as she drove, his snout thrust out the open window. Since neither of them wore seat belts, Sky didn't put his on either. It felt like one of the more insane rides he'd hitched, and he couldn't help gripping the door handle.

They drove in silence. He tried to ask one of the many questions that were bugging him, but she just grunted at him. She leaned forward to peer at the road, dimly illuminated by her headlights—there were no other lights beyond the city limits—and she was obviously concentrating hard. So he sat back, stiff and uncomfortable, and stared out at the vague shapes of the peaks, at the pressing rock faces that the car shot between, only the occasional metal direction sign or billboard breaking the continuous darkness.

They'd only driven for about fifteen minutes before she slowed, then turned a sharp right onto a track of stones of all sizes that caused the car to buck and lurch. Amlet gave a slight growl and climbed onto the rear seat, while his mistress actually pushed her nose into the windshield. Sky peered, too, at the little the headlights revealed—larger rocks, which she steered around, the edge of the track lined in shrub. Ahead was a looming darkness that he realized must be yet another mountain. Then there was sudden movement, the beams reflected in a pair of eyes. Pascaline braked hard, swerved. Sky thought he saw a flash of teeth, had an impression of a large shape moving away into the darkness. Pascaline swerved back, went on.

"What was that?"

"*Sanglier*," she said. "You call them 'wild boar.' It is a good sign."

"What is?"

"That we see one now. That they are near. We have something to hunt."

Sky looked at her, startled. "You mean we're hunting real animals?"

She nodded.

"But I thought . . ."

"Thought what?"

"That the Mazzeri were spirits. That they only hunted in dreams."

"We do. But our spirit moves within a body as solid as you are now. A body with great powers. That runs faster, sees sharper, hunts better, kills swifter. How is it you think that we old ones can hunt?" She glanced briefly at him, and he could see the hunger in her eyes. "And the beast we kill is real. So watch out for its teeth."

Ah, so a Mazzeri is the bodily Fetch, Sky thought. Like his had been, more than once. "Uh, what do we kill it with?" he asked nervously. He'd never hunted

57

anything in his life, apart from taking a few shots at birds with his air rifle.

"Wait, nephew. And you will see."

Almost immediately she swerved again. Sky saw a wooden post, a broken gate clinging to it by one hinge. Headlights briefly lit some sort of structure. She passed on its left side, stopped, turned the key, flicked off the lights. The engine wound down in a series of cracks and gurgles, the dark swallowed them, and then there was silence.

"We're here?" He was surprised how loud his voice sounded.

He felt her nod. "Welcome to the house of Marcaggi."

58

She opened her door and Amlet leapt out, vanished. The scent she'd talked about, the sweet spiciness of the wilderness they called the maquis, filled his nostrils and lungs, making him giddy. He got out of the car as Pascaline reached to the backseat, pulled out a flashlight, stepped out herself. She flicked it on and played the powerful beam over a wooden structure. He caught a glimpse of shuttered windows, steps leading up to a porch. "Bring the box," she said.

His eyes began to acclimatize to the dark, and there was a faint glow that brightened when a cloud shifted; a sliver of moon appeared.

He followed Pascaline into the hut. She went directly to a table and put the flashlight down on it, standing it on its end so that its beam pointed straight up. In its spill he could see she was again struggling with matches, so, placing the box on the table, he reached into his pocket. "Shall I?" he said, holding up the lighter.

She nodded, pointed. An oil lamp stood on the table, an old brass one with a glass shade she'd taken off. Sky flicked the lighter, dipped the flame. The wick caught and Pascaline placed the glass globe onto the base, then turned a screw beneath it. The center of the room brightened, though each of the four corners was still held in shadows.

She lifted the box, carrying it to a curtained-off alcove. Sky stared at the table. He had seen it before, and it wasn't a feeling of déjà vu. Then he realized where.

"The photograph," he murmured. "This was where my grandfather was sitting. But the table was outside."

She returned, carrying a tray, paused, nodded. "We put it out to eat, if the weather was fine. Luca was often here. Hunting. By day . . . and night."

She put the tray down, and he saw that the provisions she'd brought were laid out, the bread in a basket, cheese and salami on plates. "Are we eating?" He wasn't sure he could.

She nodded. "Soon. But first you must make a fire."

He turned. A fireplace was behind him, logs in a neat stack beside it, a wicker basket of kindling. "Are you cold? I'm not."

"It is not for warmth," she said. "There are things I

must heat up. And we have some time. Firelight is pleasant, no?"

He started to ball sheets from a yellowing newspaper. "Are you going to tell me more now?" he called over his shoulder.

She was busy herself. She had an ancient iron pot on the table and was crumbling things into it. The walls were lined with dangling bunches of what he supposed were herbs. "What do you wish to know?" she said.

Everything, he thought but didn't say, in case it put her off. "Uh, what time do we . . . go?"

"Midnight. It is the best time."

Of course it is, thought Sky. Sigurd had always done his . . . stuff at midnight. Sent Sky back in time. Killed a man. What had he called it? "The moment that is no longer today, not yet tomorrow." Sky shivered as he broke up some kindling, layered it on the newspaper. "And how do we go? And what happens when we get . . . wherever it is? And what if I can't . . ."

He snapped a stick, winced as a splinter dug into a finger. Sucking at it, he looked at her. She stood staring at him, a spray of lavender in her hand. "I know you have the gift. But it can be difficult to make the first . . . jump." She began crumbling dried petals into the pot. "But that is why you are to be my apprentice. I will help you. And as for the rest . . ." She sighed. "You will have to wait to see." She tipped her head. "Is it done?"

He looked down. He'd made a pyramid as his

father had taught him. He laid a final log, then nodded. She picked up the lighter and tossed it to him.

An edge of paper caught. The kindling began to crackle, flame climbing to the bigger pieces above. Shapes danced in the spreading flame and, just for an instant, two points took fire. In their flaring he saw an animal with dagger teeth, challenging him before it turned away.

"Come, Sky," she called softly. "Let us begin."

She'd made him eat, even though he wasn't hungry; made him drink the red wine she'd heated in an iron pot over the fire, even though he told her he wasn't much of a drinker. He thought it would make him sleepy, but something about the herbs in it had the reverse effect. After the second mug, he felt like he could go out and run a race. They didn't talk much, at least not about anything important. She put his questions aside with a "wait and see" that could have been infuriating but, perhaps because of the wine, wasn't. He was aware of time slipping away but had no watch to tell it by. No clocks ticked, no bells sounded. In England there was always some noise, a car in the distance, something electrical whirring. Here there was nothing save the crackle of burning wood. Outside, silence— and darkness—pressed in. He tended the fire relentlessly to counter both until she told him to stop, to let it burn down. After a while they just sat, staring at the dying flame.

61

The scratching at the door made him jump, so loud did it seem. Terror held him until Pascaline rose, went to the door, opened it. Amlet stalked in on stiff legs and went immediately to the fire, slumping down before it.

She bent to him, scratched the obviously exhausted animal at the neck, murmured something that Sky partly understood.

"Did you just ask him if the . . . the hunting paths were good?"

"Yes."

"But he can't hunt, can he?"

"Why not?"

"Well . . ." Sky studied the animal that was barely lifting its head to the caress. "He must be ancient."

"As old in his years as I am in mine. Yet I hunt." As she said it, she came back to the table and he could see something different about her walk, her look. She had seemed relaxed as they ate, almost dozy. But as she stood above him at the table, he could see her eyes were glowing, far beyond any reflection the dwindling fire could produce.

He rose too. "Now?" he said, his voice quaky.

"Soon. Oh, yes. Very soon."

It was strange. Though she stared at him intensely, it was also as if her eyes were glazed. As if they were looking through him. "But first . . . we lie down."

He could not have been any more surprised. "Sleep? I can't sleep. I want to . . ." He raised his hands before him, his fingers curling into fists, uncurling again.

She reached out, placed her hands over his. "You can. You must. And you will . . . with my help."

She dropped her grip, and he swayed slightly as she moved past him to the fireplace. On its edge was a metal rack on legs. Earlier she'd placed an earthenware jar on top of it. Now, pulling the sleeves of her dress down to cover her hands, she lifted the jar, brought it to the table, lifted its lid. A scent both sweet and rancid hit him. He gagged, turned away. "You don't want me to drink that, do you?"

"It would kill you," she said softly. "This will not." She dipped two fingers into it, then raised them to his nostrils. He sniffed tentatively, got that acrid tang again, had begun to turn away . . . when suddenly she thrust the fingers into his nostrils and, before he could escape her, dabbed them into the corner of each eye.

"Bloody hell," he said, reeling back, tripping over his chair, sitting down. His nose, his eyes stung and he wiped both, succeeding only in rubbing what felt like oil deeper in. "You might have warned me! What did you do that for?"

She smiled down at him. "To help you come to the hunt."

He watched her as she put the jar back by the fire. "Aren't you . . ."

"I do not need this help. You will not, one day. But your first time . . ."

He rubbed his fingers together. "It's greasy."

"Once, they say, the base for this . . . medication

63

was made from the congealed fat of a baby who'd died unbaptized."

He winced, shrank from her. "That's *so* gross."

She laughed. "Do not worry, nephew. These days goose fat works just as well."

Sky shuddered. "So this . . . this is another herb, eh? Like in the wine."

"A plant, not an herb," she replied softly. "And not like in the wine."

Was it him, or were her smiles getting less friendly? And his nose and eyes had gone beyond itching. They were burning. He rubbed them again, and it made it worse. His stomach bubbled and twisted; he felt as if he was going to vomit. What the hell was he doing? Where the hell was he now? In the middle of nowhere, with an old woman who'd just shoved some sort of . . . of drug, he supposed, into his nose?

He stared at her. She stared back. What if she wasn't even his aunt? Maybe he should run? He tried to move but his legs wouldn't lift him.

She rose slowly, as if each of her joints was clicking into place. Yet it didn't seem like it was due to her age. For Sky, everything was slowing down; he could barely detect movement, like frames were missing in a film. She was in front of him. She'd crossed to a chest. She'd opened a drawer. She was standing there with a knife.

He forced himself out of the chair. "Wha . . . ?" he tried to say. His mouth didn't seem to be working any better than his legs.

She'd turned back to him. Her voice seemed to come from miles away, echoing as it reached him. "Come here, nephew. Help me."

"How?" he drawled.

"Sleep."

"Sleep?" An old, bald crone stood there clutching a carving knife, asking him to sleep. And the worst thing was . . . he wanted to! Had never been so tired. Words came into his head. "But in that sleep of death what dreams may come?" *Hamlet,* he thought. He'd studied it at school last term. And Amlet the dog had risen before the smoldering fire and stared at him now with eyes like a wild boar's, eyes as big as his mistress's.

"Come here," she said again. Loudly.

He didn't want to. But his legs gave him no choice. They were obeying her, not him, lurching him forward, toward the old woman with her knife. One step, two steps, and he was there. His hands were pinned to his legs. He couldn't stop her doing—whatever she was going to do.

He watched her raise the knife. "No!" he wanted to scream but couldn't.

Then, slowly, slowly, she turned the weapon, twisting it in midair, lowering the grip into his right hand, which, like his legs, moved without his choice. Somehow he grasped it, and she reached back into the drawer, pulled out two more knives, a pair of huge old scissors. Her voice came again, almost at a normal pace. "Place your knife before the door, the blade toward the night."

65

Speed reversed. All that had been slow became fast. He moved, but not as quickly as she did. She laid a knife on the front windowsill, its cutting edge toward the glass, and a second at the back window the same way. Sky placed the carving knife, blade out to face the door, then turned to watch her rake the embers of the fire into a flat surface before she lay the scissors, its arms spread wide, atop the ashes.

"Why?" he said, or thought he did.

"So the Dead will not disturb us," she said, "for they will not cross an open blade. They fear it."

His mind flashed onto the night before. The Squadra had left him alone only when he had a knife in his mouth.

66   She beckoned him back to the table and he went to it. "Sit, Sky," she said. "And sleep."

"And then . . . ," he whispered.

"Then," she said, "we hunt."

"But how . . . ," he began before the darkness and the silence swallowed him.

CHAPTER SEVEN
HUNTING THE DEAD

He'd been asleep in a straight-backed chair. It should have been uncomfortable. It wasn't. He'd never slept better, never woken with more delight.

He stood straight up, looked around. The only light came from the lamp, yellow, intense. It lit his aunt, still seated, her head resting on her arms on the table; and Amlet curled up on the rug before the fire.

Sky looked down . . . and gasped!

In the chair, head thrown back, mouth wide open, eyes shut, sat Sky. He was looking at himself.

His gasp echoed round the room. It roused the animal before the fireplace—one of them, anyway, for now one stood on four paws, staring up at him, beside the other dog, still asleep.

"Welcome, Hunter."

He turned. Pascaline stood beside her seated self.

He couldn't help himself. He laughed. "This is fantastic!" he shouted.

"Oh, my nephew. You have seen nothing yet."

She moved past him. At least she must have done, because she was now standing at the open door. Immediately Amlet was through it, running growling into the night.

"Come," she beckoned, her voice soaring. "To the hunt."

He looked down at his own sleeping self, then at Pascaline's slumped body. "Will they . . . *we* be okay?"

His aunt nodded. "The blades protect us from the Dead. And as for the living, this place is so hidden, no one comes here. You are safe, Sky. Come!"

He was about to obey . . . when he remembered something. Sigurd, warning him that when his Fetch traveled, his body must never, ever be disturbed. Yet Sigurd had only hinted at terrible consequences. He had never spelled them out. "What would happen if I was disturbed?" Sky asked.

"You will not be."

"But if I was?"

Pascaline shifted from foot to foot in the doorway. Sky could tell how desperate she was to be gone. He was too, had never wanted more to just . . . run! But his question held her. She took a breath, then words tumbled out. "I have only heard of it once. A Mazzeri, a man I knew. He couldn't wait to . . ." She gestured impatiently outside. "He didn't take precautions." She shook her head. "Some children found his body under a tree. When they couldn't wake him, they called their parents, who called an ambulance. The doctors thought he was in a coma and took him to a hospital far away."

Sky swallowed. "What happened to him?"

"You will see—later—that you need a moment, one quiet moment, to reunite your body with your Mazzeri spirit. He didn't have this moment. He . . ." She closed her eyes.

"What?"

Eyes shut, she continued, "He never found his way back. Body without spirit wastes away. So does spirit without body. Both . . . fade. Eventually the body dies. But the spirit . . . lingers on. Barely heard. Scarcely seen. Reducing slowly to a shadow at the edge of vision."

"A ghost," Sky murmured. "You'd turn into a ghost."

69

"Yes." She said it softly. Then her eyes flew open, and instantly he could see the hunger there again, feel the energy crackling off her. She had restrained it as long as she could. Now she shouted, "But that man was stupid and we are not. We are safe here. Safe to do anything you desire. Do you understand me, nephew?" She laughed. "Anything!"

Her excitement, her certainty, swept all doubts away. He marched to the door, glanced back at sleeping Sky. He had seen his body once before when he'd left it, that time to become Sky-Hawk. But then he'd been part bird, had a raptor's instincts, its desire to seek out prey, to kill. Now he felt so entirely himself, in a way he never had known before, as if every part of him, every cell, was vibrating at once. Yearning filled him like an ache, for something he hadn't had since . . . since Bjørn had first gone berserk, lifted his ax, and hurled himself at his enemies in battle.

"Anything?" he echoed. "Then let's go." He knew exactly what he wanted to do. And he wanted to do it now.

She closed the door, the bottom edge just clearing the knife he had placed. Her hand dropped onto his shoulder, stopping his impulse to pursue Amlet. "Wait! I know you feel as if you could kill with your teeth and nails. And perhaps you could. But if you are fortunate enough to make a kill tonight, your first time hunting, then it would be better for you to use one of these."

She stepped off the porch. Under it was a tarpaulin. She grabbed an edge, threw it back. Moonlight flashed on a hoard of weapons. "Choose," she said.

He bent to inspect. There were daggers of all sizes; two rusty swords with curving blades; an ax, which he immediately picked up and swung through the air. But it was meant for mere wood, had none of the heft of Bjørn's Death Claw. He laid it down. "What's that?" he asked, pointing.

She bent, lifted something made of rope and leather. "In Italian it is called a *fionda*. I do not know it in English. You put a stone here"—she pointed at the leather pouch at the center of the entwined rope— "and you . . ." She whirled it above her head, releasing one end of the rope. "Like David and Goliath."

70

"A slingshot." He reached. And as soon as he touched it, something surged through him. When he slipped his fingers through the loop at one end of the rope, it felt as familiar as a glove. When he grasped the knot at the other end, he felt he had grasped it before. Immediately he wanted to look for stones, knew just the kind he would need: smooth pebbles from a riverbed, a little rounder at the base. The weapon tempted him. But it looked ancient, its ropes and leather fraying. Besides, it was designed for projectiles, for the distance kill. And just now he wanted something more direct.

Then he saw it. Laying down the slingshot, he snatched up a piece of polished wood, lifted it high. It was about the length of his arm, heavy, at one end a thick ball of knotted wood, tapering to the worn end that seemed crafted for his palm. He swung it. "What is this?"

71

"A vine stock, cut from an old grapevine."

He swung again, loved the song it made in the air. "I'll take it."

She smiled. "A good choice, nephew. For it was your grandfather's. And the blood of his kills lies thick upon it." She bent, selected a long knife with a thin, jagged blade. "This for me."

She straightened and he noticed that none of her movements were now those of an old woman, nothing slow or pained about them. And looking closer, he could see that her skin was no longer pasty white but glowed with color, while the blue of her eyes only showed at the edges, almost blocked out by her huge black pupils.

"Your eyes are amazing!" he cried.

"All the better to see you with, my dear," she said in a croaky crone's voice. They both laughed, and she went on, "You should see yours."

"Is that because of the . . . whatever you gave me?" He pointed at his nose.

"Yes. And the belladonna also pushed you across the threshold. Back there"—she pointed into the house—"I am sure you are having good dreams. But out here, the drug will have no other effect." She looked up at the moon. "Tonight there is a little light. But even in the deepest black, these eyes would let us see."

Out in that darkness, they heard a howl, then a series of short barks. She turned. "Amlet has found the scent." She took a step. "Come," she said. "For it begins."

She led him rapidly away from the dwelling, downhill, to where the trees began. Soon they were treading the faintest of paths through an olive grove, fallen fruit squishing under their shoes. The path led to a stream, and Pascaline grabbed his arm to halt him before he threw himself across. She pinched him—it hurt. "Remember, we are flesh *and* spirit, Sky. And we hunt real animals that can hurt us with their teeth." She smiled. "If they mark you, your body back in the hut will bear the scar forever. So be wary."

He laughed. There was nothing a wild pig could do to him. Not when he felt this good, armed with his grandfather's club. He swung it high, brought it down to thud onto the forest path. "Let's go," he yelled. But before he could step into the water, his shout was answered and echoed by others, some animal, some human. "What's that?" he whispered.

"Did you think we were the only Mazzeri to hunt this night?" She grinned, shook her head. "If we want to kill, we will have to beat others to the death. It is hard, for as the years pass, there is less game and it gets more cunning. Some nights, many Mazzeri hunt, and none kill."

"I will." He clutched the club tighter. He had never been more sure of anything.

73

"Then come!" She bent, picked up a stone, threw it into the stream. "To scatter the spirits," she said, "for they gather by water." She followed it with her feet. The dark liquid rose to her knees as she strode across, beckoned him over. As soon as he joined her, she turned and began to run toward a gap in a cliff face.

He caught up with her where she paused, stared ahead. They stood at the entrance to a small valley, cliffs sweeping away into the distance, their granite sides rising sharp on either side of them, studded with stunted trees, windblasted and bent.

"A fine place for a kill." She cocked her head to the sounds that came. "And others think so too."

The howls they'd heard before intensified, doubling

in volume, the voices coming from animal throats—he thought he recognized Amlet's among them—and from human, though these were as close to animal as human could get. He saw movement at the valley's far end, black shapes flowing over the cliff tops, beginning to descend by treacherous paths. "Farcese and their allies," Pascaline grunted, "for their ancient village lies there. Ours, here!" She pointed with a jerk of her dagger over her shoulder. "We have always disputed this valley."

Two paths forked before them through the thick brush that made the maquis. "There, Sky, there!" She gestured to the left-hand path. "And I am for here. Good hunting!" Without another word, she was off, sprinting into the dark.

He paused, but not because he was frightened. He wanted to take into his lungs the fragrance that arose from the tangled wilderness ahead, wanted to feel what that did to his heart. He tipped back his head, opened his mouth, and a sound came out, akin to the others he was hearing still, his own a cry made up of both the hunter and the quarry he sought.

He began running down the path, careless of roots reaching for feet that scarcely seemed to make contact with the earth. Then he saw movement ahead, a black shape, low to the ground, moving fast.

"Not fast enough," he grunted, and began to close the distance.

The path twisted and swept through the maquis,

intertwining with others, separating for a space, rejoining again. Suddenly a black shape burst from one beside him; he swerved, stumbled in the knee-high brush, regained the flat ground. He looked to his side . . . running shoulder to shoulder with him was Jacqueline Farcese.

"Did I not tell you I would see you later?" she yelled.

He'd thought she was pretty before, but here she was radiant. Her dress, the same one she'd worn when he'd met her with the Squadra, clung tight to her form. Moonlight shot through her blue-black hair where it showed under her veil, while her eyes—like his aunt's— were huge globes of darkness bursting with flame. And her smile was not like the one she'd mocked him with at the bench, but more like the one that had invited him to their home before she knew who he was.

They fell into step, effortless running, easy breathing. "Is it not wonderful?" she asked.

"Fantastic!" he yelled. "I've never . . . this is . . ."

She laughed. "There are not words. In French or English, no?"

"No! Yes! But I don't know them." He smiled at her. "Do you come here often?"

He meant it as a joke, a mock pickup line. She took it seriously. "My fifth time. But I haven't killed since my first. Tonight, I must." She looked away from him, ahead. "And I follow . . . her."

Sky looked. It was the beast he'd been chasing

75

since he entered the valley. "She's mine!" he shouted, increasing his pace. Redoubling hers, she matched him stride for stride. Then, quite casually, she reached down and stuck her club between his legs.

He stumbled, fell, smashing into the rough path, slipping sideways into the prickly vegetation. His aunt had been right—it hurt. But not as much as his pride.

"Hey!" he shouted, was up in a moment, running flat out the next. She was twenty yards ahead of him, the path they hammered down dipping, rising, then twisting hard left. Twenty paces past the bend, it widened into a cleared space, thick maquis at its sides, a wall of sheer granite to the rear. Backed against this was the beast. A wild boar, panting, facing them. Sky had only ever seen one in books, hadn't appreciated the size. It came to his hips at least, the bristle raised along its back, its hairy pink snout thrust between two enormous curving teeth.

Jacqui had halted at the bend, and he only just missed crashing into her. "Mine," she said, throwing her club aside, drawing a long-bladed dagger from her belt.

"No," he cried, raising the club in the air. "Mine!"

They glared at each other. And it made them move slower, slower certainly than the one who rushed between them with an ax raised high. The weapon fell—once, twice, and again, stunning the squealing animal with the first blow, severing its spine with the second, smashing its skull with the third. Blood spattered against the cliff face, poured onto the dry earth, squirted into Sky's face.

He reached a hand, touched the wetness, looked at it on his fingers. Then he looked up to see the black figure fall onto the dying animal. "What . . . what's happening?"

"Did the bald one not tell you, English boy?" Jacqueline had sunk onto the ground. "This is what it is all about—the chase, the kill, everything! This moment. Look!"

Sky followed the pointed dagger. The black-swathed figure had twisted the beast's head around. Sky watched transfixed as Jacqueline continued, "As the animal dies, the Mazzeri looks in its face, listens to its last cry. And in them we see the face, hear the voice of someone we know"—she turned to him, her eyes aflame—"someone now marked to die."

There was no question—the Mazzeri was trying to look into the animal's eyes! As the boar was turned, it gave one last spasm, a kick of its front hooves. One dislodged the veil the figure was wearing, and Sky could see the white hair, tightly coiled, on the head of Emilia Farcese.

"But she's blind," he whispered.

"Not here," the girl replied.

Her grandmother raised her head to the night sky, cried out a name. He wasn't sure he heard what it was— "Francesca" perhaps. But in that moment he knew that the last name she had howled was "Lucien Bellagi."

She turned to them, her face covered in blood, her hands still clutching the dead boar's head. A savage delight lit the no-longer-misted eyes. Then they recognized him. "Marcaggi!" she hissed.

But it wasn't her hatred that disturbed Sky. He didn't feel threatened by her here. And he wasn't horrified by what he'd just witnessed. The only thing that frightened him, and then only for a brief moment, was his terrible desire to do the same.

He lifted his head to the night. Elsewhere, dogs still drove beasts up the valley. Other Mazzeri still hunted. Beasts could still die.

He turned, sprinted back along the path, Jacqueline's cries, Emilia's curses fading fast. He twisted left, then right along barely seen trails, his instincts leading him. And almost immediately he saw a thick blackness, standing foursquare upon the path ahead of him. He'd thought the boar he'd just seen killed was big . . . but this one dwarfed it, tusks like bayonets shining on either side of its huge head. The animal turned, charged away from him. Other paths joined the one they took, but it disdained each one, kept ever straight. As he ran, Sky became aware of those paths disgorging other dark figures, felt the vibration of a growing pursuit under his feet, a pack of Mazzeri after this one beast.

The path widened, opening into a valley's end, flowing through a gap like the one at its head. Sky suddenly found extra speed, though his lungs were laboring now at last. The burst took him close, closer; the beast swerved to avoid a bush . . . and Sky struck, bringing the whole weight of the club's head smashing down upon the animal's haunch. It let out a terrible shriek, more human than animal, went sprawling, its own speed causing it to roll over and over, its momentum finally halted by the trunk of the tree it crashed into. It tried to struggle up, then fell back, panting.

The sounds of the hunt, which had lasted for so long, were gone. Only the harsh breaths taken by hunter and hunted violated the silence of the valley now. Until there came a shuffling, footsteps behind him. He looked back, watched hooded, faceless shapes crowd into the little glade, a dozen or more. All were shrouded in black, veils pulled across their faces, and he only distinguished Jacqui because of that tight dress and her grandmother because of her red-stained hands. Then one of the others stepped forward, and he heard a familiar voice.

"Do it, nephew. For the Marcaggi blood that drives your heart. For the Mazzeri whose apprentice you now are. Do it. Kill."

Echoes came, whispers. "Kill. Kill. Kill."

He turned back. The beast's sides were heaving still, a little whimper emerging from its throat. He stepped toward it.

"Kill. Kill. Kill."

It would be so easy. Gravity would do most of it, the vine stock's hardness the rest. He raised the club, his ancestor's club, above his head in a two-handed grip.

Kill.

The animal had begun to turn toward him, raised its tusks to him, some last fighting instinct driving it. Yet as soon as he saw a glimmer of moonlight reflected in the dark orb of its eye, the club fell from Sky's fingers, dropped onto the ground behind him. He bent, reaching to the head of the beast, and it twisted in his clutch, raking the razor tusk against his right hand. Yet he couldn't let go, not now, not when he held the face toward him, for that moment before the pain came, and could look into the eyes.

He had only met a few people in his short time in Corsica—a bus driver, a girl, a blind woman, his aunt. None of these looked back. But Jacqueline's cousin did.

"Giancarlo," he whispered, but not so quietly that all didn't hear. He knew they had when he heard someone behind him begin to sob.

CHAPTER EIGHT

THE PRICE

However much of a struggle it was for his Fetch to leave his body, coming back to it had always been effortless. It was as if there was a limit to his travels. Not set in time—as he'd discovered, time was meaningless when he traveled, an hour in one life could be a week in the other—but in goals. He'd learn something, achieve something—kill someone!—then he'd return. Have that "one quiet moment," as Pascaline had termed it, to slip into his human form.

Leaving it at will was the problem, the one he'd come to Corsica to solve. Returning was easy.

Until now.

"What are you waiting for, Sky?" Pascaline said. "The Mazzeri are hunters of the night. Dawn comes. You must return to yourself."

He glanced out the window. The dark was . . . less so. "I want to. Believe me." He did. The euphoria he'd felt, the joy of the hunt, had vanished when he'd looked into a wild boar's eyes. Now he needed sleep. As himself. Not as the figure still slumped before him at the table.

If only he hadn't lingered outside! His great-aunt had preceded him into the hut. Huntress and ex-teacher had blended instantly. Only one Pascaline stood there now, staring at the two of him impatiently.

That was it! "I think I know the problem," he said. "You. Here . . ." He paused, suddenly embarrassed.

Her voice was mocking. "You are *shy*, nephew?"

It did seem weird. Especially considering what she'd just watched him do in the valley. But that was the point! It hadn't been *her* who watched. It had been her Fetch. Now . . . well, it was more like back in her apartment, when he'd changed into his black clothes. He hadn't done that in front of her! He wouldn't do this.

"If you could just, you know, give me a moment?"

She failed to hide her smile. *"Bien sûr,"* she said, and left.

Relief came, tiredness doubled. He stepped forward, touched himself—his other self—on the shoulder.

One quiet moment. All he needed.

Sky stepped onto the hut's porch. His aunt was sitting at the wheel of her car. "Finished?" she asked.

He nodded, got in. The rubber-band engine started up.

They drove back to Sartène in silence, Sky slumped with his head against the window. His body ached, legacy, no doubt, of the drug Pascaline had smeared on him, the pain of his fall on the valley floor, and the agony radiating from his hand where the tusk had slashed him. The skin there was not broken, but there was a livid red line down the center, throbbing like the cuts Bjørn had received from sword or spear, that Sky had then carried.

Dawn's light was cresting the ridgetops when the car entered Sartène. Pascaline parked, and the three hunters—the old woman, the ancient dog, the exhausted young man—limped to her block and up the stairs. In the apartment, Pascaline changed from black into her normal clothes, then made coffee. Sky held a mug in two hands, relishing the heat more than the taste. He hadn't stopped shivering since the valley. He envied Amlet, prone and twitching before the hearth, where Pascaline had built a fire. Exhausted though he was, he knew he couldn't sleep. Not yet.

"I don't understand," he said, his first words in an hour bursting out.

"What, nephew?"

"Any of it." He looked up at her, in her purple blouse with the woolen shawl thrown over it, her trousers, the patterned scarf on her head. She looked so normal. Yet a few hours earlier . . . "What is it for?"

"The hunt?" He nodded and she frowned. "You

83

can ask this? You, who this night took the first step to-ward what you always were?"

"But I don't want the inheritance." A flash of Olav's chest, split by Sigurd's ax, made him shudder. "I've enough murderers in my family already, thank you!"

"Murderers?" Pascaline lowered herself into a chair. "The Mazzeri do not murder; they—"

"I saw it," he interrupted. "And Jacqueline Farcese explained it. Her grandmother . . . slaughtered that an-imal. Looked in its face as it died. Saw the face of someone she knew who would now die as well." He slammed his mug down, slopping coffee on the table. "If that's not murder, I don't know what is!"

"No. Listen to me." She rose, grabbed a cloth, tot-tered over to the sofa, sat beside him with a sigh. The hunter of the night was gone. The old woman was back. She mopped up his spilled coffee. "We are not . . . assassins, Sky. The animal we strike, the person that animal represents, has already been marked. We do not choose whom we kill. Death has already chosen them. All we do is bear witness."

He stared at her, stunned. "But . . . why?"

"Why? You can ask this, you who have felt the Mazzeri's power?" Her astonishment matched his. "You hunt because you have to. Because, like me, like all of us, you are compelled to!" Her eyes shone, with almost the same fervor of a few hours before. "Be-cause you never feel more alive than in that moment of a death foretold."

84

He shook his head. "Not 'why do we do it?' I felt the urge, trust me. I just don't see the point."

"That's because you are thinking here, with your English brain"—she touched his forehead—"not here, with your Corsican heart." Her hand passed before his chest. "We of this island are born staring into our own grave. Fate has already set down the date when we will fill it. A few of us—a special few—have been chosen to bear witness. To testify. We are the Mazzeri. We are the Dream Hunters of Death."

Her voice had soared, almost as if she were singing one of her laments. His question was a quiet contrast. "How long have they got?"

"It is never the same. Yet always on an uneven number of days. Some die almost straight away. Others live for a while. But never for more than a year."

"Do you tell the . . . victim?"

She shrugged. "No. But they find out. A Mazzeri passes them in the street and makes the sign of the cross. People talk. Eventually the Squadra d'Arrozza start to gather about the intended's door, murmuring his name, bearing his coffin. Mazzeri can hear them come."

"And the person who . . . who has killed, who has recognized this 'intended'? Do they always go and see the Squadra call?"

"No!" Her cry was full of repugnance. "Only Emilia does this. Only that *Farcese* gloats on death."

And what about Jacqui? Sky thought. But he said,

85

"Why not just leave the poor sod to find out for himself?" His anger was growing with his confusion. "I reckon if you tell someone he's going to die and he believes it, he will."

"He will . . . but not because he's been told. Because he's been chosen."

"But how do you live your life, knowing you are going to die?"

She reached again, this time managed to take his hands. "But we all know that, Sky. Each one of us is born to die, our name already cut into a gravestone. This way, at least, the person has time to prepare."

"Is that what it's for, then? To warn people to prepare?"

86   At least that made a little sense to him. But Pascaline shook her head. "No. We do not hunt and kill so as to warn. We are just there to testify to the inevitability of death. If the person chooses to make amends, well . . ." She frowned. "But you must remember, Sky, most people in Corsica, in the world, believe that this life is but a stage on a longer journey. They should always be preparing for the next stage, whether they are called by the Mazzeri or no."

There was still so much he didn't understand. "So if I'd killed that boar . . ."

"You didn't."

"I could have."

"No, nephew." She shook the hands she held. "I have told you—it is not in our choice. If Giancarlo

Orsini was marked to die, you would have killed him. As it is, he will be injured, or perhaps grow sick. But he will survive."

His mind whirled with all she'd said, all he'd done. "I saw Emilia Farcese when she killed. I looked into those eyes and knew that if she could've, she'd have gutted me quicker than she gutted that boar." He shook his head. "Lucky for me she was just a messenger, eh? That she can't choose me, kill me in that world?"

"No, she cannot." Pascaline dropped his hands, turned away. "Well, not usually."

He went cold. His hand, where the boar had raked it, throbbed. "What do you mean, 'not usually'?"

She rose, crossed to the fireplace, lifted the picture of her brother, Sky's grandfather. The black crepe cloth that covered it slipped off and floated to the floor. "I should tell you, Sky, now that you have become an apprentice to the Mazzeri, just how your grandfather died."

Their conversation from the previous night came back to him. "That's right. You said Emilia's family had been warned not to restart the vendetta and that she found another method?"

"Yes." She laid the picture back down, stared into the mirror. "It was an ancient part of the Way of the Mazzeri. No one had done it in the memory of anyone alive. But Emilia remembered that, every year, for one night only, all the laws that govern us are suspended.

87

It is the night when apprentices can be made into full Mazzeri, if their teacher chooses to initiate them, free to leave their body at will, to hunt when they choose. . . ."

She paused and Sky held his breath. Her promise was clear, in her words, in the way she looked at him. Then she went on. "It is also the one night when the quarry does not have to be only the beasts of the valleys. When we can hunt . . . other Dream Hunters."

Sky shot forward. "What?"

She nodded. "Yes, nephew. That night is known as the Battle of the Mazzeri. Only then can we choose who we kill. And just like the beasts, if we kill them there, they will die here too."

88

Sky's mouth had become very dry. "What night?"

"Here we call it Jour des Morts. The Day of the Dead. I think the English call it All Souls'. It is when all in Corsica honor their dead."

"And when is this?" Sky had no spit in his mouth and his voice rasped.

"November second. A month and a half away."

"Remind me not to go hunting that night."

She shook her head. "You may not have a choice. Your grandfather didn't."

He thought, I will have the choice because I won't bloody be here! But then he remembered what she'd just said. It was also the night of initiation. The one night he could learn to free his Fetch. Torn, he muttered, "Tell me more."

"There is not much more to tell. Emilia had two brothers, both Mazzeri. They waited for the night, went on the hunt. Luca had forgotten the old tradition. Or he didn't think the Farcese had the strength and the will to catch him." She sighed. "But they did. Ambushed him in the very moment when he had made a kill himself, was turning the animal to see who was marked. And he saw!" Her voice dropped to a whisper. "He saw himself! His own face in the boar's, even as the axes plunged down into his back."

Stunned, Sky blurted out, "Couldn't you stop them?"

"I was not there," she said stiffly. "I was living in Paris. He wrote to me and told me what had happened. What he was going to do."

89

"What did he do?" The dread was clear in his voice because he already knew.

"All he could. He did not know how long he would have. He knew he was already dead. So he took his wife and baby to England, hid them under another name. . . ."

"March."

"Yes. Then he came back to Corsica and avenged his own death. He killed both brothers—not in a dream, but in daylight, with a shotgun, up in the maquis. He was arrested as he marched to the Farcese house to kill Emilia."

Sky felt ill. His grandfather, the killer. Both grandfathers, for he had watched Sigurd kill too. Was this what he'd come here to learn? Was this the secret whispering in his blood? A killer's legacy, on both sides. He shuddered. "What happened to him?"

"He died in prison, waiting for his trial." She came to sit beside him again, and her hands reached up, took his head, pulled him toward her. He could have broken her grip easily. He knew what she was going to say, what ancient curse she was about to pronounce. "He died. But he has no rest because the Farcese still live. Only you can end the vendetta. Only you can avenge your grandfather. Only you can kill . . ."

"Emilia?" he croaked.

"Jacqueline." Sky gasped but Pascaline's grip tightened, preventing him from turning away. "It is not usual to kill a woman. But they brought that on themselves by violating the hunt world for vengeance in this one!"

He saw a way out, a slightly less terrible choice. "What about Giancarlo?"

"Giancarlo is an Orsini, not a Farcese. A distant cousin."

He searched again, his exhausted brain reeling. "But how is Emilia still a Farcese? She'd have taken her husband's name. Unless . . ." He stopped when he noticed the gleam in Pascaline's eye.

"Yes, Sky," she said. "After Luca refused her, she would not take any other husband. But that did not mean she would not bear a son. She needed her bloodline to continue . . ." Her eyes gleamed. ". . . for vengeance! Her shame was as nothing to that."

Sky swallowed. "Jacqueline told me her parents died in a car crash."

"They did. But their daughter survived, to bear that cursed name, and Emilia raised her." She squeezed his hand even harder, till he thought one of her brittle bones might break. "So now you see, nephew, Jacqueline is the last of them. Kill her and she will give birth to no sons. Kill her and the vendetta is over. Kill her and the Farcese are truly finished."

"You're mad," he said, pulling away, standing, almost running to the far side of the room. Out beyond the shutters, the normal world lived. He could hear car horns, a radio, rock music coming from the street. Someone talking about something unimportant. Football scores? Growing asparagus? That was his world. Not this . . . this ancient blood feud! "Why don't *you* kill her?"

Her sigh turned him—in time to see a single tear running down her face. "I want nothing more. But in this world I am old. And even if I can still hunt . . . out there, I am not as fast as I was. The Mazzeri spirit diminishes. Not as much as this body but . . ." She sighed again. "I have not killed in six years. I go because I have to. I try. I fail. And besides, on Jour des Morts they would be ready for me. Both of them."

Sky stared at her. Silence held them. Finally he said softly, "I can't do it."

Pascaline rose, angrily wiping her cheek with the back of her hand. "Then your grandfather will walk the world crying for vengeance forever." She stared at him, and her voice changed, went from a shrill summons to revenge to something more subtle. "And you will never learn what you most desire—to leave your body *at will*."

He looked away. "How do you know that is what I want?"

"Your hunger is as clear as the one eyebrow on your face."

Sky swallowed. "So you won't . . . initiate me."

"I will not. Why should you, English boy, get to pick and choose from our ancient traditions? If you want to learn the Corsican ways, you must take them all."

She watched the turmoil on his face for a moment, then turned, began to walk slowly toward her bedroom. "You will have to think on this, nephew. Consider the cost and the gain. All Souls' is more than a month away. You have time."

She was almost at her door when his words halted her, the disgust in them clear. "All this talk of death. Is that all the Mazzeri are about? Is there nothing about life?"

She stared at him. "They say there was once a time . . ." She broke off.

"What?" He saw a softening in her face.

She leaned into the doorway. "It is just a story. That once . . . once there was a type of Mazzeri who did not just kill. Who could also heal."

His heart started beating a little faster. "Heal?"

"It is legend more than story. Older even than the story of the killing on Jour des Morts."

He swallowed. "Tell me."

"They were called Mazzeri Salvatore." She sought a word. "Like 'salve.' They could strike an animal. Kill it. Then . . . 'salve' it. Bring it back to life." She smiled faintly. "If they chose to do so. The only Mazzeri who could choose."

"Mazzeri Salvatore." He intoned the words, almost like a prayer. Then he crossed to her. "How can I find out about this?"

"Find out?" Her voice echoed him, mocking. "I told you, boy. It is a legend. If ever it were true, that knowledge is lost. It is no more than a whisper from the distant past." She turned toward her bedroom. "So unless you know a way of traveling through time, I suggest you forget it . . . and begin planning for your departure . . . or your revenge!"

93

The door clicked shut. Sky stared at it for a moment, then went to the fireplace. He bent and retrieved the fallen black crepe, draping it over his grandfather's photograph again. Perhaps it was the light, perhaps the whirl of thoughts in his head, but he noticed something now he never had before about Luca Marcaggi—there was a yearning in his eyes. He recognized it because he saw the same in his own mirror every day.

"It wasn't death you wanted, was it, Grandfather?" he said softly. "It was life. Life with your wife, your son. You'd turned your back on vengeance . . . so you never saw the axes fall."

He went and lay down on the sofa. So many wounds, he thought, closing his eyes. A man murdered in the dream world dies in this one, the only way to heal him—the way of the Mazzeri Salvatore—lost to the ages. Lost, like the source of this ancient vendetta.

He turned on his side. Had he ever been this tired? Yet sleep wouldn't come. His mind whirled with images, the knowledge he'd been offered, the price he'd have to pay for it. Then suddenly all thoughts cleared, except one—Pascaline's last mocking words, urging him to vengeance . . . unless he could somehow travel in time and recover what was lost.

He sat up. "But I know how to travel in time," he whispered.

CHAPTER NINE

THE CHALLENGE

There were two things Sky needed: somewhere remote, where he would not be disturbed; and somewhere he could search for stones.

He began searching—in the library. The guide-books were okay for tourists, described the sites, the routes, the cheap hotels, the cafés where the best chestnut flour fritters could be found. Surprisingly, they didn't list the prime spots for contacting one's dead. The local maps the old librarian had given him proved both more useful—and confusing! There was no shortage of wilderness in southern Corsica; indeed, there were lots of valleys with scarcely a village marked, scores of mountains covered with nothing but maquis and goat poo. He was looking for a river valley; what he needed would be found in a streambed. But there were loads of those too.

Too many options, he thought, chewing at his lower lip. Might as well just stick a pin in!

He sat back, sighed . . . and saw the librarian behind his desk look up from his newspaper and glare. Old French coot, Sky thought. This is a library, not a church. I'm allowed to breathe!

Sky had hardly seen the man move from his newspaper in the hours he'd been there. But now perhaps his annoyance galvanized him. He got up and turned to the wall behind him. There was a calendar on it, and, because the man now reached up to it, Sky noticed it was still on *août*—August—and had pictures of bathers on a pretty beach. The librarian took the calendar down, turned a page, rehung it on a hook, then sat again, picked up his newspaper, his work for the month done.

96   Bit late, mate, Sky thought, since it was already mid-September. And then he noticed the photograph for the month.

It was a standing stone. Immediately Sky knew he'd seen it before, once, in the flame of a cigarette lighter. Even if there was no wolf howling by it now.

He reached for one of the guidebooks on his desk. He'd searched them before, looked at scores of stone photos, never seen the one from his vision. The book told how hundreds of the standing stones had been hewn from granite and erected in Corsica, probably around the same time as Stonehenge, in the Megalithic Age, about 2000 BC. And probably for the same purpose, though no one knew for certain—the worship of the Dead.

He searched again through the photos in the books. Not one of them was the one on the calendar. He got up, crossed to the desk. Closer to, he could see that a rough figure was cut into the rock, a man's face near the top, and beneath it what looked like a sword.

The librarian lowered his paper with a grunt. Sky put on his winningest smile. *"Excusez-moi, monsieur,"* he said in his best schoolboy's French, *"où est là?"*

The man turned, looked at the calendar, grunted something as he turned back to his reading. *"Pardon?"* said Sky.

"Filitosa," the man said.

"Wasn't so hard, was it, pal?" Sky muttered in English, turning away. He knew the name, had read about the site, one of the most famous on the island. It wasn't far from Sartène.

"Attendez!" Sky thought the man must have heard him. He turned back, expecting a reprimand. But the man was squinting at the photo again, at some small writing Sky couldn't quite make out. *"Non,"* he said, turning back, picking up the paper. *"Pas Filitosa."* Then he said something else unintelligible.

"Comment?"

The man irritably scribbled something on a scrap of paper, thrust it at Sky.

"Merci," he said brightly. He went back to his desk. The word on the paper was "Cauria." He looked it up in his guidebook. It was about ten kilometers away.

Sky folded up all the maps, stacked the books,

97

picked them all up at once, and dumped them on the front desk. The librarian *tsk*ed, shrugged, began sorting. He murmured something, but Sky was distracted by the photo again.

"It's not a sword," he said, staring at the standing stone. "It's a spear. It's *Isa*."

"*Comment?*"

There was no point trying to explain the runes to the man. They were difficult enough in English, let alone French. It was enough that he knew it himself. *Isa,* the challenge.

He looked at the librarian. "Thanks for all your help."

The man spoke some English. Just didn't get the subtleties of sarcasm.

"Where you go?" he said.

"Cauria," Sky replied.

How was the problem. The guidebooks talked of tours. But they had probably ended with the summer. Anyway, he could hardly climb onto a tour bus with a pack stuffed with provisions and then not get back on when the visit was over. They'd search for him—the English youth gone missing. The normal buses, as he knew, were terrible and irregular. He could hitchhike, as he'd often done back home, but he'd not seen anyone doing it here, which maybe meant that Corsican drivers just didn't pick people up.

And then he heard a roar, the sound building up

behind him. He turned, stepped to the side . . . and a scooter thundered past him.

Sky smiled.

The young guy at the rental agency barely glanced at his ID, didn't notice that his license was for a learner and that the name on it, which was real, didn't match the name on his bank card, which was false. The guy was too busy flirting with the secretary to care, handing him a copy of the agreement, tossing him the keys, pointing to the mechanic outside. This bloke grunted unintelligible instructions at him, but Sky wasn't worried. When he was thirteen, he'd gone to stay with Kristin at a big country house her mum had rented. There'd been a scooter in the garage, and, under strict orders to do nothing of the kind, they'd spent two weeks driving it like lunatics over the paths and through the woods of the extensive grounds.

As soon as he straddled the silver machine, drove it out of the garage, those memories came back—and brought others. Where are you right now, Kristin? he wondered. He'd last seen her when she'd come to get the runestones and the journal back. And he'd seen at least *part* of her later in the woods—her Fetch, the lynx, that Sigurd had "borrowed." The word had made Sky's skin creep then, and it did again now, just as he swerved to avoid a woman who stepped off the pavement without looking.

Sky, zipping along the edge of a traffic jam, shook

his head. He'd begun a whole different journey that had taken him off into this world of Dream Hunters and ancient feuds. He had stumbled into a vendetta and discovered another ancestor crying out for redress, just as Bjørn the Viking had done. Well, in the end and after a lot of scary stuff, he *had* found a way to help Bjørn. He would find a way to sort this mess out too. And he had to believe that the twisting route he took— as twisting as these narrow streets of Sartène—was somehow leading him back to free Kristin.

He pulled up outside the hostel, glad again of his decision not to remain at Pascaline's. She may not have talked anymore about what she was offering, what she was demanding in return, but even her silence spoke. He'd left as soon as he'd woken up. And what could he tell her now of what he was planning?

He went into the hostel. Strapping his bedroll and sleeping bag to his backpack, he checked that he had a change of clothes, a sweatshirt, his knife, a flashlight, his grandfather's lighter. The hostel manager let him leave the rest in bags in a left-luggage room.

There was a supermarket on the edge of the town. He bought bungee cords to strap the backpack down and enough food to last a week, filled the bike's rear box with cheese, crackers, salami, chocolate, tinned fruit. Water he figured he'd find wherever he went.

Gunning the throttle, he roared off down the road to Cauria.

⚞⚟

He'd not gone far. The bike was bigger, heavier than the other he'd ridden. And these were not forest trails and muddy tracks where, if he fell off, it wouldn't hurt too much. These were roads that bent and swooped and had unexpected patches of gravel on them, so he took it fairly slowly. It had gotten chillier the last few days, summer finally slipping away, but he was gripping the handlebars so hard that he was soon sweating inside the snug, full-face helmet that muffled even the spitting roar of his engine.

So he didn't hear them coming. Concentrating on what was ahead, he hadn't checked the side mirrors in a while, so he didn't see them either. Not until a wheel nudged in on his right and, shocked, he turned to see Jacqueline Farcese riding beside him. Her long black hair streamed behind her; her helmet was slung on her handlebars. He swerved slightly away from her. "What are you doing?" he yelled. She was almost on the gravel verge, not even looking where she was going, looking at him; and there was a bend coming up.

She tipped her head as if she hadn't heard him, which she probably hadn't. "Do you want to talk?" he shouted, louder.

She heard him this time; he could see in the shrug she gave. Then, after they'd both taken the bend, he swinging wide to give her room, she jerked her head again, indicating something on his other side. He turned . . .

Giancarlo was riding on Sky's left, in the middle

of the highway. Helmetless also, though his black greased-down hair barely moved. He was staring, as Jacqueline did, though in his eyes something fiercer burned.

Sky swerved again, away from him, forcing Jacqui onto the gravel; he swung back, overcompensating, and Giancarlo jerked his bike left, into the middle of the road. A car, coming the opposite way, coming fast, hit a long protest on its horn, flashed its lights. Giancarlo accelerated, nearly clipping Sky's front wheel as he roared past, cut in.

Crap, thought Sky, throttling down. This was insane! Jacqui had slowed even more, dropped in behind him. He was stuck in the middle. Then the rider ahead jerked his hand three times toward the verge, braking as he did, forcing Sky to do the same.

You bloody idiot, Sky thought. But he had little choice, following onto the patch of gravel that separated the road from an almost vertical rock face. The three pulled up, engines were turned off, bikes lifted onto their kickstands. Sky had his helmet off in a second. "What are you playing at?" he yelled.

Giancarlo had a big leather jacket on, all chains and studs. He sat on his bike but facing backward, a smile twisting in mockery, mouthing something.

"What are you saying?"

The reply came from behind him. "He says you ride like an old woman. And you do."

Sky turned. Jacqui was walking toward him, her

arms wrapped round herself. "Oh, what, and you're the Corsican chapter of the Hell's Angels?"

She stared at him. "You should go," she said.

"I was trying to."

She shook her head. "Go. From Corsica."

"I will, don't you worry. There's just something I have to do first."

"What something?" Fear showed for just a moment in her dark eyes.

"Nothing to do with you."

"It is!" she shouted. "I know why you are here, Marcaggi. I know why you hunt with the bald one. I know what it is you try to learn."

"You do?"

"She has told you, yes? About Jour des Morts? About what happens then?"

"The initiation? Yes, she told me." He glanced behind him. Giancarlo was still sitting on his bike, still glaring. He looked back. "Do you become a full Mazzeri that night?"

She nodded. "But she tell you something else also, the bald one? About that night?"

He couldn't keep the knowledge from his eyes. Suddenly she was shouting, "You go, English boy. I ask you before. I tell you now . . . now you know. You must leave Corsica."

"I can't," he replied. "Not yet. There's something I have to do first."

She stared at him for a long moment. Then she

jerked her head. Not at him. Past him. He heard movement and turned. Giancarlo had left his bike and was walking toward them.

"I tell him," she said, not moving.

"What?" Sky asked. Giancarlo had stopped a few feet away, and now Sky could see his eyes clearly. They weren't friendly. "You told him what I saw in the hunt?"

"No. I told him you touched me . . . here." She brushed her hand over her left breast.

"You did what?" he said, just as Giancarlo ran toward him, both hands reaching for the front of Sky's jacket.

It was a mistake. Moving and changing schools every couple of years as he did, Sky had had to fight in every new playground he went into. He'd learned fast, especially when his attackers were usually taller and older than him, as Giancarlo was by two inches and probably as many years. Lesson one: don't wrestle with the bigger boys.

Sky ducked fast, twisted to the side. Then he punched him—short, sharp—in the stomach and stepped away.

Giancarlo bent, winded for a moment. But Sky knew he was going to come again. "Tell him you lied," he yelled at the girl.

"Tell me you will leave."

Her cousin came. Not reaching now but with one fist thrust before him, the other at his hip, some martial arts stance. Sky had studied a bit himself. Not much. But enough to recognize when someone else also hadn't studied enough.

Giancarlo kicked, his rear leg shooting forward, aimed at Sky's head. Sky swatted it aside, ducking toward the wall, then realized his mistake, darted back. He needed room, couldn't get pinned against rock. Giancarlo advanced in a flurry of blows, kicks, punches. Sky kept moving. One caught him on the shoulder and hurt, but he managed to dodge the others. He could see Giancarlo was tiring, and he waited till his breaths were coming in whoops. Then, instead of dodging away as he had been doing, he stepped quickly in. Another thing he'd learned in all those playgrounds was that if you caught someone on a bone with your fist, it bloody well hurt—you as much as him. You could even break something. So instead, he used the butt of his hand and hit Giancarlo hard on the point of his chin.

He went down, onto the gravel, sprawled there, stunned. Sky stepped away, turned to the girl, shouted, "Can we stop this now, please?"

She was biting her lip, and Sky saw something different in her eyes now—a sort of desperation. One he recognized. "Please," he said, more quietly. "Can't we work this out?"

She was about to speak, when her eyes went past him, then widened in fear. *"Non!"* she screamed. *"Giancarlo, non! Arrête! Arrête!"*

Sky looked back. Her cousin was rising off the ground. In his right hand was a knife.

"*Arrête!*" she cried again, but he wouldn't stop, came forward now with the knife thrust out before him. And there was nothing clumsy about him now. The man knew how to handle a blade.

"*Tante,*" the man jeered, flicking the knife up as if beckoning Sky onto it. Instead, he stumbled back, away, hands feebly thrust out. Giancarlo was driving him toward the rock face, and Sky was almost mesmerized by the knife.

Then something changed—and it was the blade that changed it, the way the sunlight caught it. In the gleam, Sky saw other weapons, ax blades and spearheads. Saw Bjørn, his ancestor, and remembered his way with killing. No! Not remembered . . . felt it, the stirring inside, like an animal gnawing its way through a bone cage. It was the price he'd paid for going back. Once you became your ancestor, your ancestor was always there somewhere, like a switch flicked on that could never be turned off. And for one tiny moment he was frightened. Not for himself. For the man before him. Because Bjørn-in-Sky was about to take the knife from Giancarlo and slit his throat.

"Come on." Sky smiled, halting, letting the man approach, his hands easy at his side, a growl rising from somewhere deep, up into his throat. "Come on, then."

Then Jacqui was there, hurling herself onto Giancarlo. "Go," she screamed, her hands wrapped around his knife hand.

106

He nearly didn't. Nearly took the blade and slaughtered them both. But then the growl faded back, the burrowing retreated, and Sky was moving fast to his bike. It didn't start the first time he twisted the key, did the second. He had it off the stand before he looked back. Somehow she had twisted the knife free; now she threw it, and it skittered twenty yards down the road. With a yelp of rage, her cousin went after it.

"Go," she cried. "Leave. Never come back."

Giancarlo had reached the knife. "No," Sky replied. "Not yet."

"Then you will die. If you are here on the night of the Dead, you will join them."

He watched the man bend, scoop the blade up, turn back, rage on his face. Still, Sky held the engine back. "How do you know?" he said.

"Because I will kill you," she said. "I will kill you, in a world where I can never be punished for my deed. A Corsican world that is mine. Mine! Not yours, Englishman. I will kill you, for my blood. And for all the lives your family took . . . Marcaggi!"

He felt something stirring within him, deep, deep down. Not Bjørn, this time. Other secrets. Different blood.

"Not if I kill you first . . . Farcese!" he said in a voice that didn't sound like his own.

Giancarlo ran at him, was just five yards away when Sky gunned the throttle. The bike rose briefly onto its back wheel, then took off.

There was no time to put on his helmet, which

bounced on his handlebars. Anyway, the wind felt good, better the faster he went. He wanted to get as far away as possible, as swiftly as he could, both from the knifeman, from her . . . and from the feeling that had burst up from some hidden place within when she'd challenged him.

No helmet also meant he could hear better. So when he craned around to see what the buzzing was, he saw the scooter was still over a hundred yards behind him. Not so far, though, that he could not tell who rode it.

He pulled hard on the handgrip throttle, pumping more gas into the carburetor, driving up the revs. He'd been going fast anyway, and now he flew, leaning into the bends, stretching forward. But even as he did, he knew that it would probably not be enough. His bike was rented, overused, last year's model, while his pursuer clearly treasured his machine. It showed in the gleam of polished chrome, the perfectly pitched whine of the engine.

Closer, closer it came. He used his mirror now in swift glances, not daring to look away from the swerves in the road. What had been a black spot in one corner began to fill it all, growing bigger, more monstrous each time a bend or dip took it briefly away. When Sky thought the man must be almost on top of his rear wheel, he did look back.

The mirror had made him look closer than he was. Still, he was close enough for Sky to see the knife clutched in Giancarlo's teeth.

The two bikes took a right corner almost together, Sky leaning so far over that he thought he would spill. Almost immediately another bend followed, a left one, Giancarlo accelerating through it, bringing his bike alongside. But the bend was sharp, Sky overcompensated, came across hard, forcing the other bike to go wide or collide. Side by side they rounded the corner, came upright . . . and saw, simultaneously, the huge truck almost in the center of the road ahead.

They split, Sky going wide right, Giancarlo forced left. The truck's horn blasted as they swept toward it, each missing it by a fraction, both crunching onto the verges on each side of the road. Then Sky lost sight of his pursuer, could think of nothing but keeping his bike upright on the gravel. The rear tire slid; he threw his weight the other way, too far, felt the front tire slipping, jerked back. Dust exploded around him, rubber shrieked, but somehow he was still upright at the end of the skid. Upright and moving forward again.

109

Sky heard the truck's heavy brakes squealing protest as they were slammed on, a glance in the mirror showing walls of dust as the heavy tires bit down. For a moment that was all he saw. And then, exploding like flame from a furnace, shot Giancarlo's silver machine.

He couldn't slow down. Sky's hand was locked on the throttle, pulling it as wide as it would go, dropping only to accelerate through the gears. Once again the roar built behind him, Giancarlo getting closer, closer, until both of them were leaning and dipping into the bends as if they were in some synchronized sport. It was like exhilarating teamwork . . . except for the dagger clamped between one rider's teeth.

Wheel to wheel they took a left bend, its sharpness forcing them both to slow, Sky leaning so far over that he could see the twin gleams, at the mouth, in the eyes, these holding his gaze with their fanaticism, their certainty. And maybe because Sky blinked first, looked back to the road, he saw it all a half second earlier—the roadworks whose signs they must have missed.

Fifty yards off, less, no distance, on top of them, the left side of the road dug up, orange cones marking the one remaining lane. The traffic light directing them turned red; the last car had just gone through when Sky slammed on his brakes and skidded to the side. Then, as Giancarlo came past, Sky kicked his rear tire. It was a glancing blow, not much. Just enough.

There was a wobble, a moment as both Sky and Giancarlo wrestled for control of their machines. Sky won. Giancarlo, caught between his speed and an orange cone, lost.

The silver bike slipped from under him. In a heartbeat, Giancarlo was lying on his back, following his machine as both slid, cones scattering like bowling pins, bouncing ahead and behind. At one point, both man and bike stood up, as if he was about to remount in some brilliant piece of stunt work. Then down they both went again, over and over, rolling, sliding, the bike finally brought up sharp, with a shriek of impacted metal, by a dump truck; the man slowed by a wooden fence, halted at last when he thumped into a pile of sand.

Sky jerked the bike onto its stand, then ran, the first of many people who poured out of the cars lined up for the light and down from the cabs of diggers and lifters.

Giancarlo was stretched upon the sand, his arms flung wide. The leather jacket was shredded but had kept most of the skin on his back. Most. Lucky in that, not so in his right leg, bent up at a ridiculous angle under his body.

Right leg, Sky thought, remembering the blow he'd struck during the hunt. Giancarlo's eyes were wide, startled by pain. Sky looked into them. And just as he'd seen this man in a boar's eyes, so now, for the briefest of moments, he saw the beast within the man's.

A crowd had swiftly gathered. One man yelling, *"Médecin! Médecin!"* was shoving his way through. In the distance, Sky could hear the whine of another bike approaching. And so he slipped away to his scooter. He hadn't switched off his engine, so all he had to do was lift it off its stand and ride off along the line of cars.

CHAPTER TEN

STONES

WITHAIN, he thought. Really, where the hell *was* he now? At a dot on a map called Cauria. At a place where no one came, except in summer perhaps and only then in a tourist bus that would stop for a photo op and depart fast. Why would anyone linger here, even when the sun was high and there were dozens of people around you clicking cameras? Even when a chill wind wasn't blowing hard through pine trees that turned it to voices, when the air wasn't rich with the rain about to fall again and the only shelter to be found was inside a tomb?

He studied the six great slabs of granite that his guidebook told him was the dolmen, the burial place of some long-dead chieftain. Apparently, it was known locally as the Devil's Forge, which was hardly comforting. He could see why, though, or feel why anyway. Maybe it was the day, that wind, the cold . . . the isolation! But the place felt most peculiar.

He sighed. He wasn't even at his destination! That, a blue sign told him, was still two hundred meters away, over the top of a hill. He glanced back the way he had come. The little parking area below at least had a bench with a sloping roof above it, a board with a brief history of the place. Words. Some of them even in English. He could go back there, eat something, wait.

For what? A tour guide? Sod it, he thought. I'm here now. Might as well check it out. Hoisting his pack, he followed the arrow.

He stepped over the crest, and there they were— standing stones, facing him in granite ranks. He took a deep breath and smelled iron. Not the metal . . . the iron taint of blood. It was only there for a second; then it was gone again, replaced by the ever-present scent of the maquis, now overlaid with rain.

He shivered, closed his eyes for a moment. When he opened them, it seemed that the standing stones had stepped closer. He took a pace back. None of the stones were taller than him, nor much wider, yet he still felt dwarfed, shrunken.

He counted them. Twenty-two stones, all roughly the height of a man, all carved from the same gray granite.

Twenty-two sounded familiar. Then he had it. Two soccer teams.

"England versus France, Three—Zip," he laughed, tried to laugh, said it out loud anyway.

He shivered, looked away, then swiftly back. Had

they moved again? Only two of them actually had faces, of sorts, hollows for eye sockets, a ridge for a nose, a gash of a mouth. One was clearly the one he'd seen on the calendar in the library. And, of course, in a vision. Taking a deep breath, Sky moved a few feet closer to it. "Are you the captain, then?" he asked, though his voice came out no bolder.

This is ridiculous, he thought. What if someone sees me talking to the statues? They'd think I was mad.

Then he had a worse thought: What if one of them answers?

His eyes traced the shapes carved into the captain's rock. There was the rough-hewn face. There was the shape that had actually drawn him there, the spear of *Isa*.

It wasn't, really. He'd never read about runes being used on Corsica. It wasn't a part of their history, even if some Vikings must have raided these shores. And anyway, these standing stones were from the Mega-lithic Age, preceding the first rune by probably two thousand years. Yet somehow, Sky felt, the idea was the same. Someone had carved shapes into stone, shapes that meant something.

"Runes," he muttered. He'd studied them over the summer, tried to become fluent with this extraordi-nary power that had come into his life. He'd read about them in books, on the Internet, slept with them under his pillow, clutched them under trees, meditated on each rune's many meanings. But in the end he'd chosen to put them aside, for they'd been Sigurd's tools; his grandfather had controlled him through them—and you didn't fight a man with his own weapons. He'd buried the runestones, denying them to his enemy—and to himself. Yet now he needed them again. No, not them. Not Sigurd's. He needed his own. And the first one was here before him.

"Isa," he said aloud, "rune of quest. Of challenges taken head-on."

He heard the rain returning before the first drops hit him, a sheet of it sweeping over the maquis. He tilted his face to receive it, seeing *Isa* as if it were a burning figure behind his closed eyes. It *was* a spear— Gungnir, Odin's mighty weapon that never missed its mark. But it wasn't just for killing, he recalled—it was for something else too.

He watched the spear behind his eye change, the iron tip dissolving into the shaft, transforming into a stout stick, a staff to lean on, to help you over the toughest terrain. And it did not stop there; the shape shift continued, curled and solidified into a shepherd's crook. A weapon sometimes, when necessary, to fight off the wild beasts that would prey on the flocks. Usually, though, it was just a tool.

His tool, not Sigurd's.

He let the rain continue to fall on him for a minute, slowly washing the vision away. When it was gone, he turned from the stones without looking at them again. He had what he needed from them, had confirmed what he'd seen in the library. The first rune, *Isa*, the challenge. The others he would find ahead, in the land beyond the stones that his map told him was uninhabited and threaded through with streams.

Hoisting his backpack, Sky walked toward the granite cliff that loomed on one side of the site, the opposite way from the road and his scooter, now hidden beneath a tree and a pile of slashed pine branches. Beyond a broken fence and the last remnants of human life, both ancient and modern, the paths got narrower, as if their main traffic was animal, not human. The maquis pressed in, snagging his thick hiking socks below his jeans, pricking through to his skin. The climb was steep, and, despite the cool rain, he was sweating by the time he reached the sheer cliff.

There was just enough open space to walk along it, one hand pressed into the stone. He chose the left-hand path and soon came to a rent in the rock face, a gash blocked by rubble and a few hardy shrubs. It looked like a tunnel, and there was light at the end of it. Having no clearer idea of where to go, he scrambled up over the fallen rocks and entered.

It wasn't truly a tunnel; the rock did not grow together above, but it narrowed enough to block out most light, and he had to bend his arms to touch both walls. He thought he heard something slithering away in the darkness, wondered if he could remember anything about scorpions or snakes in the guidebook. But, swallowing, he kept going until the walls started to separate.

He emerged into light. It had stopped raining. He stood, staring at what had opened before him. The granite cliff he'd just come through was a screen. Beyond it a valley lay, widening fast from his feet, spreading out to other peaks in the distance.

That's where I need to go, he thought. To the high country. The mountains, as they had in Norway, stirred something deep, something ancestral within his blood . . . and yet he couldn't get his feet to move. He looked down at them, at the one still in the shadows of the tunnel, and the other in the sun of the valley. He was straddling both worlds, needed just the one step to leave one behind, move into the other. Behind him, the path led, eventually, home. To his old, normal life. It waited there, could be reached with a simple, single turn of the foot.

He nearly turned. Didn't. Couldn't. Because what was there for him? His parents, yes. But normal life? That was no longer possible. That had ended when a sack of runestones dropped from a secret compartment in a sea chest and his grandfather's Fetch had come to call—and then stolen his cousin's life. If he went back, Sky would have no choice. He didn't know enough to beat Sigurd; he'd have to join him. Them.

Sky shifted his weight. He was equally balanced between his two feet, between two worlds. Ahead lay uncertainty and solitude. Behind lay family . . . and someone else making all the decisions.

"England Three, France Zip," he said, and took a step toward the unknowable. All that was clear was the

117

runestone in his head, the first one he would carve, the only one he knew so far. His rune, not Sigurd's.

Isa. Rune of the quest.

The climb was steep and ever upward, mainly along narrow, twisting goat paths. He passed groups of stunted pines after an hour, the last hope of shelter from the cold rain that came, soaked him, and went. Then the last of the trees were left behind and grassland began to take over. After another hour, as he got ever closer to the peaks, he could see that even this vast green sea ended, surrendering to granite.

And then he saw it. And the feeling of déjà vu that had never left him from the moment he smelled blood at the standing stones, that had not faded in seconds as it always had in his past but had grown with every step he took along the paths up the valley, now doubled.

A stone fold thrust out from the rock face, looking like one side of a long tent. Yet this tent's fabric was not canvas but one solid piece of rock, hollowed out of a granite outcrop by a billion years' worth of wind and rain thrown against it by some strange thrust of the landscape, some caprice of current. It was strange enough in itself, like something a dwarf would have carved in a fantasy tale. But its strangeness only increased when he looked at the rest of it.

The long front and sides of the rock tent were filled in with irregular blocks, roughly trimmed and bound together with mortar. Someone had made use of the overhang, raising walls to meet it. There was an open square halfway up the side wall nearest him, a type of small window. Almost directly below that was an open rectangle, with a rough wood-slat door wedged into it.

He was looking at a house.

"Hello?" Sky called, his cry immediately taken and shredded by the wind. "Anyone there?" he cried, louder.

There was almost a staircase leading up to the entrance, though whether man or nature had made it he couldn't tell. He climbed it, paused at the top, called again. "Hello?" This time he thought he was answered, stepped back in fear. But it was only another quirk of wind and rock, an echo. Breathing deeply, he pushed. The door gave.

The stench! It engulfed him, excrement and urine and sodden wool. He had trodden on goat droppings all the way up, had read that goatherds still used these uplands for their flocks in the summer. But the reek here was as much human as animal, had him thrusting a sleeve across his face, gagging. Then, just as quickly as it had come, the smell vanished. He sniffed cautiously. Nothing! Or rather just the faintest trace of mold perhaps. Dust. Of a place not recently occupied.

He lowered his arm. It was the weirdest feeling. It was like he'd just had a . . . a nasal déjà vu.

It took a moment for his eyes to adjust to the poor

light. Then he saw he was standing at the end of one long room. Stalls, made of woven wood, divided up the front part of it. He moved down the passage between them, to a slightly larger area. The wall opposite the entranceway was granite, as was the long one at the back. Both were actually part of the cliff face, like the curving roof, while the other two walls were made of the mortar blocks. Half man-made, half natural, then—part house, part cave.

On the floor was a circle of stones—a fire pit. He looked up to see a beam of light entering from a hole in the roof—the chimney.

He looked around. There was nothing to show whether it had been deserted an hour or a hundred years before.

He turned to the inner wall, the cliff face. Squinted. There was something there. Dropping the pack off his shoulder, he reached inside for his flashlight, flicked it on, trained the beam onto stone.

There were carvings all over it. Graffiti, Corsican words. A rough sketch of a man doing something illegal with a goat. Slashes, some sort of calendar perhaps, as if a prisoner were keeping track of the days. They all looked relatively modern—within the last fifty years, maybe. But there were fainter marks beneath, obviously older. He moved closer.

He saw a chestnut tree. About two feet high, it had been traced in extraordinary detail, down to the furred fruit pods on its boughs. It rose from a sea of carved maquis, the various plants clear within it, the lavender distinct from the myrtle, the rosemary from the thyme.

Whoever had done that work was quite the artist. But there couldn't have been much else to do up here, tending the goat herds for the long grazing season— unless you followed the other artist's example! He supposed there was time for art.

Then he noticed something else. It rose from the maquis below the tree, like a mast on a ship. It was a shepherd's crook, the ram's-horn handle curling out of the staff. It was similar to the vision he'd had at the standing stones.

"*Isa,*" Sky murmured. "There you are again."

He peered closer. Someone other than the artist had defaced part of the beautiful engraving. But the crook seemed to be rising from some sort of box, half concealed by the shrubs. A strange sort of box, it had curved runners on it. A sled? No.

"A cradle," he said, tracing his finger along its blurred edges. Seemed a very odd thing to draw in a remote cave. Some old shepherd missing his grandkids?

He glanced around. The place may have had an earthen floor and little in the way of comforts, but the rune confirmed it: this was where he was meant to be.

He unrolled his sleeping mat and bag, bent to place them alongside the inner wall. As he did, he noticed something else there, a deeper darkness just above where he planned to lay his head. The flashlight showed

121

him an indentation in the rock, almost square in shape. It sank to quite a depth.

It's like a cupboard, he thought. I'll keep my food in there.

Something glimmered in its depths. Reaching down, he was surprised that he had to turn sideways, had to thrust his whole arm in before he touched the bottom. He felt along; his fingers grazed something. He half lifted it before it slipped away with a faint tinkle. He reached again, stretching, his fingers finally wrapping round . . .

The shock surged along his arm, threw him backward. He landed hard, his back thumping against the masonry of the cave's outer wall, and he crumpled beneath it, his breath sucked away by the force and by what felt like an electric shock. Yet what had thrown him he still clutched in his right hand, his fingers clamped around it and immovable, as if it was welded there. Not by heat, though, as a rune-stone had once clung to him. This was the binding of ice.

At first he thought he was clutching an icicle, so chill did it feel. It had the same shape, tapering to a fine point, was nearly as white as ice. But what he clutched was stone, not frozen water, though light passed through it.

Something was moving within it; shadows, slowly resolving into form. Shapes, two of them, joined, parting, only to join again, almost merge into one . . . then separate, one falling away into darkness, the other dissolving into white. The light departed, stone returned to stone.

Sky let it slip from his hand. He had held objects before that had shown him visions of what had been, what might yet be. Runestones themselves were compressed energy awaiting release; his grandfather's lighter too, bringing him to this island with its flashes. Just as humans retained something of everything they'd been through, so did objects. A recording, like the digital writings of a CD, needing the right method to release the information again.

Bjørn's ax, Death Claw, had retained the memory of every enemy killed, a life force captured and held in its shining steel planes. But Death Claw had been a weapon; those who had fallen to it had fallen in battle, in honorable combat.

123

And though the images he'd just seen were vague, unclear, of one thing Sky felt absolutely certain. This rock was an implement of murder.

He picked it up again. No form shifted now inside it. Nothing flashed. It was just a cylinder of stone again. Some kind of quartz, he thought.

He took it over to the cliff face. On a blank piece of rock, he pressed the point in. It took hardly any force to score the granite with the single line of *Isa*. In that moment he saw how all the carvings, over all the years, had been made.

He hadn't known quite how he was going to

carve himself a new set of runestones. Now he did. Even if the tool he would use had once been dipped in blood.

No, he thought, *because* it was once dipped in blood.

CHAPTER ELEVEN

THE RUNES OF RETURN

The sun was just setting when Sky returned to the cave. It was the latest of many trips he'd taken over the five days he'd been there, several to gather firewood, the last and longest in search of stones. He'd frozen his ankles in three streambeds, taking his time. Not because he was searching for the perfect set—there was no such thing; they didn't need to be utterly uniform, could have slight variations in shape and shade of gray. And he didn't have to linger over each one sensing vibrations. For now, they were merely stones. It was what he did with them that would transform them into . . . something else.

He knew he could have chosen the stones more quickly, begun the quest that *Isa* promised almost immediately. But after all he'd already been through in his brief time in Corsica—and after all that had gone before it in England—it felt so good to just . . . chill! Even now he hesitated crossing the threshold, sought some other delay. For once he was inside, once he closed the door, there would be no choice. He'd have to begin. He'd have to try to send himself back in time.

And he didn't have a bloody clue how to do it!

Taking a deep breath, he went in, walked past the stalls to the rear, stared at the area before the fire pit where it was all going to happen. It was not quite true, of course. He did have some clue.

"It's not like I haven't done it before," he said aloud. The speaking made him smile. He'd begun to talk to himself already. He understood now why so many old people wandered the streets muttering. He saw himself doing the same thing.

"Probably before I'm twenty," he muttered.

The grin faded. He *had* time-traveled, entered the body of an ancestor, lived as Bjørn for a while. But he had done very little for himself. It was Sigurd's runecast he'd followed, Sigurd's runestones he'd used. Even when he thought he was acting on his own, his grandfather had controlled everything. Only once before had he carved runes himself, in the graveyard in England when he'd sent the draug Bjørn had become— another victim of Sigurd's schemes—to his rest.

"I sent someone else back. I didn't go myself."

He sighed. There was one other thing he'd used in his travels—his caul, the skin that had covered his face at birth, that his mother had pulled off and saved because it marked him out as someone special.

He didn't feel very special. And he didn't think he should use the caul, though it was still in its leather pouch, tucked in his backpack. It was the skin that had joined him to his mother in the womb. Through her, it linked him to everyone who had gone before her. It might help him travel, but he'd be plunged back through *her* bloodline. Where Sigurd waited.

He'd come to Corsica seeking other secrets, in different blood. He picked up his other grandfather's lighter and thought again of the visions he'd seen when he'd held it that first time. He'd met the bald singer, wailing her lament. He'd found the standing stones, though what the wolf meant he had no idea. Wolves had been hunted to extinction in Corsica centuries before, he'd read. And as for the dying lynx . . .

He shivered. It was cold, and he had a practical use for this inheritance—he could use it to light the fire he'd already laid. He opened the arm and flicked the wheel, swiftly igniting the smaller kindling. Flames licked at the dry branches of the dead chestnut he'd found. It spat and he flinched as an ember shot by his face. Then the flames settled, brought a growing warmth and light, brightening the immediate area around the fire pit, reducing the rest of the dwelling to shadow, a cave of light within a cave of darkness. He stared into the flames for a while, watched little worlds catch, brighten for a brief moment, then collapse. A log split in two in a shower of sparks, its sharp crack stirring him. "Here goes," he said, and reached for the leather pouch he'd bought, now filled with the stones he'd collected.

He'd always used a cloth before. But then he had cast on floors—on surfaces that had chemicals, paint or polish, across them. This floor was raw earth. The stones didn't need a screen here.

He tipped them from the bag. Twenty-four lay before him. Nearly identical, same size and shade—each a granite round that would fit snugly into the valley of his palm. He needed five, because five made up the runecast he'd worked through before, the one he understood best. He passed his right hand over them, then pressed down, his fingers spread, felt them grow warm under his hand. He knew it was his flesh doing that; they had no life yet. They were waiting for him to bring that.

The ritual began with a simple request.

"Odin," he called, "All-Father. Guide me now."

They weren't sophisticated, his ancestors whose tools these were. They were a practical people who required practical solutions. Even in magic, which to them was just another way of approaching life's challenges.

So the ritual had to continue with a simple question. Like all simple things, it had been hard to fix upon. He'd thought about it for five days as he wandered the peaks and waded in streams. He'd wondered if it should be about Kristin, his plan to go back and free her. But that was too complicated, too bound up in other things. It was his ultimate destination, but the path to it had first to be made clear.

Within all the darkness he'd encountered so far on the island—the Squadron come to collect their dead, the Dream Hunters pursuing those marked to die—there had been only one hint of light, of life—the Mazzeri Salvatore. Those who had once salved. The Healers, their healing art lost to man, just as Kristin was lost to him.

The stones were warm. He whispered his request. "How do I recover what is lost?"

He felt something pulse under his palm. He lifted the stone that spoke to him, placed it on the large flat rock he'd brought in for the purpose. Then he drew the white quartz chisel from his pocket. He held the stone between two fingers of his left hand, brought the ice crystal's sharpened point down. Slowly he carved a single line from bottom to top, letting the words come, chanting as he cut.

Isa

Ice spear

Melting

Blade becomes staff

Weaponless

We advance

To the challenge

He sat back, lifting the stone, turning its fresh-scored surface to the firelight. It was right that it was the first one. It was the rune he'd seen from the beginning, on the bench before the hostel, on the calendar in the library. It had brought him to the standing stones of Cauria, and here, beyond them. And it was in this cave too, beautifully incised on the wall facing him.

Isa. Odin's spear, but here transformed into a staff, a shepherd's crook. A tool to be leaned on, used. But not for killing. "There is aid in this challenge," Sky murmured. And he set the stone down beside him.

He reached again. Felt a surge of energy, lifted and placed the stone. He didn't think, just spoke, just acted. His blade fell upon the rock, slashing:

Berkana

Birch and birth

Atonement

For the crime

Suffering

To survive

Redemption awaits

Sky sat back, stared at what he'd created. It was a "B," for *Berkana,* the birch tree. And he knew that atonement was what it meant. He looked again at the tool he was using, remembered again the feeling he'd had when he'd first held it, the blood trapped within the white. There was no doubt—it had been used for murder. Was that the crime that must be atoned for before he could get what he wanted? Or was it his grandfather's crimes? Or even his own?

He set it beside the other. A runecast was an unfolding story. He only had the first part of it before him. He had three stones yet to cut.

Another surge, another stone, another image, this almost as simple to cut as *Isa*.

Gebo

A gift

But to receive

You must give

To gain

You must lose

Knowledge is loss

An "X" marked the stone he laid down, like a kiss at the end of a written message.

"*Gebo*," he said. "Gift."

From his reading, Sky knew *Gebo* to be a positive rune. Who didn't like receiving gifts? Yet his incantation talked of loss.

Of course! Rune magic always implied sacrifice of some kind. To gain, he must lose. But what?

Sky shivered. Explanations had to wait for the whole cast. Each runestone lived in relation to the others. He only had a part of the story so far.

He placed the stone beside the ones already cut. There were two more to find.

He reached, placed, laid quartz to granite again.

Kenaz

Burning clean

Purified by flame

A torch lit

Passed on

The Initiate

Transformed

Two more simple cuts, a "V" on its side.

"Kenaz," he said again. The firebrand. The torch. When humanity lived in caves like the one he was in now, it was fire that separated them from the beasts outside, that raised them up. When you passed the torch on, you passed the ability to banish darkness. To illuminate the world.

It was knowledge Sky saw there. He was the initiate, and Pascaline had promised to teach him how to leave his body, "as easy as breathing out." But the price she demanded for that "gift" was another murder.

He shuddered, looked again at the other runes. They were all linked—the gift of *Gebo,* the atonement of *Berkana.* Now *Kenaz,* the fire that burns clean. Wasn't that atonement too? Being purified made you ready for initiation. Ready to receive the torch.

He stared down at the stones, those as yet unmarked. One of them would bear the final rune of the cast. One of them would complete the story that would take him on the next stage of the journey—or leave him to despair.

His hand was so tight on the chisel now it hurt, but he couldn't release it. Not now, not when he was so close. He looked into the fire pit. The flames had softened, their light had retreated. He was back in the dark.

But not alone. Something was guiding him still.

His other hand rose, hovered over the stones, swooped, like the hawk he'd once been swooped on prey. His chisel fell.

132

"*Naudhiz,*" he cried.

Two more slashes—straight down, diagonally across. Simple.

There was nothing simple about it.

Naudhiz
Rune of All Need
All conquering
Glory's rush
Harness the force
Channel the power
To destiny

Sky didn't know how he was standing. Couldn't remember snatching up the runestone he now clutched in his left hand, as tightly as he held the ice stone in his right. He didn't need to unclench his grip; he could feel the rune's two slashes imprinting themselves on his flesh as if they burned. The straight line down. The diagonal slash bisecting it at the top. It was the rune that brought the rest together, fusing them in the power the whole runecast contained. The cross of *Naudhiz* echoed the cross of *Gebo,* though *Naudhiz* was more a crucifix, with the sacrifice that implied. It was also *Kenaz's* flame harnessed, *Berkana's* atonement justified. It was the straight line of *Isa,* crossed with the power to meet the challenge.

It was his destiny Sky held in his right hand, the end of the tale written here in stone. Stone was the key, stone everywhere on this granite island. Standing at this valley's end, twenty-two sentinels guarded a dead king. Ahead of him now, in intricate carvings on

133

a wall, was *Isa,* his challenge. Carved there—and of this he now had no doubt—by the same stone he gripped so tightly in his right hand. The murderer's tool.

Yet Sky discovered, as he pressed his face into the very heart of the challenge, that stone was not as hard as he'd always believed it to be. That even it would soften, would yield to the rush of destiny. To his face pushing through it, dissolving into it . . .

It had happened each time he'd gone back into an ancestor's body—a moment of consciousness before Sky dissolved. But this time he was still outside somehow, floating, sinking slowly down. There was stone again, but blocks of it, shaped by human hands.

In the cellar, haunches of meat hung from the ceiling. Huge barrels stood on the floor. The remnants of a fire glowed in a small hearth. And near that, but pressed against the rear wall, lay a body. Sky began to accelerate toward it, to merge into the sleeper's form. It was as easy as pressing through rock, to slip inside.

Yet when that final moment of consciousness came, Sky's last thought wasn't to wonder why he was becoming a woman. It was to wonder why that woman was chained to the wall.

CHAPTER TWELVE

TZA

She was used to spirits moving within her. But this one felt different from the moment he—she was certain it was a male spirit—entered her. Perhaps it was to do with the moon, still a day off its zenith but a powerful pull anyway. When she opened her eyes, there was a touch of him still, lingering in the ember glow. Beyond it.

Tza blinked . . . and whoever had been there was gone. She was alone, as always, dawn's light filtering through the cracks in the flooring above. She turned . . . and cried out in pain. She'd managed to twist over in the night, and her right arm was stretched above her and at a bad angle. It felt like it had no blood in it, but that was not true. She could see blood at the wrist where the iron links had cut into her.

She had told him they were too tight! And that there was no need for the precaution, with the moon still a day off full. But he had insisted, commanded, daring her to contradict him one more time. She had smelled the brandy on his breath when she'd arrived at the house the previous noon. She would have enough pain in the night without his further attentions.

"Papa," she called. "Papa!"

A grunt came from above, a slight stirring, as of someone rolling over in bed—then nothing. "Papa!" she shouted, much louder, and this time there was some muttering, a thump on the floor, dragging foot-steps, a series of slurred curses. There was a jangle of keys, a lock screeching open, then a rectangle of light as the trapdoor was lifted.

"Shut up! What do you want?"

Tza couldn't see his face; he was just a black shape silhouetted against the light. "It is dawn, Father."

The shape turned away. "Dawn?" came the mutter. "You dare to wake me . . . so early!" The trapdoor began to lower. "Let me rest."

"Father!" she yelled, desperate. "The chains! They hurt."

The door paused, then lifted again. "Damn girl," he said, then began to descend the steep stair. He missed his footing, slipped the last few steps, bang-ing his heels. He cried out in pain, cursed them, cursed her.

She could see him now. His eyes were filmy, streaked with red. White flecks lined his lips, bright contrast to the unshaven chin, the black, tangled hair.

136

He bent, but not because the roof was low. "Stupid girl," he muttered, rubbing a hand across his mouth. "Why do you not let me rest?"

"They hurt, Father," she said, raising her wrists to him, jangling the metal links. "Free me and I will leave. You can go back to sleep."

He squinted at her, then nodded at the shackles. "Well?" She shook her head and he grunted. "I was taking no chances." Swaying, he stared down for a long moment, his hand now pressed to his head as if trying to push something in. Finally he said, "I need to talk to you."

"Yes, Father, of course." She shook her wrists again. "After . . ."

"Later." There was a wine barrel to his left— empty, Tza was sure—and he staggered to it, sat heavily. "First, you listen."

She felt her quick rage coming, fought it back. It would gain her nothing except more pain. What she needed was to get free. Only obedience would get her that. Swallowing rage, she nodded. "Yes, Father."

He was staring at her again. "Tizzana," he finally said, and she looked at him more closely, alarmed. He was the only one who ever used her full name and only rarely, usually when he had something bad to say. He had named her for the town she was born in, Tizzano, when he'd moved there to develop the new olive press he'd invented. Like all his schemes, it had ended badly, the family chased back to Sartène by men who were owed money. She always thought that when he said her name, he was thinking of yet another failure.

"Tizzana," he repeated. "How old are you?"

She frowned. "I . . . I don't know, Father."

"Let me see. You were . . ." He scratched at his stubble, staring above her. "You were born the year of the early frost, when the olives died. And because they died, no one wanted my new press!" He glared at her. "No one."

His anger was always such a sudden spark. It had to be dampened, deflected. "And what year was that, Father?"

"Year? Hmm!" he grunted. "It is burned onto my heart. It was . . . 1568. 1569, I mean. 1569."

"And this year is . . . ?"

"You do not know the year, you dull child?"

She shook her head. She did not care about years. Only seasons.

He sighed. "It is 1583. So you are fourteen."

She hadn't known. It didn't seem so important a fact.

Yet it did to her father. "Good," he muttered. "Old enough." He got up, began to move to the stairs, as if she were no longer there.

"Father!" He turned, and she raised her chains to him. He didn't move toward her, and she had to keep him there. He could lose himself in a bottle, and she'd be there all day. "Old enough for what?"

"To be married," he said.

"What?" she gasped. Of all the things he could have said, none could have shocked her more. "Married? But if I am only fourteen . . ."

"What does that matter? Your mother was fourteen when I married her."

And she was scarce twenty when you buried her, she thought but didn't say. Tza had been five when her mother died. All she recalled was a woman bent double with drudgery and from having five children in six years—and losing two of them. Her mother had once been fourteen? It was impossible to think of the old crone Tza barely remembered as her own age.

Her father had stepped back. "Do you bleed?"

She looked away. "I do."

He grunted. "Then you are old enough."

"But . . ." She strained toward him. "Who would want to marry me?"

A smile came to her father's mouth, twisting it in unfamiliar lines. "Someone will. Emilio Farcese will."

Another gasp came. She did not know much about Sartène. When she was eight years old, her brother Franco had died. The eldest, Lugo, was already in a school in Genoa, for he was the favorite and destined to fulfill his father's dreams of scholarly success. Her elder sister, Miranda, was weak in the chest. So Tza had been sent to tend the goats, the family's one regular source of wealth. She lived in the mountains year-round now, even returning after the animals were brought down in October. A winter in her secret stone *oriu*—not even her family knew its location—was better than one spent with her father. But even she knew of the Farcese. And Emilio had been pointed out to her by a giggling Miranda on one of Tza's rare visits.

"Why would he want to marry a Marcaggi?"

It was a mistake to wonder this out loud. Her father swooped back, his bunched hand catching Tza hard on the ear. "The Marcaggi are a famous family—scholars, inventors, statesmen. It is an honor to be allied with them—even for the newly rich Farcese." He glared down at her; then something died in his anger, and he slumped once more onto the barrel. "And we have land that they want, just outside the town, land that links two parts of their estates. I will give it to them as your dowry. In return they will . . . help me with a plan I have." A gleam came into his eyes. "A new type of dam."

You're selling me, she thought but again didn't say. Instead, she did say, desperately, "But my herd, Father. I must return to it." She had come down to bring cheese and myrrh to sell at the great market. She only came to Sartène when she had to—and rarely this close to a full moon.

"You will return with a Farcese servant. He will manage all that now. The herd is another part of your dowry." He sniffed. "Marcaggi should not be goatherds anyway."

For the first time in a very long while, tears came to her. To give away Jezebel, Indiga, the old ram Crespo, and the rest? Her only friends? It was unthinkable, horrible. Tears were not natural to her. Anger was natural. She growled. "You cannot do this, Father. I will not—"

Another blow came. Because she was ready for it, she was able to turn her head, so his hand caught the top of her head. It hurt her . . . but it hurt him too. "You dare . . . dare . . . ," he shouted at her, rubbing his fingers. "You will do what I command you to do. You are my property, just like those goats you love so well. Mine to dispose of."

She wanted to snarl back. If she had her hands free, she'd have fought him. She was big for fourteen, and strong. In the mountains, she fought wolves for her herd, hunted and killed boar . . . and not just in her dreams. But she was still chained. So she said, "I am not the eldest. The Farcese will want Miranda." It gave her a surge of hope. Miranda with the weak chest, Miranda the pretty. She was a seamstress, a weaver . . .

"Miranda is dead."

The moment before, he'd been glaring down at her, readying himself for another blow. But saying this caused him to crumple. "Miranda is dead," he said again, whispering the name. "My sweet! My lovely!" Tears came and he made no effort to block them, let them run down into his whiskers. "A good daughter, sweet, kind, so pretty . . ." He sighed. "She was betrothed to Emilio. They were to be married in September. Then a cough came and . . ." He wiped the snot from his nose, pulled himself upright. "So they have agreed for you to take her place. My last daughter. My last . . ." He hid his face in his hands, sobbing.

She had no time for the tears of a drunkard. All she needed, for now, was to be free. And her chains reminded her of something else—an argument her father would be unable to deny. "But, Father," she said, "what about . . . ?"

He looked up, saw her raised hands, came over. From the chain of keys, he selected one, fitted it into the lock on her left wrist. It gave. "Sweet daughter. So pretty."

Tza knew he was still blubbering about the dead one. No one would call her pretty. And if she'd ever been sweet, that had ended when, on the first full moon after her first bleeding, she had discovered . . . "Father," she said quietly as he reached for the second lock, "you know I cannot marry." She lifted her wrist and, as the chain came off, shook it. "This is why."

His eyes had finally focused on her again, not on his dead. "Why? Because of a curse? This curse that struck you in the mountains?" He laughed, a laugh that was all bitterness. "Every family on this Devil-plagued island is cursed. Cursed when they were born here, to this world of pain." He lifted the shackles and waved them before her. "Besides, every husband has to get used to his wife being . . . special, once a month. Emilio Farcese will just have to get used to your particular specialness. And chain you up, just like I do!"

He laughed again, a grating, ghastly sound. Then

he stepped back. Tza rose quickly, moving away from him, putting a foot upon the stairs. He watched her preparation and made no move toward her. "Go on! Run, Tizzana. Take to the maquis, live on roots in your cave. Bring ruin on the Marcaggi. Because you are contracted to marry a Farcese and if you do run, they get everything anyway. This house, our land, your beloved goats. Everything!" He bent, snatched up a bottle, pulled the cork out with his teeth, drank deep. "Everything!" he yelled, spraying wine.

His terrible laughter followed her as she bent, snatched up her hat, slingshot, and satchel, threw open the front door, and took off down the cobbled street.

She had not gone five paces before something warm and wet was thrust into her hand.

"Colombo," she cried joyfully, squeezing the dog's snout, stooping to throw her arms around its head. The vast pink tongue soaked her face in moments, little squeals erupting somewhere in that huge throat. The dog was at least part wolf, though with a coat that was a mix of black and red rather than gray. There was white in the muzzle, for he was as old as her, old for a mountain dog. He had helped her fight off many of his distant cousins to protect the herd in their years on the mountain. He had taken on boar, had scars and slashes in his thick coat to prove it. Old battles and age made the limbs move ever slower, but people still crossed the street to avoid getting too close to Colombo,

143

crossing themselves as they stared into his reddened eyes. Yet, after a night spent curled up outside the house where he knew his mistress was trapped, he was as loving and gentle as a puppy.

"Oh, Colombo!" She pressed her face into his furry neck, sniffed that sweet smell. She supposed he was another thing she would be required to give up if she married into the Farcese family.

If? Wine and brandy has rotted his brain, she thought as she strode off, Colombo a shadow at her heels, both of them careful to avoid the gutter of sewage filth that ran down the center of the cobbled street. No one would want to marry her, no matter her worth in land. She had been told many times that she was more animal than human—a joke she never appreciated. And even if this Emilio was undoubtedly the fourth or fifth son of the house—they would not waste an heir on a Marcaggi—as soon as he saw her, he would reject her. Any man would.

Her rapid pace had taken her into the town's main square. Since it was the day of the great market, people were already bustling across the cobbled space, setting up their stalls. To her right, she saw that the church doors were open, admitting those who sought blessing on their labors this day. She crossed to its steps. "Colombo, wait," she said, and the great hound settled right in the center of the staircase, causing more than one townsman to step hastily to the side.

She took off her thick-brimmed leather hat,

entered, bent at the knee, crossed herself. The altar was far in the distance, its rail crowded with supplicants. But there was a smaller chapel off to the side that, on the rare occasions that she'd been able to come there, Tza preferred. She moved up the east aisle. A small crowd was gathered where she wished to be, and mewling cries came from the center of it. A baptism was taking place, so she stood to the side, watching the weeping mother, supported on either side by black-garbed relatives. She presumed the sadness and the early hour meant that the child was due to die and its soul was being saved before it did.

Tza shrugged. It seemed a lot of fuss. On the mountains, if a baby goat was sickly, it was just put out, an offering for the wolves. Perhaps they should do the same with humans.

145

The crowd cleared. The baby had stopped crying, but the weeping had doubled. She moved forward, looking up at the statue of the Madonna. She had always liked this one because, unlike most, unlike the woman who had just left, she did not weep over the child in her arms. Did not seem to pay him much attention at all. He was just there. Like all children. There.

She glanced left. The font that the baptismal water had been drawn from had not had its heavy wooden cover replaced. Distracted from devotion, she stepped over, looked down . . .

There! The reason that no one, not even one

ordered to by his family, would marry her. Thick eyebrows joined above the nose, eyes recessed below them like holes in a rock face. Hair, the front hacked about with wool shears to get it out of the eyes, the rest bound tight with a goatskin strap, thick and black as the soot that lined her chimney hole. That nose, broken in a fall while chasing a stray. That mouth, thick, chewed lips curled in a permanent snarl. She tried to smile, but she looked like some malevolent creature about to leap from the water and rip someone's throat out. She shook her head and the reflection shook back.

"Married?" she said, turning from the vision. "*Pfa!*"

An old woman was approaching, a candle clutched in her gnarled fingers. She was about to take the space before the altar, so Tza stepped up quickly, shouldering her aside, and threw herself down to sprawl beneath the Madonna, her arms spread wide in imitation of the crucifix. She heard the old woman grumble, move away. But what did she care? She was there first. And what was the old hag going to do anyway? Pray for life? Tza's need was more urgent. Her prayer was for death.

Let death take Emilio Farcese and she wouldn't have to marry him!

The stone floor was freezing under her. She stayed there long enough to suffer, to offer that suffering for her prayer. At last she rose, lit a candle, then moved away.

The old woman stepped up, muttering. "Too late,"

146

Tza laughed, jerking her thumb at the Madonna. "She's all used up!"

She was still smiling at the shock in the old woman's eyes when she emerged from the church, into the already hot September sunshine. But the half smile vanished fast, for, at the bottom of the stairs, a group of youths had gathered around Colombo. They were jeering, jabbing booted feet into the black-red flanks. One of them had a stick and was poking it into the dog's chest.

The youth with the stick was Emilio Farcese.

Pulling the wide brim of her hat well over her face, she ran down the stairs. "Leave him be!" she shouted.

"Why should we? This Devil hound snarled at us good Christians as we were trying to go to church." Emilio hadn't removed his stick, so Tza did, taking the end, jerking it out of the young man's hand.

"Hey!" he cried, grabbing it back again. "Where does a goat boy get the balls to interfere with a Farcese?"

"Who says he tends goats?" one of the other youths laughed.

"The stench gives it away. *Pfa!*" Emilio turned and spat close to Tza's feet.

"Who says he's got balls?" said another, in a quieter tone, flicking his eyes downward.

All looked. In the struggle over the stick, Tza's loose jerkin had fallen open at the neck. She seized the lapels, pulled it to. "Come, Colombo," she said, tried to push through the circle. But a hand delayed her.

"So . . . a goat girl! The stink is just the same."

"Not just any girl, Emilio," said the boy holding her. "Do you not know who this is?"

Tza looked from the hand to a face dabbled with oozing spots, eyes that were partly crossed, teeth that jutted out at strange angles over the lips. And she knew him. "Let me pass, Filippi," she said.

He had once been a playmate, when she'd lived in the town and when there was still play. But now Filippi Cesare had other sport in mind. "And miss the chance to present my old neighbor to her new husband? What kind of friend would I be . . . to either of you—Tizzana Marcaggi?"

Tza looked from Filippi to Emilio, one face a complete contrast to the other. Emilio's skin was smooth, unblemished, of a color like the second pressing of the olive. The hair was blue-black, a thick wave of it worn long, bound back with a silken tie. The blue eyes were all the brighter for their dark setting, the teeth similarly sparkling, totally even. It was a handsome face, beautiful even, a model for marble—were it not contorted in a look of absolute horror.

Tza knew her misfortune of a face. But knowledge could not stop tears welling up for the second time that day. She broke away, running immediately, head bent so they would not see her weakness. She did not look back, but if she could not see them, there was no protection from their voices. *His* first.

"She even runs like a goat!"

"And you the ram, Emilio."

"At least the wind blows the other way."

"Perhaps she'll bathe on your wedding night."

The jibes and laughter faded with a turned corner, with her sobs.

There was a tower she would go to on the battlements if she was forced to be in the town overnight. Ruined, it was unpatrolled, its crumbled steps a deterrent to all but the most agile or desperate.

Closing her eyes, she turned her face to the breeze. Gregorio, the old Mazzeri whose flock was in the next valley, who had taught her many things, had taught her the names of the winds that swept their island: the Sirocco, bearing those scents of pure darkness, sweeping from Africa. The Mistral, the dry wind from Spain. The spice-laden Levante, rider from the east. The Grecale, borne over the seas from Lombardy, that had once brought their people to these shores, latest in a line of conquerors come and gone. But what stirred in her nostrils now, what cooled, at least a little, the heat of her running and her terrible shame, was the wind Gregorio named the Transmontane. It blew from the north, over their own snow-tipped mountains, from other mountains far beyond. It meant that summer was soon to pass. And this pleased her. In the spring, summer, and autumn she traversed the land with her goats, seeking forage, always tending, warding, breeding, birthing, raising, milking, shearing, combing the gum from the goat's beards as they foraged in the maquis, to be transformed into myrrh. It was all work. But the winter, the season heralded by the Transmontane, was hers. To sit in her *oriu,* safe in its stone walls, with only Colombo and sometimes Gregorio to talk to. To never worry, during the full moon, that she would be disturbed. To hunt the wild boar with her slingshot—by day, across the winter-held land; by night, in her dreams. Then to carve both her day and night visions upon the granite walls. She'd recently had one that would take her most of the winter. A chestnut tree in full fruit. Her shepherdess's crook rising from its core.

She reached into her satchel, pulled from it the stone she'd found only the last month. It was the perfect tool for what she envisioned, a sliver of pure white, a point of such sharpness it could be a dagger, with a blade that would never dull, even when she drove it again and again into granite.

She did so now, reaching out to the crumbling block of the battlement before her, lulling her as the carving always did. And then, in an instant, she slashed a line down the middle of the bush she'd begun, dropped the stone back into the pouch, leaned over the parapet.

Tears! Tears again! She'd become a weeping woman!

There would be no winter of glorious solitude. She would be here, in Sartène, walled up in the Farcese mansion, dressed in black, stitching needlepoint with their women, visited occasionally by her husband, drunk like her father no doubt. Drunk to overcome the horror that had been so clear on his face when he looked upon her. If the contract had been agreed, it was binding on them both; they could not defy it. It was the Corsican way. Perhaps it was the way the world over. Even in the lands where the Transmontane first blew.

A sound intruded into her despair. A clink, a jingle of harness, a snort. She rubbed her eyes to clear them of tears, scanned the ground before the walls. A horse appeared for a moment between two arbutus trees; she saw the rider's leg, the lower branches obscuring anything else. It was unusual to see anyone that high up above the town. The ways were steep. Besides, everyone, by law, had to enter Sartène through the main gate farther down the valley.

The next tower was a hundred paces down the slope. She had worried that the Genoese soldiers there might spot her, might come over to trouble her. But from the faint shouts emerging, they seemed too intent on some game of dice.

Another horse entered the gap. But this one didn't just pass through. The head was turned, off the path, toward the city walls, the rider ducking under the low branches, reining in. No more than fifty paces away, he looked up . . . and saw Tza immediately. Each regarded the other for a long moment. Then, raising a gauntleted finger to his lips, he whispered, "Shhh!"

The trees on either side of him, up and down the slopes, began to shake. Men emerged, bearing ladders, stepping out in the same time it took Tza to rise from her crouch.

She recognized the rider and his men, knew them by their turbans, their curved swords, their shining breastplates, their small shields. She had never seen any of their kind before. But she knew them. It was the Sirocco that had brought them there, sweeping them out of Africa.

"Arabs!" she screamed, just as the men began running toward the walls.

CHAPTER THIRTEEN

SLAVERS' RAID

Tza had never seen pirates—but she knew them. The latest invaders, emerging from their lairs in North Africa to row their galleys all over the Mediterranean. Most summers they'd come, their raids turning every seaport in Corsica into mausoleums for the dead. Every summer the townsfolk worried that, having picked the bones of the coast clean, the raiders would come inland, to Sartène.

This summer they had.

Tza looked to the next tower. The guards had tumbled from the open back of the bastion, were already running screaming into the town. Cowards, she thought—but could she blame them? They were from Genoa, the island's most recent conqueror. Why should these foreigners fight for Corsica? As ever, Corsicans would have to fight for themselves.

The first ladders hit the parapets on either side of

her; men were scrambling up. "Colombo, go!" she shouted, slithering after the dog down the crumbling stair. There was nothing to be done here, except become the first prize of the raid. If there was to be a stand, it would be in the town.

No, not *if,* she thought, running flat out from the moment she reached the ground. There would definitely be a fight. The Arabs had not come for such meager goods as Sartène could offer—the wool, cheese, and myrrh from the goat, the blocks of granite for building—but for something as valuable as gold. They had come for slaves, the currency of the Mediterranean Sea. And no man of Sartène would be turned into a slave without a fight.

No woman either. As she ran by the townsfolk, mouths agape, eyes wide and staring at the white-clad, turbaned figures swarming over their walls, Tza reached down into her pouch. There her hand closed around the comfort of stone. She had twenty-four, each one chosen for its perfect shape, which she could just curl a palm over. Each had lines incised on it, prayers to spirits older than the Madonna, for the accuracy of flight. Twenty-four raiders could die. And then she would find more stones.

The church bell was sounding when she reached the square, not with the gentle chimes of mass but with a summons to arms. And people were answering. The barracks doors were open, the Genoese guard marching out, all thirty of them, an officer in shirttails

154

mustering them, sword waving, while others brought out muskets and pikes. The market carts were being pulled to face the street that led to the town gate, for the enemy would have seized that to let their main forces in.

Tza ran through the square. She had to find her father. Despite everything, he was still her blood.

"Papa," she cried, flinging the door in.

"Leave me be." He was on the bed, neck arched back, an arm flung across his eyes.

"The Arabs have come!"

The arm dropped; he turned to her. "Do you jest with me, child?"

"No, Father. Listen!"

The bell was still clanging the alarm, rhythmless, harsh. Her father pushed himself up on one arm. "Slavers?"

"Yes."

He swung his feet off the bed, sat there for a moment staring down. Then he raised his eyes to her. "My crossbow and my sword," he said.

He may have been a drunk brute. But he was still a Marcaggi.

They descended to the square, through a crowd heading the other way, mainly women who had grabbed what little they could carry—sacks of food, candlestick and crucifix, babies in slings—children running before them, all fleeing for the town's eastern gate.

At a corner, a dogcart had spilled, tipping an old woman onto the cobbles, possessions scattered around her. The way was narrow, and people, careless of her cries, were pushing past her, treading on her. Tza saw a man in a beautiful linen shirt waving a sword over his head, organizing others to clear her out of the way.

"Emilio," she said. Her father took a step toward him. But bodies blocked, the obstructions of woman and goods were tumbled brutally to the side, the mob swept through. At its center, in a tight circle around a cart laden with goods, were Emilio and at least four other Farcese men.

"Cowards!" Tza yelled, but if any heard her, they did not turn. They were gone, lost in the mob, with Tza and her father struggling against the flesh tide toward the square and its insistent, summoning bell.

Not all Sartenais were intent on saving themselves. Many had rallied and were now grouped in the square, behind the slim protection of the drawn-up wagons, staring toward the west. Some held muskets or the more primitive arquebus, the lit ends of rope coils glowing at their belts; a few, like her father, hefted crossbows. Most had whatever they'd been able to grab—boar spears, skinning knives, axes. They were a loose fringe to the more ordered center—thirty Genoese soldiers, their captain behind them. He'd managed to find his armor, the sun gleaming off his burnished black breastplate, his feathered helm, his long Spanish blade.

He noticed them as they came up to the barricade. "Do you and your son want for weapons, sir?"

It was not the time for an acknowledgment of who she was. Her father, in the walk down, had tried to persuade her to join her fiancé and flee, but she had refused and he was too distracted to do more than shout at her. Now he just grunted, waved sword and crossbow.

The officer looked down. "Will your dog fight, boy?"

Tza didn't look up from beneath the brim of her hat. "Yes, sir."

"Good. We'll need all the teeth we can get." There was a brief smile and then he was gone, summoned by a sentinel on top of a wagon.

Whoever had been ringing the bell must have grown tired. Instead of the continuous clanging, the strikes now came intermittently, with long spaces between, some loud as if struck with force, some so weak they were like a whisper of metal. All at the barricade had fallen almost silent, save for the prayers muttered under their breaths.

"Forgive me, God. God, forgive me. Forgive me, God, forgive my sins."

The bell, with a final weak toll, ceased. There was one last plunging wail of despair from the area ahead of them that led to the main gate. Then silence.

They waited. Something moved in a doorway; a shutter was lifted by an unseen hand. Then they heard it—the clop of hoof upon cobble. Closer it came, and closer, from beyond the bend in the street. One corner nearer. One more.

"Wait for me," the captain breathed, his sword rising. "Wait."

Something emerged from the shadows under the eaves. And all let go their held breaths, exhaling as one. For all had expected a turbaned warrior astride a charger. What they got was a donkey.

It stood there, blinking in the sun, jaw moving, chewing some last piece of cud. It looked so unconcerned, so normal, so . . . donkey-like, that Tza laughed. She couldn't help it, and she was not the only one.

158   The donkey stared for another moment before it turned to one side, distracted by something, and all saw what its face, twitching ears, and long neck had previously concealed. There was a man on the animal's back. He wore the uniform of a Genoese soldier. And he had no head.

Something flew from a window, striking the animal on its haunch. It jerked forward, braying loudly, bucking its hind legs, dislodging the corpse that fell onto the stones, limbs twisted, neck thrust down as if the head was buried in the earth. Then more laughter came, but no longer from their side of the barrier. From the man who rode slowly round the corner now. He was the vision all had expected to see—tall, booted, robed in flowing white, a turban atop his head, a thick, styled beard tumbling onto a silver breastplate that dazzled with reflected sunlight. He was the same man Tza had first seen at the walls; he raised his hand again now. Not to say "shhh," though. To roll a severed head into the square.

He laughed again. Then he drew a long, curved scimitar from a sheath on his horse's flank and raised it above his head. *"Allah u Akbar,"* he shouted. The cry was taken up behind him, issuing from hundreds of throats.

"Allah u Akbar," the Arabs cried, warriors on foot, pouring past their leader, running toward the barricade.

It was a credit to the men—and one girl—of Sartène that only three of them broke, dropped their weapons and ran from the square. The rest raised musket, arquebus, and crossbow.

"Wait! Wait!" cried the captain, and his soldiers did but the townsfolk couldn't. Bullets and bolts flew, and a few Arabs tumbled shrieking, or already silent, onto the stones.

Tza waited. The targets were still eighty paces away, out of her range, and the stitched leather cup of her slingshot still rested cool against her neck. There was little use fitting a stone into it, to be held there while men ran at her shrieking. She would only shake, lose her concentration, miss. She had learned, from a thousand days and nights of stalking on the mountainside, the order of these things. For when you came

159

upon a hare fit for the pot, or a wolf readying itself to slaughter a goat, or a boar whose eyes you wished to gaze into, you usually came upon them suddenly, had but a moment to load, aim, kill. A moment to do and not to think.

"Fire!" yelled the captain. The guards discharged; many more of the enemy fell. It was what she had been waiting for. Through the smoke she rose, climbing onto the wagon before her, ignoring the command of her father to get down. Crouching there, she raised both hands to lift the leather oval from her neck and press the stone into its center. Stretching out her hands, both ropes taut, she rose in the same fluid motion, releasing her left hand, swinging her right, her thumb pressing down the knotted end of one rope. The stone needed no flesh to hold it firm now; the first twirl around her head and its own weight did that. At the third circle, the drone began—*voo voo voo*—like bees in a hive. At five, it was going as fast as it ever would. Her right shoulder had built twice the muscle as the left for this reason only . . . to fling a killing stone.

Enemies shredded the smoke before her. The man on the horse was not one of them, to her disappointment. But there was another leader, running just ahead, urging his followers on.

Voo voo voo. She sited on the space of flesh just above the eyes. Breathing out, she flung the knot at it.

The man stopped shouting, stopped running,

160

knocked backward as if someone had him on a rope and jerked him. Tza barely saw, dropping behind their side of the barricade just before the first pirate hit it. Despite the noise, the screams of terror, pain, and defiance, the shock of blade on blade, for just a moment there was a quiet space inside her.

So that is what it is like to kill a man, she thought. That easy!

An Arab disturbed her contemplation. Leaping onto the wagon above her, he swung a huge two-handed sword down. Tza jumped sideways; the blade splintered wood beside her face. Then her father thrust his sword up, driving it straight into the man's groin. Giving a high-pitched squeal, he fell over them, to Colombo, a blur of fangs, waiting below.

There was nothing for her here, her skinning knife no match for scimitars. She needed room for her brand of killing.

The barricade had withstood the first shock. But she could see more of the enemy massing at points where they would break through.

"Colombo, come!" she yelled, dragging the beast away from the dead pirate he was savaging. Twenty paces back stood the town well, its stone rim wide. She ran to it, leapt up, reached into her pouch.

There were enemies atop the wagons, and these were the ones she aimed for first. Some she missed, a sudden movement, a lucky stoop saving them. Lady Fortuna protected a few; others she did not. Tza lost

161

count of how many stones she had hurled, in the drone of whirring rope, in the death cries. Until she reached into her pouch and found it empty. And just as she gazed, incredulous, at her fingers, the barricade imploded.

Men who had fought, fought well, were running. Even the guards, disciplined till then, broke. She watched as their captain, turning to try to halt them, took a spear in his back. She saw her father stumble back, his sword knocked aside by a scimitar swipe from above him.

"Papa!" she cried as the scimitar rose again—and fell, slicing into her father's flesh, his falling body lost in the swirl of combat. There was no time now to consider that the man she barely knew, who had beaten her that morning, who was going to sell her in marriage to a coward, but who nevertheless was her father, was undoubtedly dead. Not when another man was running at her, spear leveled, yelling, so fixed on her and the slingshot slowly lowering to her side that he did not see the crouching dog, a black and red fury, till it had leapt up and sunk its teeth into his throat. His yell drowned in blood, the man was already close to death before Colombo had him back on the ground.

"Come," she called, and, as ever, was instantly obeyed.

The fight was over. Most of the men of the town, those not running, realized it, lowering their weapons to the ground. Cutting edges were leveled at their throats. But no further blood was shed. The slavers had not come to kill, after all. And no one wanted to mark the merchandise.

Perhaps they thought she was some gargoyle, perched there to guard the town's water, but no one looked up at her, nor at the body and hound beneath her. Not until a breeze came, clearing the powder smoke, and a horseman rode through the wisps. He looked straight at her, as he had done before. Pointing with his sword, he shouted a command.

Tza leapt off the well and ran.

She was faster than men in breastplates—and she knew the streets. A few others were still fleeing upward, uphill toward the eastern gate. Beyond it lay some vineyards and then the maquis. Make that, and the Arabs would not catch them.

Then there were as many people running downhill as up, screaming in panic. Tza saw one she knew, stepped into a doorway, and grabbed his arm as he ran past.

Filippi Cesare cried out in terror, one hand rising to ward off the ambush. Then he saw who it was. "Let me go!" he shouted, squirming in her grip.

"The east gate?"

"Taken . . . Arabs . . . there." His breath came raggedly, in great whoops. "They're in . . . all the towers too. No getting . . . over walls."

She could smell the urine on his breeches. The brave boy who'd tormented her not an hour before was gone. "Where do you run to?"

163

"I don't know . . . hide in a cellar."

"They'll find you."

"Maybe not. I saw a soldier . . . rode for Bonifacio . . . for the garrison there."

He tried to jerk free, but it was her strong right arm that held him, and she pulled him closer. "It's a day at least, there and back."

"So?" He squirmed in her grip. "What else can we do? Listen!" He wrenched around, stared up the hill.

She looked. The screams rose in volume, in terror. She glimpsed a turbaned head.

There was an alley to their left. "This way," she said, dragging him toward it.

He resisted. "Where?"

164

"The Devil's Mound."

He gasped. But then he nodded, followed. In a line they went, girl and boy and dog, threading alleys that wound ever upward.

They stood at its base, necks tilted back, gazing up at the granite wall. No watchtowers stood near it, for no invader would be able to climb down it into the town. It was five times the height of a tall man, maybe more, crowned by twin outcrops that looked like horns and gave the rock its satanic name. At least they had at the beginning. Over the years there were many other reasons why it was believed that the Devil ruled there. For many lives had been snatched away among those who had tried to climb it. It was forbidden to do so, the penalties severe. The townsfolk of Sartène no longer attempted it.

But their children did.

"Have you done it?" Filippi was hopping from foot to foot, his tooth-crammed mouth agape.

"Once," Tza lied. She had watched it done by older boys when she was eight and had been about to follow when the town guard arrived and chased the children away. "You?"

"Never." He shuddered. "Emilio has. He was going to take me next week. . . ." He trailed off as he obviously recalled Tza's betrothed and the recent encounter in the square. He looked at his feet. "I can't."

"You must. Unless you want to end up chained to a bench on a slave galley. Look!"

165

The boy followed her pointing arm. They were high up at the extremity of the town, and they could see down many of its streets. The Transmontane wind was blowing strong from behind them, so some of the awful sounds, the shrieks, the wails of agony, were carried the other way. Some of them. But they could see turbaned figures smashing in doors, could see terrified men, women, and children being dragged from whatever hole they'd been trying to hide in. They could even see as far as the main square, where the pirates' booty was being collected—lines of people already in chains. Three columns of smoke were rising from different points in the town.

"They have a day before the Genoese come," she

said urgently. "Maybe more. They'll search every nook in the town. There is nowhere to escape them. Except up there. Beyond is the open land, the maquis. They'll never find us there."

He looked up again, snot streaming from his nose. "But how?" he asked.

"I know the way." She knelt, put her arms around Colombo, whispered endearments into his ear. Then pointed and said, "Go!" The dog turned immediately and ran in the direction of the Marcaggi house.

Tza took a step closer to the rock face, her hand resting on it, squinting up. She may never have scaled the Devil's Mound, but in her high valley there were many others she had climbed, as sheer. There was always a route. . . .

166

And then she saw it, the first part anyway. A shallow fissure ran with the grain of the rock, slanting diagonally to a bulge about halfway up.

She turned back to him. "Take that off," she said, pointing at the leather apron he wore, the uniform of the tanner's apprentice he was. Her own loose jerkin and breeches would be no encumbrance. "And those," she added, waving at his thick-soled boots. She kicked off the clogs she only wore in Sartène because of the sewage in the streets. In the mountains she always went unshod, her feet as tough as any hide.

She reached fingers as high up as she could, dug them into the slight crevice. She planted the toes of one foot, knee bent. "Do as I do," she said, and levered herself off the ground.

Filippi fell at his first two attempts, reluctant to leave the ground behind. But more anguished cries and smoke from the town drove him, and he was finally up and following as Tza crabbed diagonally across the cliff face. It was slow and painful—nails ripped, skin chafed, fingers and toes both bled as they were wedged into the rough granite. But then they reached an outcrop as wide as their feet and could stand on it, leaning into the wall for a rest. "Don't look down," she said, but she did, or at least back toward the town. The town square was filling with people. Sunlight glimmered off the chains that linked them.

Again, she searched the rock. But there was no other diagonal to take them across its face. It was straight up now, on finger and toe holds she could barely see. "Halfway," she said.

167

"I can't . . . can't go further."

She looked at Filippi. His eyes were shut tight, though that didn't prevent the tears squeezing between the lids. She glanced again toward the town, but her attention was caught by a movement closer to, between the nearest houses, fifty paces down the slopes. She realized it was the top of a turban, emerging from an alley, and she realized that the man who wore the turban was mounted. "Then stay and die," she said simply, looked up, and began to climb.

She heard him follow, still weeping. But then all sounds faded save for the pounding of blood in her ears as she reached for the next handhold, thrust her toes into the next slight fissure, pulled and heaved and dangled. Twice she slipped, stuck to the wall by nothing but her own sweat and blood. Then, somehow, she forced herself on, up.

Someone was shouting from below her, way below. She'd reached a point of balance. She could see the cliff's edge, her own body length above her, just below one of the Devil's horns. She could see no handhold to let her reach it.

Something bounced off the rock by her face. There was laughter. Someone down there had thrown a stone at her. At her! Anger surged through her, or fear, or both. But whatever it was, she used it to somehow find outcrops that weren't there and haul herself within an arm's length of the crest.

"Need some help?"

The voice came from above. A hand was reaching down. It was only when she grasped it that she realized whom the hand belonged to.

Emilio Farcese.

CHAPTER FOURTEEN

THE PROMISE

Between his pulling and her feet kicking against the rock face, Tza scrambled up the last few feet. As she slithered over the crest, she heard the whine of something flying past her. She let go of Emilio's hand, turned, threw herself down so just her head stuck over the edge.

The bearded man on the horse was a few paces before the base of the rock. He was directing three other Arabs who were stretching back to hurl stones. They were all laughing.

The boy on the cliff face was weeping. "Help," he pleaded. "I can't move."

Tza turned. "Hold my legs," she shouted at Emilio. He bent, grabbed them as she whipped the slingshot from around her neck. "Lower me," she cried. He did, and she reached. Not with the whole weapon, for the stitching of rope on leather would not hold the weight. So she reached with the looped rope. "Grab it," she called to Filippi. "Quickly."

It did not look as if he would be able to prize his grip from the rocks. But then a flung stone caught him in the back. He squealed, slipped, grabbed. "Pull!" she yelled. And somehow, between Emilio and her pulling and the boy's desperately scrabbling feet, they hauled him up and over. But just as they did, the rope slipped from her blood-slick fingers. Filippi had let it go to grasp earth, and it fell over the edge.

They all lay there, gasping. For a long while there was nothing but the relief of the ground beneath her, the solidity of rock. Then, as her breath started to come a little slower, she heard a familiar sound.

Voo voo voo.

She began to pull herself to the edge. "Don't," she heard Filippi cry, but she did, peered over.

A pirate was whirling the slingshot above his head. As she looked, he let fly, but the stone—misshapen, no doubt, and flung with no skill—smashed into the cliff face before him. He laughed, stepped back . . . and the man on the horse said something to him. He bowed, tipped his head, and called up.

"Hassan Pasha says he saw you down there, with this." He raised the slingshot. "You killed many of his men. He says you are a fine young warrior."

It was strange to hear an Arab speaking Corsican. But she knew that many who had been taken as slaves before had converted to Allah, been freed, then led the raids on their former home. And everyone had heard of Hassan Pasha, the Dey of Algiers. He was the worst of the slavers, the cruelest, the greediest.

So that was the bearded man! He was talking again, the man nodding, bowing. Then he looked up. "Hassan Pasha says you should come down, young sir. Join him. He likes fine warriors. After you convert to Islam, you can fight with him, get rich with him. Your friends there can be your first slaves."

There was more laughter below. She heard Emilio grunt something. And then her rage, never buried deep, came welling into her throat, so strong she could hardly breathe.

"Well?" the man called. "What answer do you give him?"

"This one," she said, standing. Her slingshot was below, and the stone she'd reached for on the ground was a jagged lump, not smoothed for flight. But her arm was still strong, and she used all of that strength and the keenness of her eye to fling it straight at Hassan Pasha's head. "Fortuna," she said as she released it, but it was the Dey of Algiers who had the luck—well, some anyway—for he moved his head at the last moment, so the stone smashed into his helmet, not his face. Still, the noise it made and his instant jerking was enough to panic the highbred stallion he rode. It whirled around and bolted toward the town, its rider struggling to stay mounted. The Corsican renegade looked up in amazement, then, wordless, he and the others ran after their leader.

Emilio had pulled himself to the edge, had seen what had happened. "You are a lunatic," he gasped.

She turned to him. "Maybe," she growled, feeling something stirring inside her. She looked into the sky. It was still only halfway through the morning. But it *was* the day of the full moon.

Filippi was whimpering, sucking at his bleeding hands. "Please! Can we go?"

"Where?"

"Into the maquis to hide."

Emilio rose slowly. "Why? They will not hunt us—despite the crazy thing she just did. Easier pickings down there than chasing us into the wilderness."

She looked back into the town. The trails of smoke had expanded into fast-rising coils. Most houses in the town were made of Sartenais granite. But there was still enough wood to feed a good blaze. "Well, you go where you like. I must return to my herd." The sun had reminded her—she had a ways to journey before moonrise.

"What?" Emilio grabbed her arm, and she jerked it from his grasp. He stared at her. "We must wait for the slavers to leave."

"Why?"

" 'Why?' " he echoed, incredulous. "They will not, cannot take everyone in the town. There wouldn't be room in their ships, and they only want those strong enough to be slaves anyway. And others will have escaped or will be up in the mountains still. We must be here to help them rebuild."

"You must. My goats need milking." She'd begun to walk away, stopped, turned back. "Filippi, find my dog; he'll be near the house. Look after him. I will return in a month or so for him." She saw the hesitation. "You owe me, for you would now be a slave without me."

The boy stared at her, wiped his nose, nodded. Emilio looked from one to the other in amazement. "Your . . . dog?" he cried. "What of your family?"

She took a step away. "Dead."

"Your father?"

The word stopped her again. He had told her that morning that the sister she hardly remembered had died. She'd had no tears for Miranda then. And there were none now for him.

"Dead," she said, and carried on walking.

173

She'd gone fifty paces when his voice came again. This time it was not full of amazement. This time it had the tone it had carried that morning before the church.

"Well," he said mockingly, "then the bride had better find an uncle to give her away."

That stopped her. Slowly she turned. "Did you not hear me? My father is dead. The contract between our families is void."

"He may be dead," Emilio said, coming forward, a smile on the handsome face, "but the contract was always between you and me."

She watched his slow approach, almost too stunned to speak. "But why," she said finally, "why would you want me?"

He laughed, a cruel sound. "I don't. I want your land. And if you are the price of it . . ." He shrugged. "Well."

She shook her head. "Is it so valuable?"

"It is. Joins two sections of ours that straddle the road to the port of Bonifacio. Lots of trade on that road, especially now when the town will need to be rebuilt." He nodded. "Lots of gold to be made."

The anger stirred in her. "You can talk like this now? With your family and neighbors slaughtered or about to spend the rest of their lives as slaves?"

He shrugged.

She spat on the ground. "You sicken me."

"I hope you will not say so on our wedding night."

Fury, disgust, threatened to overwhelm her. If she'd still had her sling, she'd have it whirring and a stone at his head in an instant. She felt a growl building, wondered if somehow it was later in the day than she thought. Then she took a deep breath, another. Rage would not help her here. She needed something else.

She looked beyond him, to the town. The wind had turned, was whipping the columns of smoke, shredding them, now wafting the scent of destruction their way. She inhaled it. It made her dizzy. She breathed out, spoke.

"I cannot give you my answer yet. . . ."

"There is only one answer. Break the contract and everything the Marcaggi own is forfeit."

She breathed, fought down her fury. "Then perhaps

that is what will be. I must think on that, on everything. And then give you my answer." She stared at
the triumph on his face. "So you will win either way.
Which way I will tell you . . . in one month."

"Why should I wait," he sneered, "if I've won
anyway?"

Breathe. Suck in the smoke.

The dizziness came again. That sense also, the one
she'd had when she'd woken that morning in the cellar, that strange feeling of someone . . . someone else
within her. It was different from the growling. Similar.

She raised a hand to her forehead. "We cannot . . .
cannot marry for a half year. Until I have mourned for
my father."

"But I still need your assent. To prepare."

She staggered. He was right before her now, and he
reached out, held her up. "Are you well?" he asked.

Breathe. Suck in the smoke. What is . . . ? Who . . .

She opened her eyes, looked at him. At a face that
would be so handsome if it were not for the cruelty in
the eyes, the downturn of the mouth. She forced a half
smile. "I am well. And I must go to my goats. Come to
hear my answer in . . ." She swayed, steadied. "In one
month's time. There are no calendars in my *oriu,* no
clocks. So come in exactly one month. The night the
moon is full, an hour before its rise. I will meet you
then at the standing stones of Cauria."

He would have said something more, would have
held her. But he had her right arm, her slingshot arm,

175

and she jerked it easily from his grasp. Strangely, though, the movement hurt. Too much sling work, she thought, rubbing it as she turned and strode off into the hills.

A dip swallowed her from their sight. She was forced to stop, lean against a chestnut tree, using it to keep her upright, sucking in air. She could no longer see the town. But she could still smell it burning.

Breathe. Suck in the . . .

CHAPTER FIFTEEN

BURNED CLEAN

. . . smoke? Where there's smoke, there's . . .

"Fire!"

Sky's yelp barely made it out of his scorched throat. Coughing wildly, he jerked his right arm out of the fire pit.

"Aaaah!" His jacket was filled with synthetic down, and waving it in the air, trying to shake out the spears of flame, only made the nylon shell blacken and crisp.

"Down!" he screamed at himself, falling to the ground, rolling over and over until his body hit a goat stall. No air was getting into his lungs, only foul plastic smoke, and he knew that if he kept inhaling that, he'd faint and probably die. So he pressed his body onto his arm. The pain was intense, his chest and stomach burned, fresh skin seared. But the flames were snuffed out. Ripping the jacket off, he hurled it away. Unfortunately, it landed in the fireplace, caught again, more foul smoke gushing up.

Got to get out, Sky thought. Groping behind him, he felt the edge of the goat stall again. Swinging himself around it, he crawled to the door.

It was his legs that drove him along the earthen floor. He used his left arm to help a little, but there was no feeling in the right. Choking, he raised up enough from the floor to flick the door latch, pull the wood back, crawl the last few yards outside.

It took an eternity of racking coughs for his breathing to settle, for him to realize that it was raining, and that the night was chill. He didn't care, lay there sucking in the sweet air. Gradually his head began to clear, though clarity brought to it a terrible, nauseating throb. Pain returned . . . and did nothing to reassure him, because it was intense on his chest, where he'd pressed down to extinguish the flames, where he was only slightly burned. But in his arm, his hand, he felt nothing.

He forced himself up so he could put his back against the wall beside the door, protected from the rain by the granite overhang. Then, stretching his left arm into the doorway, he groped, found metal. Blessing his good fortune—he'd left the flashlight there when he'd needed the toilet in the middle of the night—he flicked the switch.

He didn't feel so fortunate now. Bollocks, he thought. His arm, from wrist to bicep, looked like roast pork, a Sunday lunch straight from the oven, the skin glistening and crisped. But the worst were the streaks of melted plastic, the same blue as the jacket, veined throughout. His hand was a more normal color, still burned and red, but it must have escaped the worst because it wasn't directly under the plastic coating.

His fingers were curled into a fist, and he couldn't make them open. Reaching over, he used his left to prize them up. Each gave with a strange crackling sound, like paper unfolding. Then, as he pulled up the last, the little finger, something dropped out.

It was a runestone.

He remembered that he'd been grasping *Naudhiz*, the final rune he'd cut, when he'd . . . traveled. But he already knew that the rune lying facedown on the ground wasn't the straight line down, with the diagonal across. He must have fallen back, snatched up this other. And he didn't need to pick it up to know which rune it was. He just had to raise his hand.

In the center of his palm, in lines of red, it was marked out, the near-perfect oval of the stone's circumference. Within it, a "V" lay on its side. *"Kenaz,"* he muttered, coughing the rest, "the torch. Burned clean."

He laughed. Well, he was certainly burned! "It's meant to be metaphoric," he yelled as more laughter threatened to take him over. That wasn't good. The situation wasn't funny. His arm wasn't funny. It was terrifying. Because it didn't hurt.

He remembered burning his finger on a stove once. It hurt a little and then it didn't much. Till later,

179

when it really did. Till the blisters came and brought true pain. That was a finger, nothing. But when the pain came for this . . .

He grabbed the runestone, the flashlight, and stood up, swayed, his head pounding, his whole body shaking, cold and hot simultaneously. He steadied himself, torn by another terrible bout of coughing. He just wanted to lie down. But if he did, he knew he'd never get up. He had to get help.

He had to get down the mountain.

Sky went back into the cave. The flashlight showed that the jacket had all but disappeared, consumed by flame. There was still that lingering stench of burned plastic, but he could breathe at least, though each breath came and went on a wheeze. His shivering had grown worse, and he went closer to the faint heat of the fire pit. He had a few spare clothes with him but . . . what if he put his sweater on? The thought of scabs forming around the wool of his sweater, of some doctor—if he ever found one—having to cut it off of him . . .

He shuddered, looked around. By the stalls, his pack leaned. He went over, reached in and pulled out his plastic bags of food. Wasn't sugar supposed to be good for shock? He wolfed down two chocolate bars. The shivering continued but his brain cleared a little.

"Wait!" He thrust his good arm through the ends of the two plastic bags. Then he carefully pulled them up over his burned arm. Using his teeth and left hand, he used the two straps that tied his sleeping bag to his pack to secure the bags on his arm.

"Brilliant, Doctor," he laughed again, waving the arm, then swayed, winced, took a deep breath, coughed violently. I mustn't start hallucinating, he thought as he struggled into the sweater. Not yet.

His canteen was full of stream water. He swigged some now, then awkwardly clipped its belt around his middle. What else did he need for his journey? What could he manage?

He looked down. Three runestones from the cast lay there. The fourth, *Naudhiz*, was by the back wall. *Kenaz* was already in his pocket—and branded on his wounded hand. Bending, he scooped the other four up, thrust them into his jeans. They were power, whether he liked it or not. You didn't leave power lying around.

181

"And speaking of which . . ." It was where he must have dropped it, at the base of the wall. The quartz carving rock was too large for his pocket—so he thrust it into his belt like a dagger. Then he turned the beam on the wall. Within the chestnut tree stood the shepherd's crook of *Isa*. "Tza's still got to carve that," he mumbled.

He found he was just staring. "Got to go," he declared. Turning, he followed the beam out into the night.

The rain had ceased, the clouds parted, and he thought he saw the faintest glow to the east, roughly the direction he was heading. His coughing had eased a little, and the sweater took the worst of the chill away.

Two hours, he thought. That's about what it took me to get up here from the stones. Must be less going downhill.

Yet as he walked, it grew darker; what had brightened the east proved a false hope, and the clouds rolling toward him promised more than rain this time. Lightning stabbed the land ahead, thunder in ever closer pursuit. He hated lightning, had ever since Sigurd had used its power and the runes to sever his own soul from his body.

Something was happening in his arm, electrical pulses running up and down it. It was not pain . . . yet; not the pain of the far less severe burns on his chest. But he knew pain could not be far off.

182

Lightning, rain, and agony hit, all at the same moment. One second, he could see the slit in the cliff face ahead, the tunnel that led from the world of Tza to the world of the present; the next it vanished, scorched from his sight by a fire spear. The lightning hit so close, the force of it knocked him back, his hair rising from his head, electricity pulsing in the air around him. Thunder threw him to the ground, his flashlight smashed, rain drenching him.

Somehow he got to his feet. Somehow he was staggering again, stumbling down a path lit by lightning, knowing when he had veered off it only by the prickly maquis snagging his ankles. Then, somehow, he found he'd fallen into the tunnel between the two worlds, stood there soaked and gasping and staring back at the storm that had tried to destroy him moving away up the valley toward the peaks.

He wanted to stay where he was, in relative shelter. He knew he couldn't, no more than he could have stayed in the cave. He was going to pass out any moment.

Forcing himself up, he slithered on, crying out as his arm brushed against the tunnel wall. Then he was through. The path along the cliff face led to the other that descended to the stones below. There was just enough light to see by now as he slid and slipped down the slick path.

Dawn's mist wreathed each standing stone like an aura, softening the hard edges, transforming the coldness of rock into something warm. Sky gazed at them, coughing, blinking, shuddering from cold, from pain . . . and saw someone step out from behind the one with the carved face.

Sigurd smiled. "Hello, grandson," he said. "How goes the ordeal?"

"No!" Sky screamed, breaking into a run that was more of a long fall. He thought he heard laughter, engulfing him like the mist did, insane, cruel. Then it was cut off, as suddenly as it had begun. Cut off by the howl of a wolf.

He stumbled past the place where he'd hidden his scooter. For one mad moment he thought of digging it out, riding away. Anything to put distance between himself and the stones; anything to find someone who would stop the inferno his arm had become. But he knew he'd get no more than fifty yards before crashing. He stumbled on.

There was something on the main road—beams of light cutting through the early morning mist. He ran, faster now the ground was level, faster with his desperation. But the beams were approaching faster too. Any moment they'd pass the entrance to the site. And if they did, hope was gone. At five in the morning, how many people drove past the standing stones?

"Stop," he panted. "Please! Stop!"

He came to the road. The beams were there, the engine roaring. He had no choice. He fell into the road.

184   There was a shriek of brakes, the squeal of tires biting. Something heavy was sliding on gravel. A stone kicked up, hit him in the face.

Funny, he thought. Maybe she thinks I'm Hassan Pasha.

Someone was shouting, words he could not understand. A hand touched his right shoulder, and he wanted to shriek from the lacerating agony of it. But he knew he only had one breath left to him and he had to use that for something else.

As the hand rolled him over, Sky looked up and said, quite clearly, "Marcaggi."

CHAPTER SIXTEEN

BACK

"Sky!"

That voice! How long had he been wanting to hear it? And here it was.

"Kristin?"

"Yes, Sky. Dear cousin. I'm here."

Here? Where was here?

"You're in the hospital, Sky."

Hospital? How did he get there? Then he remembered. A car. Terrible pain. Then nothing. And here he was. No car. No pain. And Kristin was here.

He could have wept. Maybe the moisture of tears would open his eyes. "You came? All this way? For me?"

"Of course I did, Sky. That's what you do for those you love."

He supposed it was. Hadn't he come to Corsica for love of his cousin?

"And I've come to take you back home."

"Home?" The word forced a tear out, but his eyelids remained glued down.

"Yes, Sky. It's time to go home. Your parents are so worried about you."

"Mum! Dad!"

"Yes! They've missed you, Sky. And so have I. We went through so much together. We were such a great team."

"We were!"

"And we can be again. You don't have to face these ordeals all alone. You have me."

Ordeals? He knew that word. Someone else had mentioned that word. "But Sigurd . . ."

"Hush, Sky. He's not important. He's just a dead old man."

186 "Yes." He wanted to see her. But still his eyes wouldn't open. "Except I thought I had to free you from him."

"I know you did. But there was no need. I'm in charge of me. I decide what I want." He felt her lean closer. Her voice came, a whisper in his ear. *"And what I want is you."*

"Me?"

"Of course. Come back to me and I'll take all the pain away. I'll help you in the quest. The old team—the Ancient Society of Wall Walkers, reunited. Oh, the things we'll do!"

"Things, Kristin?" He could feel his eyes slowly unpeeling, past the gumminess that held them. There was light, bright neon. Silhouetted in front of him was a shape. "What things?"

"Anything, Sky. Everything. Because . . ."

His eyes opened. The shape resolved into form. Sigurd was smiling down. But when he spoke, it was in Kristin's voice. "We're going to conquer the world."

A hand stretched out, the fingers blue-veined and bony, a claw reaching for Sky's face.

Sky was screaming but he didn't seem to be making any sound. And he couldn't keep his eyes open; talons were forcing them shut. "No!" he cried as loud as he could. "No!"

A voice came, not Sigurd's, not Kristin's. It took him a while to understand, because the language spoken was French. He forced his eyes open, expecting more horror. But this face was young, female, and under a white cap. *"Bonjour,"* the nurse said. *"Ça va?"*

He tried to speak, coughed. "Water?" he croaked.

The cap dipped out of his sight line, reappeared. A glass was raised to his lips. He drank but she took it away before he'd drained it. He had asked in English, so she spoke in the same, her accent heavy. "You are better?"

He nodded. Even the slight movement shot pain down his arm, and he cried out.

"You need more medicine, Monsieur Marcaggi. I will return."

"Wait!" Sky coughed again, halting the nurse's turn away. "What did you call me?"

"Marcaggi." She gestured to the chart at the end of his bed. "Your aunt was here. She just leave." He must have looked puzzled, because she continued, "You give name to man who found you."

"I did? I don't remember."

"Yes. He bring you, the man who owns the wines out there. Then we find your aunt." She bent to look into his eyes. "How are you?"

He coughed and the movement again brought pain. Despite it, he raised his head to look. His arm was resting on top of the sheets, covered in dressings. He let his head fall back. "You tell me."

"You are burned. They are going to operate. . . ."

A lurch of panic. "Amputate?"

"No, no. It is not so . . . terrible. A . . . how do you call this? A transfer of skin?"

"Skin graft." Sky didn't know how the phrase came into his fuzzy head.

The nurse nodded. "Exactly. But first, something for the pain, yes?"

She picked up a vial with liquid in it, then a syringe—and someone began shouting. Sky lifted his head slightly, saw that there was a screen of curtains opposite his bed, concealing another patient. The voice continued, a man's, a rapid combination of anger and pleading Sky couldn't understand. The nurse sighed, put the vial down. *"Un moment,"* she said, and went through the curtains opposite.

Sky looked around. The hospital room had four beds—two unoccupied, plus his and the curtained one. A door led out to a corridor to his right. To his left was a side table; the water jug was upon it. The nurse had only given him a little for some reason, but he was still so thirsty. Awkwardly, he raised himself, reached over . . .

His hand never made the jug. Because, on the table, sat whatever had been in his pockets. A few euro notes and coins. A pen. The quartz chisel. And five runestones.

Someone had put them into a plastic bag. Awkwardly, with another rip of pain, he reached with his uninjured left hand, snagged the bag, tipped it out onto the blanket, the stones clinking as they fell together. He placed them into the cross of his runecast, stared at this journey in stone.

What was the question he'd asked before he carved? "How do I recover what is lost?" He'd wanted to return to the past to seek out the lost art of the Mazzeri Salvatore, the Dream Hunters who could heal. But his trip to his ancestor hadn't answered that question. All he had really learned was that Tza, like the other ancestor he'd "lived," Bjørn the Berserker, was a killer. He had killers on both sides of his family. And he seemed particularly drawn to them. How delightful!

He shook his head. There had to be more to it than that. But, of course, he hadn't had a chance to explore his question fully, to seek his answers, because he had been interrupted. There was a good reason why the traveler should have a guardian to watch his body when the Fetch left it, as Kristin used to do for him. There were too many dangers in being alone—as he'd discovered. He supposed the shock of the burning had been enough to drag him back.

He peered at the lines incised into rock. He

had barely begun to work his way through the cast. *Isa?* Well, his challenge was clear. *Kenaz,* the firebrand? He'd been burned, all right. But insight did not come with it; no torch was passed to light the darkness. Only pain.

He prodded the "B." "*Berkana,*" he muttered. He knew it meant atonement. But a burned arm was punishment, not the righting of a wrong. He still had to atone. But for what? And how?

He shuddered. It had to do with Tza and Emilio, he felt sure. With what he was certain was the beginning of the vendetta between Farcese and Marcaggi.

He looked down again. If he atoned, the gift of *Gebo* awaited. He stared at the simple "X." Then remembered what he'd chanted as he scored the lines.

To receive

You must give

To gain

You must lose

Knowledge is loss

If the gift was recovering the healing art he sought, what did he have to give up? Or, perhaps worse, what did he have to take in? There was a price for traveling back into an ancestor. You retained some aspect of them forever. He knew he now had a berserker inside him somewhere, itching to kill. He had felt that terrible desire when Giancarlo pulled a knife. But what would be the price here? And would it involve Tza's fear of the full moon's rise?

He looked down again, at the last rune he'd carved, the end of the stone journey. *Naudhiz.* A declaration of intent, of extraordinary power. Once he had mastered *Naudhiz,* he'd be able to do anything, anywhere.

Even go back to England and free Kristin?

He sighed. That might be his ultimate goal, why he'd come to Corsica in the first place. But the route to it wound through all the other stones and somehow— he wasn't certain how—was bound up with the lost art of the Mazzeri Salvatore.

Sky lowered himself back, his head throbbing as much with the questions as the pain. There was only one place where they could be answered, one time. And he felt sure that something dreadful waited there for him along with the answers, among the standing stones of Cauria. Anyway, how could he return there, even if he wanted to?

And then he saw the how.

The nurse emerged from the curtains, came over, picked up the vial, inserted the needle into it. "Ready?" she inquired.

He stared at it. "Will it make me sleep?"

"Oh, yes. And dream too. Good dreams."

"You know," he sighed, "somehow I doubt that."

He reached down. He didn't need to look. He knew which runestone would come into his hand.

"*Gebo,*" he murmured. "The gift. Odin. All-Father. Guide me now."

"Comment?" the nurse queried, sliding the needle into his skin.

The jab was a tiny pain, negligible after all he'd been through. Almost immediately numbness spread over his arm and chest, darkness into his eyes. He began to drift away.

"Yes, yes," the nurse said impatiently, in answer to yet another call from the other bed. She began to push its curtains along the rail.

Sleep sucked at Sky, sleep . . . and something else. There was light in the dark too. He began to drift toward it.

A cry pulled him back, eyes struggling against huge weight to open. He looked to the bed opposite.

Giancarlo lay in it, one leg raised in traction over the sheets, an arm in plaster, bandages around head and back. On a chair beside him sat someone else Sky knew.

"Marcaggi," Jacqueline said, rising in shock.

"Farcese," he replied. The shock didn't make him rise, though. He could only sink, folding into the mattress, through it, down . . .

. . . on and down. In. And there he was, looking through eyes he'd looked through before, out onto a valley he'd stumbled through only yesterday, burned arm thrust before him.

Sky waited. There was always this transition, this moment of sharing. It never lasted long. Soon he would dissolve, become Tza. . . .

It didn't happen. There was no dissolving. No darkness. There was Tza, rising from the shadows of the tunnel where she crouched. There was Sky, rising with her.

This was wrong. So wrong. He should have been gone by now. He was not meant to be standing, stepping out of the cleft between two valleys, running immediately, flat out and effortless. Arms driving either side of the body—*My body! Our body!*—each hand clutching the end of a rope.

Someone howled. No! He howled—*they*, the two of them, howled, head tipped back, to a waxing moon perhaps a day off full. And instantly the howl was answered, echoed. Other shapes were in the side of his . . . their vision, black-swathed, flowing by different paths, giving out the same cry that they gave again now.

"Ai-ai-ai-ai-ai ah!"

And beasts reacted to it, the snuffle of wild pig, their squeals of fear, the crash of their feet through the brush.

What is happening? Sky thought.

And then he knew. Knew why his consciousness had not dissolved. Why he was still there, as Tza was there. It terrified him. It thrilled him.

His Fetch had not entered Tza. His Fetch had entered hers. For she was a Mazzeri. And she was hunting.

He looked—*they* looked. On every side, the Dream Hunters ran, pursuing the fleeing boar. And he felt it, even if he didn't know exactly *who* felt it—the yearning

193

for the kill, the bloodlust he'd had that first hunt with Pascaline.

Tza's sure feet drove them on. This was her valley; she hunted it by day and night. There were paths she could take that none could know, that were scarcely wide enough for a foot; yet she placed hers easily, and they flew between and over the maquis shrubs, away from the main hunt.

"There!" yelled Tza in glee.

With every sense exploding, Sky heard the animal before he saw it crash onto the path, hooves gouging the earth as it scrambled away. But a Mazzeri did not merely run. The beast was fast. They were faster.

It knew it too, stopped, turned as they—Sky could not shake the feeling that there were two of them, not side by side, far closer than that, indivisible—as *they* burst into the small clearing. It was a giant male, bigger by far than the one he'd struck before, huge savage tusks transformed to sharpened steel by the moonlight.

Sky might have hesitated—Tza did not. A hand dropped into a leather pouch, a stone was pulled out. "Fortuna," she said. In a moment the slingshot was whirring, that sound like a hive of bees came, speeding up, speeding up, building to its low roar.

Voo voo voo.

"Yahh!" Her voice urged the beast to charge. And it did, no coward animal, running at its tormentor. Fifty paces, forty. And still the roaring of leather and rope.

194

Sky would have shot. Tza held.

Thirty, twenty, bayonet tusks lowering, death on their points.

Shoot! screamed Sky, though he couldn't.

"Now."

Her arm flung forward, the knot was released, the stone flew, taking the charging animal right between its great black eyes. It staggered, tumbled, its momentum carrying it forward, on, nearly up on its feet again, like a scooter rider Sky had seen in another life, ending on its back, sliding the last ten feet, in a shower of pebbles and dust, to stop less than an arm's length before the feet of its slayer.

For a moment there was only the sound of the animal's heaved breaths. Then Tza reached, turned the great head round. She pressed her knife into the flesh just beneath the jawbone, jabbed in hard, a slit made and extended round to meet the other ear. The light that the stone had failed to extinguish in the beast's eyes began to fade now. And in its fading Sky saw a face that he had known in another life.

"Filippi Cesare," the whisper came. Marked now for death.

But then Tza's hands reached again to the knife-slashed throat. "Peace," she said. Her fingertips touched where the blade had ended its terrible work, then began to run along the lower, torn flap. And where they ran, the bloodied rent closed behind them.

Sky had felt it all! His Fetch within hers . . . had

flung the stone that felled the beast. Had slit its throat. And now his fingers vibrated along the hideous gash, sealing it as if he were soldering steel to steel, healing it. His fingers reached between the boar's eyes to pluck out the stone embedded there, rubbing the fur until the last trace of blood was gone.

The boar lay still for a moment, then rolled onto its stomach, and finally up onto its feet. With a grunt and many a step to the side, the animal staggered away, blending into the maquis.

Sky stared after it. Filippi Cesare would be hurt, like Giancarlo was, he thought. But he would live.

Eyes lifted to the sky. There was a touch of red in the east. Dawn's coming, he realized. A new dawn— for I am now a Mazzeri Salvatore.

Tza began to run up the valley, toward the great granite cliffs. And with his keen Mazzeri sight, Sky saw, from miles down the valley, the distinctive shape of the slanting rock, Tza's *oriu*. His cave.

When they entered it, when Sky saw Tza's body lying on a pile of goatskins, Colombo stretched out before it, he knew what was going to happen. Tza's Fetch would have her quiet moment, would sink back into her body and sleep. His would return to his own body in the hospital. There, clasped in his hand, was a runestone— *Gebo,* the gift. The gift he now had.

As Tza's Fetch slipped inside, Sky's consciousness, his sense of separation from Tza, began to dissolve. But as it did, he had no sense of returning to himself in that bed.

No, he thought in a scream. No! Let me go!

But he had no choice where, when he went. And time would flow at its own pace in each world.

Tza rolled on the skins, eyes fluttering. And Sky realized *when* he was. Remembered it in the waxing moon they'd hunted by, a day off full. Remembered that an hour before it rose again, Emilio Farcese would come to the stones of Cauria to hear Tza's answer. And, with his last thought, realized that the price for the gift of healing was yet to be paid.

'97

CHAPTER SEVENTEEN

THE HOWLING

Tza straightened, rubbed at the small of her back. She'd been bent before the wall for some time and was stiff. But the ache was a small payment for what she had accomplished. A few last strokes and she'd be done.

Glancing up to the chimney hole, she was startled by the color of the sky. She had lost herself again in her carvings, lost track of the sun's progress. It was nearly time. But first . . .

Touching the very tip of her quartz chisel to the wall, she completed the half circle of the ram's horn on the top of the crook in one fine stroke. Bending, she blew the dust from the track. Beside her, a hollowed stone held red clay mixed with rock shavings and olive oil. Dipping her finger, she rubbed the fresh lines till all the white granite scars were gone.

"Perfect," she said, stepping back. The visions from

her head had again been transferred to granite. The chestnut tree full of fruit. Her shepherd's crook, rising from its trunk like an extra branch, its base centered in the thing it must protect. The cradle.

"Perfect," she repeated. "And I'll seal it later with ladanum gum."

Her finger was still wet with red dye. She raised it and ran it along her lips.

A whine came from behind her. "Peace, Colombo," she said, crossing to the dog before the fire pit, rubbing the thick fur behind his neck. He had returned a week after the pirates' raid, finding his own way back from Sartène. He had done the journey often enough with her, so she was not surprised when he appeared. She wouldn't have wanted to wait long with Filippi Cesare either.

"Filippi," she muttered, biting her lower lip, tasting the dye there. Choices were strange. As herself, in Sartène, she had chosen to save him from the slavers, even though she loathed the pox-faced little toad. But last night, as a Mazzeri Salvatore, she *had* no choice. She was compelled to kill, yes. But she was also compelled to heal. And Fortuna had spared Filippi yet again.

She glanced over to the pile of goatskins she slept on, to the dress laid out upon them. It reminded her of other choices she had made. The things she could control, and the things she could not.

She went across, leaned down to touch the white

dress she'd worn so reluctantly two years before, when, on one of her rare visits to the town, her father had insisted she come to God. She had hated it; her sister had worn it before her, and Miranda was taller, wider. It had felt like a sack, and she had scowled throughout the entire ceremony, ached to flee to the mountains again and get back into the breeches and jerkin she wore all year. Her father, with the sentiment of a drunk, had tearily insisted she take the dress with her. She had nearly thrown it down the first ravine. But, for some reason, she hadn't. Now she was glad.

She looked up through her chimney hole again, to a sky shading toward sunset. Soon she must set out for her rendezvous with Emilio. He was coming for her answer. She would give it. And then he would have his own choice to make.

She pulled off her jerkin and breeches, dropped the dress over her head, shoved her way into it. It was a struggle now; she filled it better, and it clung where once it had shrouded.

Her thick black hair hung in a braid down her back, still wet from the bath she'd taken a few hours before in the nearest rock pool. She loosened it now, spread it out over her shoulders; it would dry in the walk down the mountain. She had a stone, a piece of clear quartz she'd smoothed into an oval. It was fixed in the center of a strip of wolf hide. The beast's skin always felt good against hers; as she tied it around her head, she gave a little moan.

She looked around the cave. There was nothing else to be done. It was time to be going.

She bent, picked up her carving stone, tucked it into her belt, where it nearly blended with the white of the dress. Grabbing her crook, she moved to the door. The dog rose to follow.

"No, Colombo," she said, turning back. "You stay."

He seemed almost to nod, nuzzled her hand, then returned to his spot before the glowing embers of the fire pit.

She walked down the slope. It was still warm in the sun, though she could feel the trace of autumn's chill in the breeze that blew on her neck. The Grecale, another wind from the colder north. To her left, a stream bubbled into the rock pool where she'd bathed; on a whim, she climbed its slight slope, peered over its rim, gazed onto the surface of the water.

The face that stared back was different from the one that she'd so loathed in the church's font in Sartène. It had no dirt on it, reddened lips such as certain women of the town wore, hair that was no longer a matted lump but tumbling thick and lustrous over her shoulders. She had a jewel on her forehead and wore a white dress, and if she would never be described as pretty, at least she was no longer a monster. Indeed, except for the tangled weave of her eyebrows, joined over her nose, she looked almost like any other girl. Almost.

※※※※

When she emerged from the tunnel that divided her valley from the valley of the Devil's Forge, the sun had already dipped behind the peaks. It had only a short way now to journey, before the moon usurped it in the sky.

It was the hour appointed for the rendezvous. But no horse stood tethered under the trees close to the stones, silent sentinels in the dusk. She stopped by one, leaned her crook against it, laid her carving stone at its base.

Had he changed his mind? Thought longer and concluded there were better matches to be made than with a lowly Marcaggi? Perhaps other land had become available, owners now dead or, as good as, slaves. He knew that she would never hold him to the contract as he had tried to hold her. She would go into town next market day and there he'd be, richer for the profits his family had made from rebuilding Sartène, a sneer for her on that handsome face, engaged to some suitable girl who did not stink of goat.

The thought brought a swift flush of relief. She would not have to go through with it! She could wait till moonrise—do what must be done—then return to her cave, her herds, her life. It would not be so bad. Her family's name would be safe, their herds, their lands—such as they were—preserved for her brother and his return from Genoa.

So why did her stomach feel like it was turning inside out?

And then she heard something—she stepped up,

202

leaned against one of the stones, two faces peering into the gloom of sunset. There it was again, the jingle of a harness. A whinny came, a horse was ridden into the clearing. And Emilio Farcese was on its back.

He reined in, looked around. "Emilio," she called softly, stepping out from behind the stone.

The horse shied at this white vision in the dusk, ears flattening, head jerking, backing away. Its rider fought for control, finally won it with hard pulls on the rein. "What are you doing?" he cried, then peered closer. "What are you wearing?"

She didn't reply, just took another step toward him.

The horse shied again, and Emilio yelled "Stop!" at her while he wrestled for control. Finally he had it, dismounted, led the animal back into the copse of trees, tied it there out of sight. When he returned, he looked Tza up and down in astonishment. "Christ preserve me! You . . . in a dress. You!"

"Yes." She studied him. He had not made the effort she had. The roads were dusty, but the dust clung to much patched breeches and an old cloak, while the fine linen shirt underneath it was spotted with mud.

"Why?" he asked.

"I thought it would please you," Tza replied softly.

He looked at her suspiciously, his mouth open. Even from a few paces away she could smell the liquor on his breath. "Please me?" he barked. "The only thing that will please me is if you give me the answer I have ridden all these damn miles to hear."

He was staring at her hard, and she stared back,

203

studied his confidence, his arrogance, looked deep within his eyes—and saw there the answer he craved. He had said on the Devil's Mound that if she married him, his family got the Marcaggi land. And if she didn't, she was a contract breaker and his family got the land anyway. He was a cur who would force her to this, and she owed him nothing.

Still, she had made herself promise that she would give him a choice. "Emilio, let me get a letter written and sent to my brother. I am sure we can sell you the land you desire. For a fair price."

"The Farcese will not pay even one small coin for it." He grinned at her. "Because we do not need to."

She closed her eyes. "So you refuse to release me from our betrothal?"

"I do."

She did not need to look at him. She could hear the triumph in his voice, and behind their lids, her eyes burned. So. He had made his choice. Now he would have to live with hers. Or not.

She opened her eyes, stepped forward. "Then I will marry you."

"What?" His mouth fell open. He even staggered. "You . . . will."

"I will."

She watched the anger and the disappointment rage on his face. "I thought you'd say no," he grunted. "Thought you'd take to the maquis and live like a bandit queen."

"And bring disgrace to the name of Marcaggi? Lose what little wealth remains and leave my brother destitute?"

"Your brother," he sneered. "A drunk student in Genoa, I heard."

"Well," she said, "you'll just have to make sure your new brother-in-law has enough family gold to drink on, won't you?"

Emilio spat into the dust. "Come, then." His tone was sour. "We will return to Sartène. It is not suitable that a Farcese woman lives out here alone. And we will find you more . . . suitable clothes." He eyed her dress in disgust.

In the distance, there was a loud pop. "What's that?" he said, startled.

205

"Hunters," she replied. "The full moon brings them out." She had looked up at the shot, suddenly noticed how dark it had become. The sun had set in the west. To the east, though, it was getting lighter.

"Let us go, then," he grunted.

She stepped closer. "Touch me," she said.

"Eh?"

"If we were not betrothed, and you touched me, it would dishonor me, would it not? My family would seek vengeance. A vendetta would begin."

"So?" He shifted before her.

"We *are* betrothed. So you can touch me."

She bent her head toward him. Confused, he raised a hand. Stooping swiftly, she bit his finger.

"Ai!" he yelped, jerking away. "What are you about?"

"This," she whispered. Reaching, she took the finger and raised it to her lips.

"What are you about?" he said again, but in a slightly different tone. "What would you . . ."

"You have touched me. We are betrothed," she said. "And is it not the custom that once that is so, we are now one?" She smiled. "Why should we wait?"

She was now close enough to smell his wine breath. Close enough for him to smell her hair, clean as a mountain pool. "We should go back to town," he said halfheartedly.

206   "We should. We will." She forced a smile. "But then you will go to your house; my mother's sister will come and watch over me at mine." She looked to the sky. "It's a nice night, isn't it? And the moon will soon be up."

She turned, began to lead him up the slope, pulling him by the finger she still held in her hand.

"Where are we going?" he said, his voice deepening.

"Not far," came the reply.

They came to the tomb. Six slabs stood upright, nearly twice her height. They supported a seventh, the biggest, like the top of a table.

Emilio stopped at the sight. "What is this place?" he whispered.

"The Devil's Forge," she replied, finding the

footholds, climbing up. She looked down at him. "Come," she said. When he hesitated, she laughed and lifted the white dress over her head.

It was over quickly enough. She spent the time staring at the rock surface, studying the shapes in it, nature's carvings. It made her think of her own, most recent one, the cradle she hoped would now be filled. She thought she knew the way of her own body, just as she knew when to bring the she-goats to the ram. And she also knew that this was her one chance, for she would never seek another man. She did not want to live behind shutters in Sartène, stitching her needle-point. She wanted to live as she always had, free in the mountains, to tend her flocks, to hunt—by day and by night. To kill. To heal. But—she did not want to live in the mountains alone. A surprising desire had come over her when her father told her she was to be wed. She wanted a child. And these moments might . . . might, if Fortuna smiled . . . give her one.

207

She looked beyond the man to the horizon, turning ever more silver.

"Come," she said, rising. "Follow me."

"Why?" he groaned. "Let me lie here."

"But I've something else for you. Much better. Down there."

She leapt off the rock, ran down the path. She heard him stumbling after, laughing, as she slipped among the standing stones.

"Here," she breathed, threading the ranks, seeking.

"Got you," he giggled, stepping around—to an empty space.

Her staff was leaning against the tallest standing stone, the one with an ancestor's face.

"Where are you?" he called.

"Here," she whispered, bending, reaching.

He turned to the sound, to that tall stone, saw its profile, the beak of a nose, the thick forehead. A tip of moon had cleared the horizon, shimmering in silver.

"Tza?" he said, moving round, reaching for her.

Hand had not yet become paw. It could still hold a knife made of stone. "I am here," she said. And slashed the blade across his throat.

208   A man dies faster than a boar, she thought, watching Emilio's body jerk and twist. Especially since no healing hands reached out to halt what flooded from the gash, so much blood ensilvered now by moonlight. But this was not the world of the Dream Hunt; she did not have that power here and did not wish for it. Besides . . . she no longer had hands to reach with.

Silver light glistened in her gray fur, shone off her huge white fangs. She bent swiftly, teeth ripping at the throat, disguising the cut the tool had made. When they found him, even if others knew of their meeting, no one could accuse her. A wolf had killed Emilio Farcese. It was a tragedy.

Even as she savaged, in her mind Tza gloated. It was what her father had not understood about this curse. He'd thought that when she turned into a wolf, she lost all control. But the opposite was true—she was never more certain of every choice she made. It was just that all the choices happened to be about what—or who—she should kill next. It made life so simple.

Her task complete, she threw back her head, opened her jaws wide, and let out a long howl of triumph.

She was so loud, so lost, she didn't hear them at first, the other cries. Then she did, and was quiet in an instant. For it wasn't just a horse that was whinnying in terror. Tza the Wolf also heard words.

"Jesus, protect me! Mother of God, protect me!"

She sprang around the stones. In the trees, struggling to undo the reins Emilio had tied to a trunk, was Filippi Cesare.

For a moment the wolf hesitated, stunned by the sight. Then, with a growl, she was running. It was forty paces, less, to the trees where Filippi had been left to spy, where he must have seen everything. She covered it in moments. But her slight hesitation had let him free the reins. He was mounted and the horse was moving by the time she reached them.

"Yahh!" he squealed, jabbing his heels in hard. Tza-Wolf leapt, rear paws powering her off the ground. But the horse shied, bucked, kicked out. A hoof caught the wolf in the chest and she went sprawling.

Somehow Filippi had stayed mounted. And the

horse needed no further urging to flee. With another whinny of terror, she galloped away down the path.

Winded, Tza-Wolf struggled to rise. When she had, she began to run, not in pursuit, but across the maquis. Filippi would spur his horse as fast as he could along the road to Sartène. Tza-Wolf would have to cut him off.

By the time she reached the outcrop above the road, she had regained all her strength. She crouched down, only a tip of ear showing above the stone. And soon the ear caught the sounds it desired—the thrumming of hoof, the whimper of man. Closer they came. Closer.

Grayness burst from gray stone into moonlight. Her front paws struck Filippi in the shoulder, knocking him from his stirrups, tumbling him from the horse's back. He hit the ground hard. The horse, with a last scream, bolted.

Tza-Wolf looked at the boy whom she'd saved from slavery, whose spirit she'd killed and healed. There was something wrong with that, because Filippi Cesare could not now live. Not when he'd seen her kill Emilio Farcese. Especially not when he'd learned the secret of her blood.

He was driving his legs into the ground, pushing himself away, snot running from his nose, tears from his eyes. "No," he whimpered, "Mother of God, please, no!"

Tza-Wolf leapt. He flung an arm up and she seized it. There was no need to go for the throat, not yet. She had the night if she wanted. She now knew how quickly a man could die. It would be interesting to discover how slowly.

And, after all, she had never liked the little toad.

She felt the bullet and heard the blast almost simultaneously. It passed between her ears, smashed into the rock wall before her, ricocheted off. It was followed by shouting, one voice, then many. She looked up the road, saw the group of men upon it, running toward her. Smoke rose from one barrel. Others were lifting.

She looked to Filippi. He was staring at her in terror. She bared her teeth, readied to spring. There could be no delay now. But then a second gun cracked, this bullet going she knew not where. Turning, leaping, gray dissolved again into rock. Beyond it lay the maquis. It was hers and they would never catch her within it.

Yet she didn't flee so fast that her sharp ears could not hear. "Tza!" wailed the boy with the mangled arm. "Tza! Tza!"

211

CHAPTER EIGHTEEN

VENDETTA

Screams had accompanied his fall into darkness; screams now brought him back into the light. At first he thought it might be his own screaming that was waking him, cries filled with the horror of all he'd just seen, just done. He could taste blood, hot in his throat; feel flesh pulsing between fangs, his whole being throbbing with the awful, terrible, exhilarating power of man transformed to beast.

But the screams were not his. His eyes flickered open, not to moonlight and blood, but to neon and white sheets. And before him two old women—one blind, one bald—were wrestling.

They grappled and shrieked, and it was clear that if Pascaline Druet and Emilia Farcese could kill each other, they would.

Perhaps they might have, given enough time. They were both so old, one or both their hearts could give out, or one could slip and brittle bones would crack on metal bedstead or linoleum floor. But a nurse rushed in and began prizing them apart. A male orderly arrived to help, and ancient arms were eventually separated, the combatants dragged to opposite corners like boxers in a ring. Each was held, each leaning over the arms that restrained them, spitting curses.

"Aunt! Aunt!" Sky yelled, and eventually Pascaline turned toward him, though her mouth still worked at insults, the bald dome of her head glistening with sweat. The eyes, blazing hate, did not take him in. "Aunt!" he said again, clicking his fingers.

She focused on him. "Nephew," she said, then pointed across the room. "Our enemy, the Farcese . . ." She'd said this in English, but Corsican came again now, her high-pitched voice rising to a scream. Emilia, who had sagged in the orderly's arms, erupted again too.

It ended with the orderly lifting Emilia and carrying her to the door. She flailed, and the nurse released Pascaline to go and help her colleague. The shrieks faded only when a door was shut farther down the corridor.

Sky looked to the bed opposite. It was empty and the sheets upon it were rolled back. "Where's Giancarlo?" he asked.

It took a while for an answer to come as Pascaline fought for breath. "Gone," she said at last.

"When?"

"I do not know. I came to visit you. She was

here. The Farcese." She leaned forward and spat on the floor.

Sky looked again. Beside the bed was a suitcase. A leather jacket, shredded by its contact with gravel, lay over it. He pointed. "That's his stuff."

"Or he died," the old lady muttered. "With luck."

"Why? He's only a cousin to the Farcese."

"Same viper. Different nest."

Sky shook his head. The woman's pit of hatred was bottomless. Yet, even as he wondered at it, he felt something similar stir inside him, coming from some deep place, a growl rising to his throat. It didn't sound like him, and he shuddered, sought something else, something normal. "My arm," he said, lifting it. He now saw that it was covered not in bandages but in a far lighter gauze dressing. "It doesn't hurt too much."

She turned back and her gaze softened at last as she looked at him. "When I arrived, the nurse had just given you more painkillers . . . through that." She pointed at his drip.

"This gauze?" He raised his arm, wincing. "Is this what they put on before they do the skin graft?"

She blinked at him. "Sky. They did the graft one week ago."

"A week?" He was stunned. "But I don't remember . . ."

"You sleep since then. They were very worried."

Sky lay back, looked up to the ceiling. He was always amazed at how time got twisted when he "traveled." Some journeys lasted days "back then," and yet he'd return to his body in hours. Others, like his most recent one, lasted just a day . . . and he'd slept for a week.

He looked at his aunt again, saw the hatred still working within her. Could he explain what he had just seen: that it was the Marcaggi who had caused the vendetta to begin? That their family was to blame for all the years of hatred and death? For there was no doubt in his mind—Filippi had survived the mangling of his arm. Tza, the Mazzeri Salvatore, had healed him in the hunt. He was destined to live—to live and to tell all he'd witnessed that night.

Filippi, telling of Tza's transformation in 1583, would have been believed. But today? The term "were-wolf" was a joke, a fantasy figure from cheap movies and comics. Yet, in those stories, the werewolf was always this wild beast, totally out of control, murdering indiscriminately. Whereas Tza *chose* to kill, quite cold-bloodedly.

No, worse than that, he thought. She made those choices as wolf *and* woman. And I was within her when she did. What has that left in me?

Sky shivered. His aunt came over, pulled up the blankets that had slipped down. How could he tell her that when she hated the Farcese, she hated a part of herself? For there was little doubt in Sky's mind about what else had happened—that . . . coupling on top of the Devil's Forge must have produced a child, as Tza hoped it would. Knowing Tza as he did now—he could still feel her in him, like an extra organ—he knew she'd never seek a man again. And she must have had a child, or Sky couldn't have been drawn back through time to her.

He chewed at his lower lip. No, he felt sure he was Tza's descendant. And Emilio's. So was Pascaline.

Yet, however it had begun, horrible crimes had been committed by both families for nearly five hundred years since. His own grandfather had just been the latest victim.

It had to end with him. Him and Jacqueline Farcese. He knew this now.

"Aunt," he whispered, "I will do what you ask of me."

It startled her, hatred banished from the face by hope. "You will . . . do what must be done?"

He took a deep breath. "I will."

"Why? Why have you changed your mind?"

"Two reasons. This vendetta will only end in death. I'd rather it was theirs."

She leaned forward, seized his uninjured hand. "Now you speak like a Marcaggi. Now your ancestors stir and beat the sides of their coffins with pride." She smiled. "And the second reason?"

"Because you promised that if I do as you bid, you will show me the way to release my Fetch . . ." He saw her puzzle at the word. ". . . my other spirit, at will."

"I did. I can show you. It is not, in the end, a difficult

thing. Not for one of us. The blood that screams for vengeance within you also flows with this inheritance. You are a Marcaggi, and you will hunt as a Mazzeri." Pascaline had risen in her joy. "And you will do it as they did, on Jour des Morts? At the Battle of the Mazzeri, when one can kill another, so that no penalty can befall you . . . here?"

She waved her arm at the room, but Sky knew she meant this world. "I will."

"Good. Revenge untouched by the law. As it should be." She reached down, patted his hand. "Your doctor wishes to observe you for a while. Your graft has taken well and it was . . . I do not know how you say this in English . . . not full skin? Not so deep. But he will let me know when I can collect you, to complete your recovery at my apartment." She smiled. "Jour des Morts is on November second. Many weeks away. So, maybe we take a little trip around the island first, yes? Our island is so beautiful in the autumn. *À bientôt.*"

Murderer one minute, tour guide the next, Sky thought, watching the door close behind her.

For a while he just stared up at the ceiling, tried not to think. He felt totally drained. Which was allowable. In this life he'd just been asleep for a week, after an operation. In the other . . .

Memories came, despite his best efforts, and he groaned. No matter how many people Bjørn had slain, he had always done so in battle, killed men who were trying to kill him. Tza, even if she had a good reason, still *chose* to murder Emilio . . . and enjoyed it as she did.

Bjørn was a killer, sure. But Tza was a murderer . . . and more.

And now, so was he. The runecast had spoken to this. The gift of *Gebo*—recovering the lost art of the Salvatore—had always come with a price attached. It was like a light being switched on, never to be switched off. He knew a part of him would always be a berserker. He couldn't know for sure if he wasn't also now part wolf. Not until the next full moon.

But the art of the Salvatore was only one of the gifts of *Gebo*. Pascaline had offered him what he most desired—the ability to leave his body at will. Sky knew it was the first step to controlling his Fetch—just like Sigurd did. But the asking price for this second gift was the murder of Jacqueline Farcese.

The door opened again . . . and in she walked. She stopped as soon as their eyes met. "Oh," she said, "you are awake."

Considering his most recent thought, Sky felt he did quite well. "Er . . . uh . . . ," he managed.

"So you are better?"

"A little, I think, yeah." He tipped his head to the bed opposite. "And Giancarlo?"

She shrugged. "At last they find another room for him. He was not sleeping so good in here. He keep trying to get out of bed."

It was obvious what she meant. "Lucky for me he was in traction, eh?" he laughed.

He looked for any humor in her. Found none. Jacqueline just tossed her head, her long black hair flicking out of her eyes. "So you will go home soon, yes?"

"To England? Not yet."

"Why not yet?"

"There's something I have to do first."

She took a step toward him, her voice dropping. "This thing. It is not to do with Jour des Morts, is it?"

His silence confirmed it for her.

"You cannot go there. To the hunt," she cried.

"Will you go?"

She nodded. "I must. For it is the only night when one can become a Mazzeri fully. When one can learn to walk alone."

"And I must go for the same reason. I need—"

She interrupted, furious. "These are *our* traditions, not yours, Englishman. And they are dying! I, a few others, seek to keep them alive. All that is good in them."

"The vendetta?"

"No! The vendetta was dead—until you came and brought it back to life. If you go now, never return, it will end."

"No, it won't. It will just be delayed, postponed for another generation." His voice was as hard as hers. "My aunt calls vengeance a fire, banked down, just awaiting a spark and some tinder to start the flames again. Sometime, somewhere, it will flame again. Your children. Mine."

She bit her lip. "You cannot know this."

"I can." He shuddered. "Believe me, I know all about the secrets that lie sleeping in the blood."

"But if you were to go away. Never to tell your children? Never to return to Corsica?"

Sky hesitated. His grandfather had tried that, hiding his son in England. But it only took Sky to show up in Sartène to start the whole thing over again.

She took his hesitation as something else. "There you are. We agree. It's over."

She reached out her hand. He looked at it. "So simple, you think? Five hundred years of hate ended with a handshake?"

"Cannot we make it this simple? Here, now?" She looked deep within his eyes, shoved her hand forward. "Shall we try?"

220

"I will go"—he overrode her cry of delight—"on one condition."

"What?"

"That I go *after* Jour des Morts. I will hunt that night, learn what I need. And you will stay away—this time. Learn what *you* need next year."

She stared at him for a long moment, her hand gradually sinking down. Finally she said, "My grandmother is old. She may be dead next year. So you must be the one to stay away."

He lowered his hand too. Kristin's face came into his head, superimposed on another. "I can't wait."

She shrugged. "Neither can I." She got up, walked toward the door, turned. "So remember this, English boy. I am Corsican. Not half-blood—full! And I have hunted before, many times. So there will be only one choice there—who is to die? And it is *my* world where that choice will be made. Mine!"

She said it almost sadly, but with a firmness that made him shiver. Then she went to her cousin's case and jacket, picked them up, and left.

Sky flopped back, stared at the ceiling again. Perhaps she is right, he thought. If I were to leave now, never come back . . .

He closed his eyes. His leaving answered nothing. For a start, how could he let Pascaline walk into the valley of the Dream Hunters to face Emilia and her initiated granddaughter, alone? And he couldn't leave without being initiated himself. It was somehow the key to saving Kristin, he felt sure. And it was the other half of *Kenaz*, the torch beyond the flames.

The runecast! He saw it again in his head. *Berkana*, the atonement. The runestone that would lead him to the final rune of the cast, to *Naudhiz* and all the power he required.

And he also saw that Jacqueline was wrong—there wasn't just one choice in that valley of death. There were two.

He said it aloud. "Tza!"

221

CHAPTER NINETEEN
THE INITIATION

She woke him before light was in the sky, while sleep's last shadows still chased each other through his mind. "Breakfast," she said, placing a glass of water on the table, then disappearing back into her room. He looked at it and shivered, not just because it was cold— it was—but because of what the water meant. On Jour des Morts, many chose to fast, to eat no food and to drink only water from the sun's rising till it set. The initiate *had* no choice. Not if he wanted to learn the secrets of his dead.

Do I? he thought. To drink was to commit himself—to the day, into his aunt's care.

He reached, though his hand did not quite make the glass. Even though it had been over three weeks since the operation, his new skin could still surprise him with its purpleness, tinged with the yellow of the antibacterial ointment. The doctors had been pleased;

the graft had taken well, and it no longer itched—the week after they'd taken off the gauze, it felt like he had a colony of ants living under there! But it still did not feel entirely his.

"Ready?" his aunt called from her room.

"Not really," he replied. But he grasped the glass, lifted it to his lips, took a sip.

The Day of the Dead had begun.

He rose, dressed quickly in the clothes she'd said he must wear, that he had worn that first time of hunting— black T-shirt, black jeans, socks, sneakers.

She emerged from her bedroom. She was also dressed entirely in black, and they looked at each other for a long moment. Ever since he'd been released from the hospital, three weeks before, they'd worn normal early-autumn clothing. And she'd been as good as her promise, giving him a driving tour of the island, staying at small hotels. They'd only come back last night. All the time away, they'd never once discussed Jour des Morts or the Farcese.

And now here they were, facing each other in black clothes.

She ended the silence. "You will carry this," she said, pointing to a metal tray on legs.

"What is it?"

"A brazier. Tombs are cold. And bring Luca's lighter for it." A brief smile came, disappeared. "But nothing else, Sky. In ancient times, you would spend this day naked—for that is the way of one about to be born.

223

The authorities do not allow this now. So you dress—but these clothes are all you may have with you."

She went into the kitchen. He heard her opening cupboards. Going swiftly to his backpack, he pulled out two objects, both stone, put them in separate pockets of his jeans.

As he stood up, she came back into the room, shopping bags in her hands. "Let us go," she said.

He followed, felt a little guilty at disobeying her, hoped that what he had taken wouldn't affect his initiation. But he remembered what it was like before, in the world of the Mazzeri. He was completely lost to the overwhelming thrill of it. He'd need something to find himself again.

224   They joined a procession as they left her apartment block. Nothing organized, no floats or banners, but from the cobbled alleys, figures emerged to join the larger street, as if from streams feeding into a river that flowed upward through the town. By the time the wall that surrounded the cemetery was in sight, in the faintest light of dawn, Sky could count at least forty people. The iron gates began to open, even as the first arrived before them, though Sky did not see anyone open them. They gave with a shriek of rusted metal, and the people poured through them, scattering down the avenues of tombs.

All were dark, save one. "Farcese," muttered Pascaline, seeing where Sky looked. "The rich are not required to wait for the dawn."

The Farcese mausoleum was huge, dwarfing those around it, granite colonnades and crenellated walls a full twenty yards broad, more long. Light flickered behind barred windows. Sky had no doubt that one of the monstrous shadows that moved was thrown by Jacqueline. Another seeker among her ancestors. Another who sought to step free from her body that night by choice, to hunt, kill.

They took the same route he'd taken when he'd pursued his aunt there over a month before. Sky could see now what he'd failed to notice then—the farther you walked into the cemetery, the more impoverished the tombs became, in design, in tending. When they halted at last before the Marcaggi tomb, he saw it was little more than a stone box. Six of them could have fit inside that of the Farcese.

225

It was as if Pascaline could read his thoughts. "The Dead don't care," she whispered. "The outside show matters not at all. It's what's within that counts." She gestured to the brazier. "Put that there."

He obeyed, placing it by a small pile of firewood to the side of the entrance. She put a key into the lock, and the gates gave off their iron protest. *"Après vous,"* she said.

He knew he could not hesitate. He stepped in and she followed, and they stood in the faint light-spill of dawn, their breaths pluming before them, their eyes adjusting to the deeper dark, their noses to the smell of wood and cold stone . . . and something else.

At last Sky spoke. "What now?"

Pascaline reached back into the shadows by the door, pulled out a broom. "First this," she replied, handing it to him. "Then . . ." From one of her bags she pulled a dustpan and brush. Other items followed—cloths, bottles.

"We're going to . . . clean?" After the dawn rising, the procession to the graveyard, he'd expected something a little more ceremonial.

"*We* are not," she said, placing a bottle of water down. "You are." She stepped toward the door.

"Wait!" he called, his voice shrill. "You're not going to leave me here?"

"I will return at sunset," she said, still moving.

"Sunset!" He looked around, swallowed. "What am I going to do till then?"

She was a dark silhouette against dawn's light, her face in shadows. "Tend to your ancestors, Sky. Clean their dwelling place. Get to know your dead."

With that, she was gone. He stood there, thinking of all the questions he still wanted to ask, resisting the urge to run after her. He looked around. The faint light was growing outside the door, but the tomb was windowless, so it had yet to reach the farthest corners. There was enough, though, to see outlines of the metal frames bolted to the coffins, which held the photographs of the more recently dead Marcaggi.

"Hello," he said, his voice tinny and small.

Silence. Yet it was not total, like there was no one

there. Instead, it seemed the sort of silence that came as someone took a breath before replying.

He lifted the broom. He'd been frozen almost from the moment he'd woken up. She'd only let him wear his T-shirt, and the stone sarcophagus he stood within was chill within chill. But the brushing began to thaw him. There was a lot to clear; the tomb was probably cleaned only on this one day in the year, and the iron grille that served as the door let in all that the wind blew. Leaves, wrappers, flowers from other graves, all rolled in the dirt that filled the cracks in the stone floor. He realized why she'd left him water for drinking but none for cleaning—it would have turned dried earth to mud in moments. So, once the worst of the surface dirt was swept out the door, he bent with dustpan and stiff-bristled brush and started on each flagstone, scraping the gaps between them, sweeping, collecting, dumping. He took his time—he knew he had plenty of that—and ever since his burning he'd tired more easily. Also, in movement there was distraction; he could almost imagine he was somewhere else, nowhere specific, just someplace other than a room that contained twenty-four bodies. He barely looked up at the coffins, so focused was he on the floor.

By late morning the corners were visible, cleared of cobwebs and some huge spiders, which, superstitiously, he refused to kill but caught in his pan and threw outside. Lizards had slithered out to blink at him, but he left them to dart back behind the coffins.

He set his brush down, lifted the water bottle, took a sip. It was already half empty. Resisting the temptation to drain it, he put the lid back on . . . and finally looked to the ranks of wooden boxes. "Let's go," he said, and stepped toward the nearest one.

Screwed into the wood was a metal frame, about the width of his hand. The black-and-white photograph within was of a woman; he had no idea how old it was. There was writing at the base of it, some dates perhaps, but time had blurred them. He could just make out a name—*Madeleine.* She wore a dark blouse, buttoned up high around her neck. Her hair was thick, piled and pinned into a tall column. It was impossible to tell her age. Anywhere between twenty and fifty, he thought. The gaze was severe, the eyes peering straight out, straight into his. Aunt? Great-great-grandparent?

"Madeleine," he said, bowing slightly. Then he reached for a bottle of polish and began to take the tarnish off the frame.

Not every coffin had a photograph; some had just a nameplate. Dates on them showed that they had been placed there before photos were possible. One, under the name Matteo Marcaggi, had lived from 1717 to 1799. He'd died an old man.

"What? No vendetta in your time, Matty? What was the matter with you, you wuss?" Then he laughed. Perhaps Matteo was just the top-dog avenger!

His laugh sounded hollow in his own ears and he fell silent. Relief, he supposed. Relief that this was the

228

earliest coffin, that they didn't go any further back. No Tza waited, curled up in a box.

There were twenty-four to get through. The sun was slipping toward the horizon when he reached the final one, the one he'd left till last. The most recent, it bore the photograph he now knew well. "Grand-father," he murmured, looking again at the man who had brought him there. As ever, the lighter rested on the table at his elbow. Sky had the original in his pocket, took it out now, placed it on the lid. Then he began to polish, first the wood of the coffin, then the frame of the photograph itself. He took even more care with this one, though he'd neglected none. By the time he was done, the wood gleamed in what he real-ized was a last shaft from the setting sun. It shone di-rectly onto the picture, illuminating the face. Sky saw his father clearly there. He saw himself.

229

"Help me," he said.

Shadow swallowed the light. "He will."

The voice was soft; yet, being the first he'd heard for an age, it sounded like shouting. He yelped, stag-gered back, turned to the figure silhouetted in the doorway by the departing sun.

"They all will, Sky. That is what they wait to do— on this one day of the year."

Pascaline stepped into the tomb, set down the huge basket she was carrying. From it she plucked a small folding table, draped a cloth over it. Then she covered it with food—a loaf of French bread, some goat cheese, grapes, a salami. Finally she pulled the lid off a thermos, and Sky got a waft of the same warm wine they'd drunk in the cabin the first time she'd taken him hunting.

"We're going to picnic . . . here?"

She looked up from pouring, a smile for his incredulity. "Of course. The Dead enjoy the company."

Having been starving all day, Sky now wasn't sure he wanted to eat. And when she broke off a piece of bread and he saw crumbs fall to the floor, he resented the mess. But Pascaline spread some cheese on it, lifted it toward him. Reluctantly, he sat down, cross-legged, took it. The first bite made him ravenous. She'd also brought a folding chair, which she set up now, collapsing into it with a sigh. "You have done well, nephew," she said, looking around.

"Hmm," he grunted, cramming more food in.

He took another big gulp of the warm wine. "Enough," she said, a hand reaching out to stay his. "This is not all for you."

"Why? We expecting guests?"

"Of course." She stood as she spoke. "Help me."

From her basket came more things—a box filled with pastries and a bunch of candles, which she held out to him. "These are for the coffins, the ones with the photographs. Do not light them yet."

He placed one before each staring face, in a little holder obviously designed for the purpose, and resisted the urge to disobey, to snatch up the lighter and

230

banish the creeping dark. Outside, night had already fallen. He still hadn't gotten used to how swiftly the sun set in the Mediterranean.

Task done, he turned back to her. She had moved the small table to the rear of the tomb, placed the pastry box there with its lid up, poured some wine into three small glasses. "The brazier, Sky. Bring it in. There's wood there for it too."

He stepped outside. The night air was chill. Light came from other tombs down the avenue. Shivering, Sky piled wood, both kindling and logs, into the iron brazier and placed it where she directed, on the central flagstone. "Make a fire," she commanded.

He hesitated. The last fire he'd made had not ended well for him. She saw his reluctance. "Make it, nephew," she said. "It is time."

He nodded, started. His arm felt a little weak from his exertions, but it didn't take long; the brazier was small, and he filled it rapidly, first with newspaper, then the dry kindling, building a pyramid of ever larger pieces. At her nod, he held the lighter to it. It caught, grew rapidly. The surrounding darkness deepened as the light grew. He felt the first warmth he had in a day, and he drew closer to it.

Pascaline leaned in from the shadows. Her head was swathed in a black scarf, pale skin emphasized by its dark surround, the bones of her face so near the surface of her parchment-like skin. Her face floated there, like a lantern. Like a skull.

231

"It is time," she said again, her voice a whisper. "Time for you to place your feet upon the path to your destiny. For on this one night, the night of All Souls', the Dead return to teach the living." She took the lighter he still held in his hand, rose, and went to one of the candles. "Do you believe that, Sky?"

"Do you mean," he asked hesitantly, "do I believe that they will rise from their coffins"—he swallowed—"to teach me?"

"We are not necromancers, nephew. We do not try to rip the Dead from their rest. But they do not have to rise to teach us. They have other ways to do that. That's what I ask if you believe."

She lit the first candle. The flame climbed high, then settled, its light reflected in Madeleine Marcaggi's eyes. She had looked straight at the camera. So now she looked straight at him.

Sky turned away. "I'm not sure what I believe."

Pascaline moved to the next coffin, the next candle. "You are young. And the young don't wish to believe in anything but themselves. They think they will live forever." She laid a hand on the coffin. "This one, within. He thought so. *She* did also." A finger stretched toward Madeleine. "And her. And him." She gestured around. "All of them believed that they would always be strong, be pretty, be brave. Be *alive*! And what are they now?"

"What?"

"Dust." Another candle lit, another ancestor summoned, peering into the half-light. "Their lustrous hair, their shining eyes, their bright teeth . . . dust. Just as I will be, Sky. Just as you will be."

"I know that. . . ."

"And do you also know that there is a part of you that cannot rot, cannot become dust? Do you believe that something survives?"

" 'Non omnis moriar,' " Sky muttered. It was what had been carved onto his other grandfather's tombstone in Norway. " 'I will not die entirely.' " He looked at her. "Yes, I believe that something survives."

She moved to another coffin, lit another candle. "So you believe in the spirit of the Dead, one that can walk. And you believe that you have a spirit in you that can also walk—"

"You know I do!" he interrupted. "You saw it. Me. We hunted together."

"And yet you do not believe this spirit can walk *free*? Why?"

"Because it never has. *I* never have."

"That is because, despite everything you have seen and done, you do not simply *believe* that you can. Belief, Sky. How strong is yours?" She came toward him. "You say you believe. But do you?" She bent till her face was level with his. "Do you?"

He did! He knew he did. He had witnessed too much, *done* too much, not to believe. "Yes," he cried.

Her voice rose. "Then, for the first time I say to you: step out of your body!"

He closed his eyes, tried to envision all the times

233

he'd transformed before, tried to will himself up, out. He rose, opened his eyes. But it was just Sky standing there, just Sky slumping down to squat before the brazier again. "No," he sighed.

She regarded him for a long moment. "So now we know—for you, belief, by itself, is not enough. Not yet. You are not of a generation that wants to simply believe. With you, the question is the thing. So." She stepped away again into the shadows between the candles, into the space between the coffins. "You need more. Very well."

The fire crackled. It had already consumed most of its small store of wood. By its fading light he watched her. "What else can there be?"

She turned. "Blood."

"Blood? You mean, like, inheritance?"

"I mean that exactly. Blood." She jabbed a finger into the dark, toward the coffins. "What Madeleine Marcaggi felt on her wedding night, I feel now." Jab! "The bullet *he* took when he fought the French invader is lodged here." She touched her neck. "The knife slipped between *his* ribs by a Farcese? It rests here." Jab! "I do not need to *know* to still feel . . . everything." Her skull-like face loomed in the flame of the lighter. "What do you know, nephew?"

"Nothing," Sky whispered.

"And what do you feel in your blood?"

"Everything!" he shouted.

"Then, for the second time I say to you: step out of your body!"

A surge came, something shifting inside him. He recognized the sucking, the pull and the push, like his bones pressing out. When he traveled, when he entered the berserker, the murderer, when he ran as a Mazzeri, it began like this. His brain swirled, dizzy and its opposite, totally focused.

Yet when he tried to rise, it was his body that rose once again, his body that fell back down, that sat again upon the stones. "I can't," he cried.

She shook her head. "You will. You have before. Remember the one quiet moment of return? It is almost like that. Almost. But to do it at command . . . well, we have discovered that both belief and blood are not quite enough. You need something more."

He lay his face in his hands. "What else is there?"

She paced away. "When you traveled before, how did it happen?"

Behind his splayed fingers, Sky thought back. There had always been something external involved. When he'd first gone to see Sigurd, it had been through the Ouija board. When he'd first gone back to become Bjørn, he'd had to sacrifice a bat. A fever took him again to Sigurd, on again to Bjørn. He'd dreamed his way into a hawk's body. The runes had taken him to Tza. And when he'd hunted as a Mazzeri . . .

"You drugged me."

She nodded. "I did. It is a way in. Quick, painless . . . at least until later. Later, when you get used to it, you begin to love the journey too much, you forget the destination. There are those who will tell you that is as

235

it should be"—she tossed her head—"they are not Corsican." She came closer. "Every century brought new enemies to our shores, new conquerors. We never had the luxury of traveling for no purpose. We developed our own ways—the vendetta is one. The Mazzeri another—and the Dream Hunters know their purpose. That's why they find it so easy to just go."

Sky sat up. "You mean my purpose will free me?"

"Yes."

"Wanting it enough?"

"Wanting it completely."

"But I do."

"No! You want it for one reason. To achieve one thing. But I say to you—want it for itself. The power of it. For what it does to your blood. For the force of it that means you will never die entirely but will live on forever in those that follow you, just as those that have gone before live on in you." She gestured to the dead ancestors all around. "What you seek is not something you choose. It is who you are, who you have always been. It is you."

Her voice had dropped, yet somehow it had also grown in power. She lifted the lighter again. "And so, for the third time I ask you . . ."

Flame. From his grandfather's lighter, tilted toward the candle that sat before his grandfather's photograph. Wick touched by fire, eyes staring out. And in them, through them, Sky saw, though he didn't see, felt, though he touched nothing, knew . . . a man dying in

236

battle, falling to a French musket ball; another seeing his life bleed away down the blade of a dagger, wielded by a Farcese in a Sartène alleyway. Felt Tza, once more upon the Devil's Forge, the pain of that, the greater one of birth, that child the next link in a chain that ran between them, flowing from beyond Tza to beyond Sky . . . Sky who was now rising off the floor, the channel, the conduit, the continuity, the focus of all that was, all that had ever been, all that was to come . . .

". . . to step out of your body . . ."

And there it was.

It required nothing in the end, no effort of will, just a lack of effort; no desire, just its absence. Belief and blood and purpose joined and then forgotten. Like breathing out.

237

Sky looked at his aunt, saw her as he had never seen her before, every part of her distinct. Saw through her eyes, beyond them, down the bloodline of his ancestors whose day this was. Finally he looked down at himself, that other part of himself, sinking gently to the flagstoned floor.

CHAPTER TWENTY

THE BATTLE OF THE MAZZERI

For a moment it was as if they were joined, a cord linking the two Skys' bellies, core to core, pure power pulsing along it like an electric surge, energy flowing and filling every fiber of him. Then that link shimmered, dissolved, and he was standing there, though it felt more like floating, his feet hardly needing to connect with the floor.

A groan came from beside him, a sigh of exhaustion that transformed to ecstasy in the moment it took for his aunt to lower herself into the small chair and rise up immediately, spring up, as if from a trampoline. The old woman's body had been abandoned; there was nothing of age in her movements now. Her eyes blazed with every candle's flame.

She looked down at Sky's body on the floor, then up at Sky standing before her. "Welcome, nephew," she said, reaching out to lay her hands upon his head.

She spoke not in English, not in French, but in the older tongue of the island, in Corsican, of which Sky understood not a word. And yet his Fetch, released by the blood that linked him to each ancestor resting in the coffins around him, understood the words well enough. They soared and swooped in the ancient song of the land, sometimes a lament, sometimes a curse, here a prayer.

"The Mazzeri have called him
Through the years they have cried
They have given a dagger
To hang at his side.
Let Fortuna run with him
Down the paths of the night
Let him slay and then see
With the Dream Hunter's sight."

239

Releasing his head, Pascaline stepped away. "Welcome, Mazzeri," she said. Then she moved past him, crying out, "To the battle!"

She appeared not to step from the tomb so much as to leap from it. Sky paused, to look once more at the Marcaggi dead. Every one of them, whether through lips on a photograph or the thickness of coffin sides, seemed to howl, their blessings no different than curses, curses formed into a single word: "Farcese!" Another surge went through him, clearing a space, a hollow that could only be filled with blood, a hunger that could only be sated by death. Five centuries of hatred were channeled into him, he the sum and total of vengeance.

"What kept you?" Pascaline snarled as he emerged. Her bald head glowed beneath her veil, as if from some internal light. Without waiting for a reply, she bent to the vault entrance and placed a pair of shears across the threshold, its blades opened and facing out into the night. Then she swung the gate, locked it, tucked the key inside her clothes. "Now we are safe from attack . . . both kinds!" she said.

Sky looked around. "Where's Amlet?"

"Home. Humans are not all who can use this night to kill. And he is a small dog." She stooped again, lifting something from the ground. "Here," she said, pressing it into his stomach.

It was his grandfather's club, the same he'd hunted with before, when he'd struck the boar that was Giancarlo. Yet now he felt its power in a way he hadn't before. It wasn't just the weight, its excellent balance, a tool crafted for a single purpose. Some trace of every victim it had claimed over the years was there in it now. Like Death Claw had been for Bjørn. "Perfect," he said, hefting it.

"Come," Pascaline said, and strode off down the path, not back toward the entrance and the town but the opposite way.

"Where do we hunt?" he asked. In another body he'd have struggled to keep up, so fast did she seem to surge along the cemetery's paths. Not now, though. It was only that he did not know their destination that kept him from sprinting past her.

"For this one night we fight in the valley that runs between two ruined villages. One is the ancient home of the Marcaggi. The other is where the Farcese used to dwell."

"Will it just be our two families who fight?"

"No." They had reached a gate in the cemetery wall. Ushering him through, she continued, "All the Mazzeri from each village around hunt there this night. All who choose to can fight."

"It will be a massacre." Sky smiled as he said it.

"It will not. It is a remembrance of a time long ago when every tenth person was a Dream Hunter and we could afford a sacrifice to Jour des Morts. But our numbers diminished, and we could no longer bear the loss. For centuries it was a ritual fight, nothing more. No Mazzeri died. That is why it was such a terrible crime when the Farcese brothers and sister hunted your grandfather to death. The vendetta is not for there, the Battle not meant to be used for such a purpose."

"Yet we're going to." It was not a question but a statement of intent.

"They began it there. We will end it there also." They were on the hill, beyond the graveyard. There was the occasional house, though the land seemed mainly to consist of overgrown gardens. "And once they hear a Mazzeri's death cry, all will gather." She looked at him, her eyes sparkling. "All will gather to witness the death of Jacqueline Farcese."

Yes, Sky thought exultantly. It was extraordinary

241

how all his doubts had been swept away. Everything was so clear, from the way he saw each place they passed through, to the reason why they were marching so swiftly to the rendezvous. The vendetta ended tonight. Five centuries of hate would be over because there would be no one left to kill. And he, Sky, was the redeemer, the avenger. This was his destiny. He'd come to this island seeking something. He'd found it, knew that from now on he'd always be able to leave his body at will. His Fetch would always walk and he would achieve . . . great things. What was a little murder compared to that?

He had heard someone say something similar before. Tza? No. Sigurd.

He broke stride. Pascaline looked back impatiently. "What is it?"

Sky shook his head, clearing it. "Nothing," he replied, catching up. And it was.

Something loomed over the crumbling town walls ahead. "I recognize this place," he said, even though he knew he'd never been there.

"It is called . . ."

". . . the Devil's Mound."

"Yes, nephew. This way, there is a gate in the wall, a path that leads around it."

She walked away; he stayed. She looked back, and he grinned. "Why go around it," he said, "when you can go over it?"

It hadn't changed much in five centuries. Tza's

hand and footholds were still there. His aunt took the path she mentioned, but he waited for her at the top.

The howl began on a low note, almost a growl that rose rapidly to a prolonged shriek. It reverberated along the sheer granite cliffs, running from the far end of the valley to where they stood.

"Is that a wolf?" he said, the hairs rising on his neck.

"There have been no wolves in Corsica for hundreds of years, nephew."

"You never know." Sky smiled. "Maybe they're making a comeback."

Pascaline ignored him. "It is the cry of the Mazzeri. From another village, not ours. It is a sign that they are ready."

"Are we?" Sky said, and was answered immediately by a wail to his left. He became aware of shapes moving, deeper shades of darkness gathering.

"So. It begins." Tipping back her head, Pascaline gave out a cry of her own.

"Yes!" cried Sky, and joined her. Instantly the valley was transformed by sound—and movement. All around, black-clad women and some men had begun to run, yelling, down the forest paths.

His aunt reached out to grab his arm. He resented it, any delay, seeing all those others stealing ahead of him. He tried to shrug her off, to escape from restraint. "Let me go!" he cried. "I must . . ."

But her clawlike grip was strong. "Do not fear, nephew. None of these here have your need. They will hunt as they always do, kill an animal if they can, fight only if they must. But you . . . you only have to trust your blood. It will lead you to whom you seek." She released him, gave him a shove. "Now . . . go, Marcaggi!"

He needed no further bidding. From a standing start he was sprinting within yards, running flat out, heedless of the darkness of the path, the threat from root or fallen branch. His arm, which had ached after his long exertions in the tomb, now clutched the club tightly, pulsing with power. His sight was so developed he could see a single chestnut lying under a tree. Each of his senses was like an instrument in an orchestra, sight, smell, scent, and sound all tuned to an ultimate pitch, all blended superbly. Only touch was missing, and that only because he could not actually feel the ground he ran on. It was as if he hovered just above it, floating on air.

A cry to his right, a wild boar breaking cover, overtaken by an old man with a youth's speed, stabbing down, the beast tumbling over and over and sliding, its tusks gouging tracks in the earth. Sky did not see its end, his eyes ever searching ahead. He heard its death squeal, though, wondered who in Sartène was marked to die in its cry.

A body burst upon him from the right, a hound, as big as a small wolf, snapping its huge jaws at him. Sky laughed, outdistanced it, didn't even raise the club he

244

cradled in one arm to strike at it. There was only one victim he sought tonight, down the path that now forked ahead of him, the left one taking him out of the shelter of the trees and along a maquis trail beaten by the smallest feet. The distant cliff face grew large impossibly fast. He was upon it almost before he realized, bending to the right now, paralleling the granite, his feet pumping in the flint shards at the wall's base. They did not lessen his speed. On he ran, letting instinct guide him.

It nearly failed. For she came at him from a hollow in the rock face, a fissure he had not seen until he was upon it. The only thing that saved him was the slip of stone beneath her feet as she lunged, letting him twist his body sharply to the side. "Die!" screamed Emilia Farcese, certain she'd struck true, her triumph blazing in the blank white sockets of eyes that, in this world, could see as well as his. But it was her certainty that failed her. Her dagger's blade ripped Sky's shirt open, but his twist caused it to slide along his chest as if its edge were paper, not honed steel. A trace of pain, of blood, and he was past, her anguished shrieks pursuing him. He could have turned back; it was tempting to kill her, as she had killed his grandfather. But Death would claim Emilia Farcese soon enough. It was Jacqueline who must not survive the night. The vendetta could only be ended when he found her.

Then he did. Another shriek drew him; he heard a woman's howl of triumph and ran into a small olive

245

glade, to see a goat with its throat slit, twitching upon the ground, a black shape slipping with exultant cries between the trees. It was not whom he sought. He knew because he looked up . . . and there stood Jacqueline, on the opposite side of the glade.

They were fifty yards apart. For a long moment they just stared silently at each other. Sky felt he was not looking with just his own eyes, but with the eyes of all who had preceded him, from his grandfather and on, back and back, man and woman, victim and murderer and those who'd cried for vengeance over their open coffins. Back and back until . . . it was as if Tza was looking at Emilio by the standing stones.

Through Jacqueline, generations of his enemies stared back. She spoke. One word. "Marcaggi."

"Farcese," he replied.

There was nothing else to say. So instead they ran at each other.

She came at him in a dazzle of twists and flips, and seeing them he remembered what she'd said, that this was her world; and all the power that burst from his every pore, she had learned to channel. She vaulted over his first, ill-aimed blow, struck down from mid-leap, caught his shoulder hard, and the only reason he was not upon the ground and bleeding was that she, too, wielded a vine-stock club like his and not a blade. The pain, nevertheless, was extreme.

She came again, twirling her weapon as if it were a baton and she at the head of a parade. The heavy club slipped past his clumsy defense, striking the other arm, his own blow slicing the air where she'd just been.

He gave a yelp of agony as she spun away. This time she didn't return immediately, but stood there watching him fight for breath, try to get a proper grip on his weapon, try to draw himself upright. Then she shook her head once, almost sadly, and came for the last time.

One blow will end it, he thought. One to his head, and if that didn't kill him, he wouldn't be able to stop the dagger he'd glimpsed flashing silver at her belt. She'd kneel and slit his throat like a hog.

So it was that flash he focused on as she spun and swerved toward him, ignoring the club that was now in her right hand, now in her left; he looked only at that dagger and the death it promised. And it was the space just above it that he hit, though it was her own leaping that inflicted most of the harm. If he was not as quick as her, he was quick enough. The blow took her hard in the stomach, and she folded over it, collapsing backward, crumpling onto the ground, all air expelled.

247

"Vengeance!"

The word came as a whisper, not a shriek, from many voices, not just one. Looking away from the girl and her agony, Sky saw that each tree in the glade now had a shadow. He didn't know when the Mazzeri had gathered. Perhaps they'd been there all along, watching the duel, waiting for one of them to fall.

"Vengeance!" The word was spoken now by one voice; spoken triumphantly by Pascaline Marcaggi, stepping out from the shadows. And then the word was echoed, wrought in rage and a terrible grief, as Emilia Farcese staggered from the circle opposite, arms waving before her as if searching, grief turning her once again into the blind old woman she was.

A black circle formed around them. They swayed there, looking much like the Squadra d'Arrozza he'd encountered his first night in Sartène, come to claim the one soon to be dead: Jacqueline Farcese.

She was still gasping at his feet—but her hand was reaching out toward the club she'd dropped. Sky kicked it away, just as Pascaline stepped forward. "Death," she said simply, snatching Jacqueline's knife from her belt, handing it to him. He grasped it, saw that it was ancient, its long, dark blade thinned by the years, by a hundred slayings.

"Death!" The cry was taken up by a score of throats, even Emilia's, tears pouring from the sightless eyes. The group swayed, shifted, began to move counterclockwise, the word taken up and repeated, again and again, on a high, keening note, a *voceru*, the Corsican lament, but with a single lyric.

"Death! Death! Death!"

Sky looked down at the girl, who had now regained some breath and was looking up at him and the weapon he held with eyes widened in terror, her heels driving her backward in the dust. "No," she sobbed. "Please, no!"

He looked from her to the blade again . . . and thought of another Farcese, long ago, and the weapon that had been used to kill him. And then he remembered.

How fitting that I brought it with me, Sky thought. The beginning and now the end. Throwing the dagger aside, he reached into his pocket and drew out the quartz knife.

It wasn't he alone who bent now and seized a hank of the long black hair, not just Sky who raised the jagged rock high. Generations of Marcaggi looked through him. Generations of Farcese looked back.

"Death!" he shouted, sweeping the weapon down diagonally across the last Farcese's throat. He felt it bite, saw the blood spurt, following in a red line as he cut. And at the sight the circle moaned, not with individual voices but like a solitary, shuddering beast.

249

He had no need to turn her face toward him. He knew his victim already. In that other world, that some called real, she was now marked to die. He'd see her in the streets of Sartène tomorrow. She'd look as normal as any other girl. But she was already dead.

The howling began, more animal than human. In its note, Sky heard another animal, the wolf. And he remembered another ancestor, who delighted in death . . . but only when she was herself. For when she was a Mazzeri, she delighted in life.

"Tza," he breathed. He looked down, saw this Farcese thumping upon the ground as that other Farcese had. The stone weapon, cause of both their deaths, was in his hand. And it reminded him that he had brought something else. Something from his other bloodline. What was it?

He dropped the quartz dagger, reached into his pocket. *"Berkana,"* he murmured as he drew out the stone, "rune of atonement."

Then Sky bent over the twitching body, reached, seeing Tza's hands reaching, feeling what she'd felt. With the runestone pressed into his palm by his thumb, his fingertips touched the end of the wound. Slowly he moved them in and along. And where they passed, the terrible gash was sealed.

Gasps came, a new word breathed out. "Salvatore!" they whispered now in amazement, in awe. "Mazzeri Salvatore!"

Jacqueline stared up at him, her eyes filled with the terror of death.

"Peace," he said, as Tza had once said. "Peace," he repeated as he closed the last of the wound.

"What have you done?" Pascaline had broken from the group, seized Sky's arm, jerked him roughly around to face her. "You . . . spare her? A Farcese! Our enemy!"

"I killed her," he said softly, rising to his feet. "You all saw me do it. So vengeance has been taken. The vendetta is finished. But now"—he looked down—"now I choose to heal her." He took his aunt's hand off his arm, held it, sought her gaze. "It is a Marcaggi who began this feud, Aunt. Only a Marcaggi can finish it.

We must atone. But not with death. With life." Glancing down, he saw that color was beginning to return to the girl's white cheeks. The wound on her throat was gone, as if it had never been there.

They looked at each other for a long moment. Then he nodded and pushed slowly through the circle of black. As soon as he was clear, though, he began to run, as a Mazzeri runs, with all the extraordinary power of his Fetch, freed. Yet when a wild boar bolted across his path, eyes widening in fear as he saw who—what—pursued him, Sky just threw back his head and laughed. "Don't worry," he said. "Hunt's over."

251

CHAPTER TWENTY-ONE

SECRETS IN STONE

She found him about an hour before his departure. Sky had been a little disappointed she hadn't sought him out earlier. Then again, he'd probably have avoided someone who'd slit his throat too.

"You leave?" Jacqueline leaned in the doorway. His aunt must have let her in, then left. Pascaline may have finally accepted the end of the vendetta, but she couldn't be in a room with a Farcese.

"I do."

"You return to England?"

"No, not yet." He hoisted his new backpack, checked the straps. They weren't quite right, and he began to adjust them. "I'm going to live in the mountains for a while."

She looked at his equipment. "Camping? In the winter? Are you mad?"

"Barking!" He circled his finger at his temple. "You should see the dreams I have."

She came farther into the room. "I wonder if they are the same as mine."

"Probably. Wild boars, throat slitting . . ." He stopped himself. He could tell by her expression that she wasn't amused.

She lowered herself onto the sofa. "About that . . . uh, that other night . . ."

He watched her struggle for words, doubted it would be any easier for her in French. "I know," he sighed. "It's complicated."

" 'Compliqué'? Oh, you and your English under-statement!" She blew out her lips. "I wanted to kill you. . . ."

"You nearly did kill me."

"And another time I would have," she said fiercely. "But you did that . . . that thing, and . . ." She broke off. "I would not have done that for you."

"Perhaps you would. You just didn't know how."

"No," she said angrily. "I did not. I do not. And why? I am Corsican, and the lost way of the Mazzeri Salvatore . . . ? It is part of my past. Mine! Not yours, English boy!"

Sky looked at her, at her black hair that fell in waves to her shoulders, her dark, pretty face now twisted in frustration. He'd have loved to explain it to her. But how? "It's . . . a long story," he sighed. "And my bus leaves for Cauria in twenty minutes."

"Cauria? The stones?" Curiosity replaced her anger. "You go to sightsee?"

"Uh, not quite." What could he tell her when he

253

wasn't totally sure why he was going himself? "I'm going to camp in the valley beyond them." He looked down. "Well, not camp exactly. There's an *oriu* . . ."

"An *oriu*? You mean a shepherd's cave?"

She said it with so much disgust he had to laugh. "It's not as bad as it sounds. And I have great gear." He pointed. From his mountaineer's backpack, through his winter-weight sleeping bag, to the freeze-dried food and gas cooker, it was all brand-new and top of the line. One of the advantages of having a big bank account back home.

She studied the large pile of equipment incredulously. "How long you go for?"

He thought, As long as it takes to learn what I need. But he said, "Dunno. I'll see what happens."

She remained unconvinced. "Where is this cave?" He explained about the cliff face, the tunnel through it, the valley beyond. "I think I know it. I have . . . hunted there with my grandmother." She shivered. "A cold place. What will you do there?"

He shrugged. "Think."

"About the Mazzeri?"

"Among other things."

She leaned forward. "What things?"

How could he even begin to tell her? There was still so much to be learned about Corsica and the secrets in his blood. But he hoped to do it without "going back" again. Each time he did, he picked up something, switched on something, in a way, that could never be switched off. One switch had saved the girl before him now. But another led to the berserker within him, the violent killing rage of Bjørn. And as for Tza . . .

The thought of her reminded him. He glanced out the window. The morning sun was bright. But it would set, and the moon would rise. The first full moon since he'd come back from his ancestor. Tonight he would discover *exactly* how much of her still remained within him.

And he couldn't do that in his aunt's apartment. "I've got to go," he said.

She studied him in silence as he strapped the sleeping bag to the pack. "Perhaps you find another time to tell me," she said at last. "You will come back to Sartène, yes?"

255

"At least once a month. For supplies. A shower." He sniffed at himself and grinned. "Don't know how many times I'll plunge into those ice-cold streams."

Dummy! Here he was, this man of mystery, full of secret powers, off to live alone in the mountains—and he was talking to her about . . . body odors? He really had to get out more!

She didn't seem to mind. "Perhaps I come to see you?"

He looked up. "I'd like that," he said.

"Good." She rose, kissed him on both cheeks, went to the door, paused there. *"Bon chance,"* she said.

"And you," he replied, adding, "oh, and Jacqueline, if you do come for a visit . . ."

"Yes?"

"Just make sure it's not during a full moon, eh?"

The bus dropped him at noon, but it was close to three before he made the *oriu*—he had a heavier pack, plus boots and not Tza's fleet feet. All the way up, an icy wind drove against him from the northeast—the Grecale, he remembered she'd called it.

The shelter was as cold as the stone it was fashioned from, an icebox within a refrigerator. But no one had been in the cave since his hasty departure; the wood he'd collected before was still there, and he soon had a fire going.

He sat for a while, chin on knees, watching the flames, imagining Jacqueline in some Sartène café, himself beside her.

"WITHAIN?" he said out loud.

No, it didn't apply. He knew "where-in-the-hell" he was. Just not "why-in-the-hell" he was there.

Disturbed, he opened the side pocket of his pack and took out the quartz carving tool, held the white rock to the light. When he'd first clutched it, he'd felt and seen the darkness within it. He'd discovered what that was—the murder of Emilio Farcese. But perhaps what he'd done with it since had gone a little way to lightening its shadows.

Beside the fire pit lay nineteen stones. Reaching into his pocket, he pulled out the five he'd taken with him after he burned his arm, laying the carved ones down beside the uncarved. That was one of his goals for the time ahead, to make himself a complete set. He would take his time doing it. He could brood for a week on each rune before cutting; make each stone entirely personal to him. Fashion them into the tools he'd need for the tasks that lay ahead.

He looked at the five runestones from his cast. He'd worked through them all now, save one.

"*Naudhiz,*" he said, reaching. And holding it tight in his palm, he knew that *that* was another reason "why-the-hell-he-was-there." This rune of power, of destiny fulfilled. And his destiny—once he'd established certain things—lay back in England.

With a cousin's hostage soul.

Looking around, he saw other reasons too. "It's all to do with stone, isn't it?" he murmured, recognizing the truth as soon as he said it. Answers always lay within stone. His own set of runestones and the tool he'd carve them with, one that had been used both for death and for life—and for making the pictures on the walls around him. Created by a murderer who was also an artist. And an ancestor.

He rose. The flame light was flickering against the *oriu*'s walls, seeming to cause the fine tracery of lines to move. Now he knew something of Tza; he could see her stories unfolding on the granite. Saw, with his memory of hers, which ones had been there on his trips back, which were born since. There was the shepherd's crook, sprouting as if from the branch of a chestnut tree. There was the cradle, whose meaning he now understood. And beyond that . . .

He noticed something new, leaned closer. *Yes!* Another artist had been at work here. The lines were not as assured as Tza's. Simpler. More . . . childlike.

He ran his forefinger along the curve of a boar's tusk; felt, just for a brief moment, another ancestor's pulse.

"Who are you?" he murmured.

Then it was gone and he sat back, stared up, nodded.

He'd brought some stiff brushes, some cloths. He planned to clean away the dirt of years, as he had cleaned the tomb of the Marcaggi. To restore Tza's art upon the walls was a huge task, but he had the time. After all, the next Jour des Morts was a year away.

258

He glanced up to the chimney hole, just as he remembered her doing, to gauge the light. The sun had almost set. The full moon was about to rise.

"Ah-ooo!"

He breathed the howl out, frightened, eager. "Here we go, then," he said aloud, and took a deep breath.

CHAPTER TWENTY-TWO

HIGHER EDUCATION

It was extraordinary the simple delight Sky got from reading an English newspaper! Not even a national, not even a local! A free handout, *University Times*. It had items from the various Cambridge colleges, notices for parties and play productions, for this club and that sport. Bits of news, usually of a somewhat sensational nature, interrupted the gossip that you obviously had to be a student to understand. The man who'd streaked around the Market Place on Saturday night was suspected to be a bishop's son and theology scholar at King's. Something dubbed "the Beast of the Backs" had struck, leaving three swans gutted on the banks of the Cam over three nights. Police suspected students who in turn blamed a jaguar or some such, escaped from a private zoo. Meanwhile, players of the Trinity 1st XV rugby team had all had their heads trimmed and colored in a pizza-slice shape to celebrate a sponsorship deal from a local Italian restaurant.

Sky laughed, picked up his cup of tea—another thing that delighted, tea from a china cup. It tasted different from the metal mug he'd been drinking from . . . well, it didn't taste of metal! And this paper, full of trivia. A year in a cave had made him a bit serious, he supposed. Even the trips into Sartène and the visits he'd had from Jacqueline in the mountains hadn't done much to shake him out of his trance. He'd been focused on one thing—preparing for his return to England. He'd carved and polished. He'd hunted. Every month he'd discovered a little more about the secrets that whispered in his blood—especially under a full moon's light.

Yet here he was, his destiny in sight . . . and all he wanted to do was sit in this café all day, read nonsense, drink another pot of tea or three and find room for maybe just one more scone with clotted cream.

He looked outside and realized he couldn't linger when he saw the goblin and witches. Halloween was obviously taken very seriously in Cambridge; every third person seemed to be wearing some sort of costume—and it was only three in the afternoon.

All Hallows' Eve. Tomorrow, November 1, was All Hallows' Day. And then the second was the day of All Souls'.

Jour des Morts.

He shook his head. In the window, his reflection, his double, shook back. There'd been no mirror in the cave he'd left only two weeks before, so it was still a surprise to see himself bearded, his hair in straggly waves way past the shoulders, and eyebrows that joined in the middle. A flash of metal at his ears showed him the gold rings that Jacqueline had bought for him as a farewell gift and insisted he put in. She'd pierced the ears herself, drawing howls and blood. "Vengeance," she'd said, and had even giggled. Then she'd held up a mirror. "Suits the image, no?"

He hadn't known he'd had an image till she'd mentioned it.

His cell phone, vibrating on the table, took away both memory and reflection. He glanced . . . but there was only one person who had his number. His mother. She'd insisted that if he was going to go off so mysteriously after a week, having been gone over a year— bumming his way around Europe, he'd told her—then he'd just have to put up with a phone and ring her every night. He'd agreed—it wasn't much to ask after his sudden disappearance, his sudden return. He'd planned to send them monthly postcards that he'd get tourists to post for him from their hometowns in Germany or Greece or Italy. He'd managed two!

It wasn't a call but a text message. "Where U Now?" he read. He'd call later. He hadn't told her he was coming to Cambridge; she'd only have worried after his previous history with Kristin, how they were supposed to have run away together to Norway. They had, of course, but not in the *Romeo and Juliet* way his mum had thought. She had let slip that his cousin had just started at the university, having done all the entrance examinations in half the time usually required. She hadn't said which college, but it didn't take Sherlock Holmes to discover that.

"Speaking of which . . ." His phone's clock read 15.15. The newspaper said that the Challenge Cup final between two of the Cambridge colleges, Trinity and St. John's, would take place on the Lower Fields at three p.m.—and that almost everyone from both colleges would be cheering on their men. It was no guarantee that she'd be there, but it was worth a try. If she wasn't, he'd have to bluff his way into Trinity itself, later.

His map told him it was about a fifteen-minute walk away. He'd miss most of the first half, but he was more a football man anyway.

"*L'addition, s'il vous plaît,*" he called. Then he remembered where he was. And wasn't.

"Bill, please."

It was warm for an English autumn day—which made him really miss Corsica. Late October there could be chilly . . . but this! Cambridge, in the flat eastern part of England, had no barriers to the winds that swept in from Siberia, and he was still dressed for the Mediterranean, hemp trousers, T-shirt, a light jacket. He even had his sport sandals on, the biggest mistake, as cold mud from the playing fields squelched between his toes.

There were several rugby matches on; most of the college teams had to be playing, but only one had drawn a crowd of a few hundred, so he assumed that had to be the final. He could see a ball kicked high into the air, hear the cries of the chase, the grunt of bodies colliding, the cheers or boos of the spectators. Most of these seemed to be wearing almost a uniform of long wool coats, scarves with bright-colored stripes trailing down their backs. If she was there, she wasn't going to be easy to find. He began to walk down the left sideline.

Then he noticed her, by sound rather than sight. Something had happened on the field, the noise had built and climaxed in loud cheers. "Dirk! Dirk! Bravo!" she yelled.

She was half a dozen paces away from him. "Hallo, Kristin," he said. 263

She looked back, smiling as if he were just someone else joining in the cheers. She'd turned halfway back again before she froze, her face in profile, her eyes aimed downward. She shook her head, as if trying to clear it. "Sky?"

Then she was running at him. He couldn't remember them ever hugging . . . no, there was that one time, after their return from Norway when she'd come looking for the runestones, when he wasn't sure *who* was hugging him. But she hugged him now, her mouth coming close to his ear, making a smooching sound. As she stepped away, his first impression was that she hadn't changed much, not in obvious ways, as he had.

He saw that her hair had a more expensive cut, the white blondness bobbed around a face that had lost a little weight, her strong cheekbones and jawline even more prominent. Her skin was less golden now, more marble. Her eyebrows were different; when he'd seen her last, they'd started to grow together, just like his did—the mark of the Fetch. But she must have plucked them, teased them into these two thin bows. Under them, her steel blue eyes still dazzled, as her gaze ran all over him, amazed.

"What have you been doing?" She punched him hard on the arm. "Your parents were worried sick, you bad boy. So was I. Where the hell have you been?"

"I've been asking myself almost that exact question," he laughed. "Here and there, you know. Round and about."

264

"I can see that." She laughed too, and he remembered how much he'd always liked her laugh, the trace of wildness in it. "We have got so much to talk about."

"You bet." As she took his arm, a whistle blew on the field of play. Spectators gathered in knots, passing bottles and thermoses between them, while the two teams went into huddles. A large man, over six and a half feet tall, detached himself from one of them and came striding over, glowering down. He had a good glower because it looked as if his forehead was about to slide into his eyes. "Who's this?" he asked, jerking his head at Sky.

"My cousin," replied Kristin. "Sky March. This is Dirk van Straaten."

"Cousin, eh?" The man made the word sound both suspicious and degenerate. He looked Sky up and down, taking in his sandals, beard, hair, brow, earrings. "Tree hugger, is he?"

Kristin sighed. "I don't know. Sky, do you hug trees?"

"Whenever possible," Sky replied. There was something peculiar about the man. Not just his accent, which was definitely not English. Then Sky got it— Dirk's hair was shaved in the shape of a pizza wedge, with pepperoni pieces dyed on. He remembered reading about it in the paper. "Nice haircut," he said.

The man could hardly be insulted, since he'd chosen it himself. Yet he managed. "Funny boy," he said, stepping closer.

Kristin stepped between them. "Dirk, save your aggression for the game, will you?" She nodded behind him. "And you are being summoned."

Another player had cleared the huddle, was yelling "Dirk! Dirk! For God's sake, come here!" Grudgingly, Dirk started to trot away. "You'll stay for the rest of the game, eh?" he called back.

Kristin shook her head. "Sorry, darling. I only promised to freeze my butt for one half," she said. "Besides"—she gave Sky's shoulder a squeeze—"I've got more interesting things to do."

Sky smiled. Dirk grunted something unintelligible, but certainly menacing, then ran on. "Charming fellow."

"You caught him at a bad moment," Kristin laughed. "His adrenaline's up."

265

"I can see that. Boyfriend?"

She shrugged, then shivered. "Come on. Let's go back to my rooms and warm up."

"Shouldn't you stay?"

She looked to where Dirk, towering above some obviously quite big men in the huddle, glowered back. "Oh, I definitely should. That's why I must go immediately." She waved, ostentatiously seized Sky's arm, and they set off. "Treat 'em mean, keep 'em keen," she said.

"Van Straaten? South African?"

"Yup."

"Name sounds familiar."

"So I should think. His father's Oz van Straaten."

Sky whistled. "The telecommunications giant? Films, TV, newspapers?"

"The very same."

"Quite the catch!"

"Yes, I am." She grinned. "This way."

They walked for a while making small talk, as if each were afraid to begin the real conversation that had to cover so much ground. At one end of a small stone bridge over a river, Sky paused to gaze. Willows drooped, reflecting themselves in the still surface. A punt went past, a male student expertly driving a pole into the water to propel the flat little boat along, a girl gazing admiringly up at him. Beyond them, two swans arched their long necks, dipping gracefully into the water to feed. Medieval buildings ran the length of the far bank.

Sky laughed. "It's like a tourism film. Could this *be* any more English?"

Kristin followed his gaze. "I know. You sort of take it for granted when you've been here a while."

"Quite the contrast to what I've been looking at for the last year, I can tell you. Four stone walls."

Her jaw dropped. "Sky, you've not been in . . . in prison, have you?" He teased her with silence until she hit him. "Will you tell me?"

But who will I be telling? he wondered as he looked at her excited face. The Kristin he loved, the Kristin he'd come back for, was there before him. Trouble was, he didn't know who else was there as well. How did possession work? Was Sigurd always around? No, he'd "borrowed" Kristin's Fetch, the lynx, to meet Sky that last time. He could be off with it again. Yet—did he have access to Kristin's memories? Could he play them back, like a recordable DVD, when he "returned"? And the last time Sky had seen Kristin, he'd told her he thought she was possessed. She would remember that, Sigurd or no Sigurd. It was all a little *compliqué,* as Jacqueline would have said. He'd have to tread carefully.

"Treading" gave him his out. He looked down at his sandaled feet. "I'm freezing!" he said. "And you promised me warmth."

Reluctantly, she led him on. They continued along the river path for a bit, then crossed another bridge, cutting up to a long building of sandstone blocks, square archways with metal grilles, and a lot of tall

267

windows filled with old glass on top. "Trinity, my college," she said. "That's the library up above."

They went through an iron gate and Sky stopped dead. Kristin, a few paces ahead, looked back. "What is it?"

He was staring at a flagstoned hall, the archways, with metal grilles in them, opening onto the riverside, the other, open side, onto a rectangular green enclosed by old buildings. But the thing that paused his breath was the rank of stone pillars that ran down the middle of the narrow hall. "What is this place?" he whispered.

"The whole thing's called Nevile's Court. Late seventeenth century," she said, then waved at the pillared hall. "This bit is—are?—'the Cloisters.' And at your feet, my favorite bit of graffiti. '*Jacobus hic erat*. 1779.'" He looked his question. "'Jimmy woz 'ere—in 1779.' Students, eh? Never change!" She snorted a laugh. Then she saw his expression. "You all right? You've gone white!"

He shivered, but not from the cold. "Tea?" he muttered.

"This way." She led him to a stairwell, disappeared up it.

He paused, looked back. The shaped and uniform granite columns were nothing like the standing stones of Cauria—and everything like them. The setting sun threw shadows from each one, and in them ghosts danced. His own; perhaps Jacobus's too.

By the end of the second pot of tea, they'd swapped some stories about their year apart. Kristin told him of the two months she'd spent in Norway—Oslo, not Lom—improving her Norwegian. Sky told her about Corsica. A small part of it anyway.

"But . . . what's the point of these Mazzeri?" she asked, blowing into her cup.

"Believe me, I had the same question." He helped himself to another cookie. "I suppose it's all tied up with Corsicans, their attitudes to death. To fate. The Mazzeri are messengers, warning of what will be. They . . . testify to Death."

"I think most people would prefer to be surprised." She shuddered. "Did you kill?"

269

Sky didn't hesitate. "No. It would have been too weird. Besides, I didn't know anyone there. I could hardly kill, turn the beast's head, then say, 'So, who the hell are you?' " They both laughed and he went on. "But I wasn't there for that anyway."

"No? What were you there for?"

He looked straight into her eyes. "To learn to free my Fetch. At will."

"What? No sacrificing?"

He put on a movie voice. " 'No animals were hurt in the making of this transformation.' "

She was too focused to laugh. "So you did it?" On his nod, she gasped. "What? Anytime you choose?"

"Anytime."

"Human Fetch or animal?"

"Either." He smiled. "Both."

She sat back, stunned. "But . . . how?"

He studied her—Kristin, the older cousin he'd always wanted to impress. And now he had, how tempting was it to keep going!

"I . . ."

"What?"

He nearly went on. But he couldn't. Partly because . . . where did he begin? In the tomb of the Marcaggi? With the girl he murdered and the choice he'd made to heal her? With the year he'd spent, almost always alone, cutting power into stone? Or with each month passing, hunting once as a Mazzeri, and once as . . .

And there was a second reason he couldn't tell her. He had his audience to consider—both of them. He didn't want Sigurd to know . . . any of it. Not until the exact moment when Sky would show him.

"It can't really be . . . be explained in words," he mumbled.

"So?" Her eyes sparkled and she moved closer to him. "Then why don't you teach me, Sky?"

He took a deep breath. "Maybe I could. I mean, there's a difference between being a student and a teacher, but . . ." He smiled. "We could always try."

"Excellent. And I don't think it will be too difficult. I'm halfway there already because . . ." She put down her teacup, grabbed his hands. "This doesn't sound quite as stunning as your revelation but . . . my Fetch has walked too!"

Surprise, surprise, he thought, but said, "Really? When did it—you—start?"

She got up, pacing across the small floor space between the bed and her desk. "Soon after that last time I saw you. It began, like, with dreams. Then walking. Before I knew it, I was outside the dormitory at school—but the girls said I never left my bed. Then I made my own set of runestones and . . . it all got much easier." She sat again, leaned in excitedly. "And then, the first night I tried them? It took a bit of time . . ." She hesitated. ". . . a bit of blood. But eventually I went into an animal."

"A lynx."

Her brow furrowed. "How could you know that?"

This damn double conversation! How could he tell Kristin that he'd already had a conversation with her Fetch before he set out for Corsica? But Sigurd, of course, already knew. "I saw it in a dream. Somehow it seemed so . . . you!"

She nodded. "It is. I feel so free as the lynx. Well," she laughed, "I don't have to explain that to you, do I, Sky-Hawk?"

The thought of his grandfather . . . *eavesdropping* perhaps, reminded him that he couldn't be too accepting about everything. "Kristin," he said. "That last time we met, I was convinced that Sigurd was still inside you."

"I know you were, you idiot!"

"So can I just ask you a few questions? For my own peace of mind?"

"Ask away!" she said, leaning against her desk.

"This . . ." He gestured around at the room. "How did you get in?"

"Trinity? I did my A-levels in one year, sat the scholarship, voilà!"

"Unusual acceleration?"

"Not for a genius." She laughed. "You always knew I was brilliant, Sky, come on!"

"True," he said, nodding. "Still, the subjects you're doing—anthropology, specializing in the Northern European tribes? Old English?"

"What about them?"

"Aren't they just what Sigurd would choose to study? If he wanted to learn even more about the runes and the people he came from?"

"Quite likely." Her eyes held nothing but pure amusement.

"And your boyfriend, Dirk," he continued. "I mean, if Sigurd was building up to some . . . I don't know, some grand revelation about the Fetch, then how convenient to have mass communication at your fingertips . . . through the son of a man who owns a TV station, film companies, and newspapers in almost every country in the world."

"Ah, yes! I see where you're going with this." She got up to pace again, hand at her forehead in mock concentration. "Sigurd's still inside me and manipulating me to study what he needs. Then I marry a van Straaten to take command of the world's media. All in my kvest for total vorld domination!" She stood to attention and shouted the last in a sort of Hitler-type ranting voice. Then she smiled down. "Sky! Dear cousin! I'm not saying that Sigurd hasn't influenced me. Doesn't influence me still. After Norway? Yes, I want to learn everything possible about the secrets in my blood . . . oh, don't look at me like that. I know that was one of *his* phrases. But come on!" She sat, took his hands again. "The runes are part of me now, and I am compelled to dig back and uncover their riches. The same with the Fetch. Can't think of anything else I'd want to do with my life."

"And Dirk?"

"Ah, well," she sighed. "Dirk's simply gorgeous. Didn't you see?"

"Not my type," Sky muttered, blushing, turning away.

She studied his change of color, his silence. "Sky, something happened to us, in Norway. Something changed us. I mean, look what you've been up to . . . Fetch Master!"

"So what's your point?"

"I have two, actually. Number one: doesn't everyone seek a purpose in life? Couldn't we just be lucky to have found such an amazing one so early?"

"*Poss* . . . ibly."

"And point two—we're not alone. We can continue the journey—the hunt—together, can't we?"

273

He saw her certainty; and just for one moment he so wanted to say yes. They'd always been such a team, in childhood and after the runestones had arrived. He wouldn't have known where to start without Kristin.

And even as he thought it, he knew they couldn't. Nothing had changed from before he went to Corsica. Unless something extraordinary had happened, Sigurd still possessed her, lived inside her like some . . . parasite, bending her will to his purposes. There wouldn't be just the two of them. There'd always be three.

He was careful not to let any of these thoughts show on his face. "You know what?" he said. "I don't care if Sigurd's inside you or not . . ."

"How many times . . ."

"... because he's also inside me. Always has been, always will be, I suppose." He took her hands. "What matters is that you and I are together."

"Exactly. 'Fetches Reunited,' eh?" At his nod, she threw back her head and laughed. "And you'll show me how to free my Fetch at will?"

"I'll try."

"Fantastic!" She stood. "Let's start now."

"I can't now. I've got to go back to Shropshire, see the folks. My train leaves in about an hour. And, if we're to do what we're planning, we'll need Sigurd's runestones. They're back there."

"And you'll get them?" On his nod, her eyes sparkled. "Oh, yes! So much more powerful than any we could make, eh? So when will you come back?"

Sky made a show of thinking it through. "I can't just go and not stay a night at home. How about . . . in two days?"

She had a calendar above her desk. "November second?"

"If you say so. I'll come back then." He went to her, gave her a hug. "We'll meet an hour before midnight."

"Here?" She gestured to the room.

"Why don't we just . . . enjoy our Fetches for a night. You say you've already freed yours?"

"Yes."

"Could you, that night?"

"Yeah. It's not easy, as you know. And there's always a price to be paid." She shuddered.

"But can you?"

"Yes," she said determinedly. "Night after next, my lynx will meet your . . . what are you? Still a hawk?"

"Yes," he lied.

"So where do we meet?"

He'd thought that the best place for what he planned would be the remotest, out-in-the-open countryside somewhere beyond the city. But he'd changed his mind. "How about down in that courtyard below? Where the pillars are?"

"The Cloisters? Why?"

He smiled. "I just like stone."

"A lynx and hawk zooming around Trinity College at the witching hour. Could be dangerous." She grinned. "I love it!"

275

He was halfway to the door when her voice halted him. "Hey, Sky, guess what?"

"What?"

She had her finger on the calendar still. "November second is All Souls' Day." She peered closer. "And do you know what the French call it?"

"Not a clue."

"Jour des Morts." She grinned. "Kinda appropriate, don't you think?"

He kept his voice even. "Definitely."

The door was nearly shut when she called out again. "And it's also a full moon. How cool is that?"

"Really?" He stopped, looked back, trying not to let the sledgehammer of the revelation show. In Corsica he'd always kept track of the moon, for a very good reason. Somehow, in the journey back, his time at home, he'd lost sight of it. He'd thought it was a day later.

"Listen," he said, stepping back in. "That changes things slightly."

"How?"

"Long story. But we have to meet earlier. Before moonrise. Does your calendar say when that is?"

"No, but . . ." She pressed a few keys on her computer. "Voilà! Moonrise, November second, is at six-forty-two."

"So if we meet a half hour before?" He chewed his lip. "But there'll probably be lots of people about then, right?"

"Nah. Supper's at six; they'll all be in the refectory. And the gates are locked to keep tourists out. So we'll have the Cloisters to ourselves. Or rather, our Fetches will." She smiled. "I can't wait, Sky. That night will be just the beginning!"

"I hope so." Of what? he thought. There was still so much that could go wrong. He could be so wrong! This was Cambridge, not Corsica.

"Tuesday, at six-fifteen," he said. "See ya." He closed the door, descended the narrow stairwell, went the opposite way from the stone pillars, through the Great Court. Pausing under the arch of Trinity's main gate, he looked out onto the street. In the gloom of dusk, the life of the university town went on. He watched the cycling students, the camera-toting tourists, the shops closing up, the bars opening, young people pouring into them. It was all so . . . normal. And he yearned to join them, to be anonymous, ordinary. Instead, he headed to his hotel. A seagull rose, cawing loudly, as he exited the college. There seemed to be a lot of them in Cambridge, though the city was nowhere near the sea.

His hotel was five star; his bank account could stand it, and, after a year in an *oriu,* he thought he deserved a bit of comfort while he waited for the Day of the Dead.

CHAPTER TWENTY-THREE
JOUR DES MORTS

He lay with his hands under his head, staring at the ceiling. It had none of the intricate tracings of Tza upon it, yet its very blankness had occupied him now for nearly two days, a screen to project his dreams upon. During the waking hours; after them. He'd thought when he'd taken the room that he would feast on room-service burgers and fries, gorge on the 140 stations on the television. He'd barely flicked it on, eaten only when necessary and sparingly then. Mostly, he'd just lain there. The bed was indulgence enough, after the bedroll spread on the earth of the cave. And he'd discovered that after nearly a year spent "seeking," lying still was actually a wonderful thing to do.

But now that time had ended. In Corsica he'd learned that, on the day of the full moon, he was aware of every moment of its approach as it made its way around to the rim of his hemisphere. He had no need to look at the clock. The pull in his blood was enough.

He closed his eyes, took a deep breath. Then he stood up. His pack was on the table. Opening it, he reached within.

The bag came easy into his hand. He loosened the leather strap, pulled the silk square out, spread it on the table, tipped the runestones he'd carved upon it. Some fell up, some facedown, some upright, some reversed. It meant nothing until he selected them for a cast, and that he was not going to do. The stones he'd carved that first time in the cave were what he needed.

Three were swiftly found. The challenge of *Isa*, the gift of *Gebo*, the torch of *Kenaz* all came to his hand as if summoned, were slipped into his pocket. *Berkana* required a little searching. When he had it, he folded it into his palm, closed his eyes, thought himself back to that valley, making atonement in the only way that could end five hundred years of hate. For a moment everything he'd felt then, done then, surged through memory and body.

279

The stone joined the others with a clink. There was one more.

He looked down. It stood out so clearly, even though it showed him its back. Though he had worked hard on every runestone, explored their every meaning, it was this one that he had concentrated on most, finally to the exclusion of all others. Holding it, dreaming on it, rubbing its cut lines with dyes he'd created from the earth, from berry and stone, as Tza had done in that same cave to create her work upon its walls. Gradually drawing out all the runestone's secrets.

"*Naudhiz,*" he whispered, his fingers reaching but not touching, hovering an inch above the polished granite surface. Rune of destiny fulfilled, rune of all hope, the rune also meant "need." And his had been so clear. If he was to free Kristin, stepping out of his body at will was only the first step. The second, as important, was to learn to control his Fetch. Body or beast, he needed to learn how to resist its terrible urgings to just run wild. *Naudhiz* had finally taught him how to do that—but at a price.

Sky sighed. Rune knowledge always demanded a sacrifice! And giving up the joyous abandonment of his Double was the one he'd made for its wisdom, for the control he would need if he *was* to free Kristin.

If! Sigurd had had a lifetime of study, Sky just a year. "Even now," he murmured, "I'm not sure it's going to work."

He would need all the help he could get tonight. He picked *Naudhiz* up, closed his hand over it, shut his eyes, spoke the invocation he spoke whenever he began a journey with the runes.

"Odin. All-Father. Guide me now."

He dropped the runestone into his pocket. His hand went once more into the bag. Out came his grandfather's lighter. He gripped it, pushed the arm up . . .

Flick. Spark. Flame.

No images came, those that had first taken him to Corsica. No bald old woman sang her *voceru* in the fizz of gasoline; no wolf howled near a standing stone; his scarred hands didn't reach deeper into flame. Yet all those images were there somehow, every time he struck. The beginning and now, he hoped, the end of a journey.

"Luca Marcaggi. Grandfather. Guide me now."

He flicked the arm down, put the lighter in his other pocket.

There was one last thing he'd need. His hand closed over the jagged roughness of white quartz, and he pulled it from the bag. He ran his finger along it till he touched the chisel's end, worn smooth by his and another's many carvings.

"Tza. Mazzeri Salvatore. Guide me now."

Reaching over his shoulder, he slid the rock blade into the holder he'd adapted from a knife sheath. He wore the belt under his shirt, high up across his chest, the buckle in front so that the weapon, in its leather sleeve, stretched along his spine.

Then he held his left hand up before him. It was shaking, and a deep breath would not still it. He studied the whiteness at the forefinger's tip, that scar left when he'd cut the flesh off there. One more sacrifice he'd needed to make so that he could send another ancestor to his rest.

"Bjørn. Warrior. Guide me now."

His hand stopped shaking.

281

He checked that the *Do Not Disturb* sign was on the handle and that the door was bolted as well as locked. Then he went to the window, climbed out onto the fire escape, and lowered the window, leaving just enough room for a body to fit through. Reaching back into the room, he picked up the clasp knife he'd left there, opened its blade, and laid it, edge outward, on the sill.

"Be safe," Sky said, looking back at the figure on the bed. But of course Sky, in the deep sleep of the traveler, did not reply.

The Mazzeri he still was wanted to run to his destiny, a blur of speed, a shadow moving through the ponderous crowds. But he forced himself to move slowly.

282

He'd timed it right. So many students were hurrying to the summons of the refectory bell that none of the porters questioned him as he walked through the main gates of Trinity. He followed the throng toward that building, entered the same door as they did. But instead of turning right into the hall and its sounds of life, he kept going, through another door, out into Nevile's Court. He let the last latecomers rush past him. Only when their echoes had finally faded did he descend the steps and walk along the passageway to the Cloisters.

Sky shivered. He was dressed, as always for the hunt, in black. But the T-shirt and jeans were useless against the river mist that slipped through the arches.

He placed his back against the last pillar, watched gray fingers of light thread between the standing stones. They were shot through with red, final glimmers of a sinking sun. Even as he watched, all color dissolved, and such light as there was now spilled from the distant refectory, such sound came only from its occupiers. The rest was silence.

She would be here any moment. *They* would be here. It was time to begin.

From his pillar, Sky moved diagonally across three flagstones, toward the back wall, halted a few paces before it. Delving into his pocket, he pulled out a runestone. *"Isa,"* he said, "the challenge." He placed the stone onto the ground. Then he moved straight across, till he reached another point at the same 45-degree angle from the pillar. Another stone came out. *"Gebo,"* he said, "the gift."

For a moment he studied this first triangle he'd made. Then he began on the second. Moving forward, he placed another runestone. *"Kenaz,"* he said, "the torch." Across he went, lifted the second-to-last stone from his pocket. *"Berkana,"* he whispered, relieved as he placed the stone, "atonement." He'd have been disappointed if it had been anything else, for it meant that the last stone he now drew out was the exact stone he needed there.

"Naudhiz. Rune of destiny," he said, laying it down, completing both the triangle and the five-pointed star, the pentangle.

And as he said it, she came. He heard her first, the faintest scrabbling of claw on metal, his hearing as acute as all his senses.

There was movement, in the deepest shadows at the far end of the pillared hall, something wriggling through the gap at the top of the iron grille gate. It paused for a moment on the ledge, before leaping to land silently on padded paws. Then, with the faintest of growls, the lynx began to move down the avenue of stone toward him.

"Kristin," he called softly, stepping out of the shadows.

A blur of fur, running, leaping. As the cat came into his arms, as he staggered back, Sky suddenly wondered if he'd made a terrible mistake, if Sigurd knew everything, and it was Sigurd who leapt, razor claws and savage teeth at Sky's throat. But the mouth that opened produced a rough tongue that licked him and a voice he knew well.

"Sky!" Kristin cried, her voice emerging from the animal's throat without the help of lips. "Oh, Sky!"

Within the lynx's eyes, light blazed. This close, he could also see something else—a deeper darkness, a stain spread around the jaws, down the neck, into the chest. His hands, where he held her, were wet.

"You're so heavy, Kristin, I . . ."

The lynx dropped, to immediately push its head into Sky's legs and purr its pleasure. "I know! And every part muscle. Muscle is heavier than fat. Every girl knows that!" The animal tipped its head back, gave a series of grunts that could only be laughter.

"What's this, Kristin?" he asked, holding out his sticky hand, though he knew the answer.

The lynx thrust its face forward, sniffed. Then licked. "Blood!" it cried. "Don't you like it?"

He wiped his hands on his jeans. "So *you* are the Beast of the Backs," he said softly.

The lynx dropped onto its haunches. "We haven't all had the luxury of training at the University of Mazzeri," she snapped, the sarcastic tones of Kristin clear. "So I enter my Double the only way I know how. Through sacrifice! Just a dumb bird." The lynx paused in its licking, looked up at him over a bloodied paw. "We'll still kill, won't we, cousin? Even when we don't have to?"

He watched her, envied her. What a rush, to be lost to an animal's urgings! As a hawk, he'd killed because that was a hawk's nature. And as Bjørn, when the berserker spirit took him? How fantastic to bury an ax in an enemy's skull. While Tza . . .

He shook his head. He'd had to give up the innocence of slaughter, for a reason that pressed him now. "We'll still kill, Kristin," he said softly, sadly. "The killing never stops."

The lynx finished its grooming, arched its back, its front paws thrust out in a feline stretch. Then it sat up. "Hey," Kristin said, "I thought we were going hunting. Where's *your* Fetch?"

285

"This is my Fetch." He saw that she was just out-side the boundaries of the runestone star. "And it's got something to show you. Come here."

The lynx rose. "You are acting a little weird, Sky. Anything wrong?"

"Nothing," he replied. "But remember I told you a little about the Mazzeri, about what they taught me?"

"I didn't get it," she said, starting to move closer. "Killing an animal just so you can predict someone's death? Couldn't they just use the runes like every-one else?" A laugh came again, from the lynx's throat. Yet this time Sky didn't hear Kristin. He heard some-one else.

"They could. Some do. See?" He pointed between his shoes.

The lynx was still a few feet away. "A runestone! Is it one of mine?" The head raised. "One of Sigurd's, I mean."

"No," he said, "mine."

"Beautiful! Which one is it?" The neck craned over. "Ah, *Naudhiz*. Rune of power. Of destiny."

The lynx was a foot away. "Exactly," he said, step-ping up to her. Bending, he placed his hand in the fur of the neck, stroked. "Destiny."

The animal turned its head, caressing in return. "Whose, Sky? Yours or mine?"

"All of ours, Sigurd, " he replied. As one hand tight-ened in the fur, his other rose over his shoulder. Quartz cleared the scabbard. He plunged the blade into the lynx's chest.

He held tight, despite the claws raking his hand, the blood and the agony there, pushing that aside by thinking of his ancestors, those who helped him here. Held tight as the power of stone surged through him, from each of the runes laid out in the pentangle that focused their energy, from the pillar before him and the granite he stood on, all channeled through him and on into the quartz he pressed into the body of the beast.

Then he lost her, powerful rear legs kicking, wrenching the fur from his grip, the chisel from his hand. The pillar halted her slide; she smashed into it, but he could see she was still within the five-pointed star. He could also see the cat edges begin to blur. Tufted ears shrank, fur contracted, claws withdrew. And then it was his cousin sitting there, or at least her bodily Fetch; Kristin, staring in horror down at the stone dagger buried in her chest.

287

"What have you done?" The words came from a throat already thick with blood.

"What I had to. I couldn't let him have you anymore, Kristin. This was the only way."

"Oh, no." The eyes raised to him were filled with horror. "You still believe . . . believe that Sigurd's inside of me?"

"I know he is."

"You've killed my Fetch," she choked.

"Killed *you*," he replied softly. "For what marks the Double bears, so the body carries. Even unto death. You'll live, you'll walk amongst us. But within a year, Kristin, you'll be dead."

Sobs were coming, gurgling with blood. She collapsed onto her side, and it began to seep onto the flagstones. The mist had continued to slip in from the river, and she seemed to float in it.

Then her body began to shudder. Her mouth opened wide, as if to form a scream, but no sound came. Instead, other lips were stretching out her lips, another face pushing out Kristin's, as if her skin was plastic film. Her whole form began to bulge, the mouth stretching ever wider, impossibly wide, as if it were about to vomit forth something enormous.

The scream that came was terrible. And then Sky was knocked backward by the force of the shape flowing from every part of the convulsing body. Dark, bloated, a huge misshapen ball, it rolled away along the flagstones, then slowly, so slowly, began to resolve into form. Legs stretched, arms spread. A head lifted. Two eyes opened.

Sigurd.

He uncurled himself from the floor, rising to glare down at Sky, who slid until stone halted him and his back was against the wall. Any triumph he might have felt was banished by the terror—for this was not the frail Sigurd of the mountains but a formidable man, tall, strong—and raging.

"What have you done?" he shouted.

Somehow Sky found his voice. "Killed her," he said. "Her Fetch is dying. Her human form will follow."

Sigurd rushed at Sky, grabbed him, threw him hard

288

against the wall. Sky had no strength left to resist him, had put everything into one thrust of a stone dagger. He waited for blows, or worse.

None came. "You fool," Sigurd hissed, his face an inch away from Sky's. "You went away, to learn . . . this?" He gestured down.

"Yes." Sky could not move, could only stare back into his grandfather's crazed eyes. "It was the only thing I could do. I couldn't let you . . . *feed* on her while you planned to work your evil in the world."

"Evil? You have never understood my cause."

"I understand this—that what starts in murder and possession is wrong. That's why I don't care about your cause. I only care about Kristin."

Sigurd shook his head, stunned. "So you've killed her?"

"Yes." Sky lifted his head defiantly. "That's how much I care."

He braced himself. He saw Sigurd shudder, as if gathering himself for attack. Then, instead, he stepped away. Sky looked at Kristin. She had slumped onto her side, lying in mist and her own blood. She didn't have much time.

"So, grandson, you have learned to control your Fetch." Sigurd's voice had lost its anger. Sky could even hear a smile in it, and it frightened him more than the fury. "Did I not say you could become the most powerful of us all? And I can guide you to that destiny. This"—he pointed at the dying Kristin—"this is

289

nothing." He stretched out his hand. "Are you ready to join me now?"

Sky pushed himself to his feet. "No, Sigurd. I am only ready to watch you die."

The outstretched fingers curled back, like claws retracting. "Die? Double fool! Did you think that I would spend a year just waiting for you?" he jeered. "Your powers may have grown, boy. But mine have become . . . extraordinary!"

And with that, Sigurd turned and ran, away from the river, back toward the college green. Yet he hadn't even reached the grass before the man blurred, running ended, flying began. A large white gull circled the green three times, then vanished with a long, drawn-out scream.

Sky bent, snatched up the runestone at his feet. In a moment he was beside his cousin's Fetch. She was shaking now, freezing to his touch. He turned her head toward him, as he would have done a boar's in Corsica. Kristin's eyes flickered open, their light fading fast.

Grasping, he gently pulled out the dagger. He had witnessed this enough, done it enough, in the previous year's hunting in Corsica to know what would happen. And sure enough, the stream of blood became a torrent. Death was moments away. Kristin began to shake.

Then, just as he had done for the first time with Jacqueline Farcese, and done again every time he'd hunted since in the valleys behind the standing stones, practicing, training for this moment, Sky pressed *Naud-hiz* into his palm with his thumb, reached down, and placed his fingertips on his cousin's chest. And the blood that was flowing there slowed, then ceased; the gash made by the stone dagger gradually faded, until it vanished altogether. And the light that had almost been extinguished in Kristin's eyes flickered and, after a moment, began to grow strong again.

"Sky . . . ," she coughed.

"Peace," he said.

CHAPTER TWENTY-FOUR

PREY

He cradled her, murmuring softly. Her breathing gradually slowed, heartbeat steadying, terror slowly fading from her eyes. Then a look came into them, one he recognized. Pure Kristin.

"You total bastard," she said indignantly. "You murdered me!"

He smiled. "Nothing personal."

"And then . . ." She shook her head. "You healed me."

"Well, I learned three things in Corsica. The first was controlling the Fetch. The second . . . I became a Mazzeri Salvatore."

"A what?"

Somewhere a door opened; they heard laughter, student voices raised in greeting or farewell. They froze. But no one came near.

"Can you get up?" he asked.

"I can try." Gripping his shoulders, she struggled to her knees.

"And you know why I had to, don't you? I mean, you saw . . ."

He didn't need to say any more. Her expression told him. "If you mean Sigurd . . . then yes, I saw him." She shuddered. "I didn't believe it at first, thought it was all part of some death hallucination. And it's true what they say, your whole life *does* flash before you! Except most of the time I'm going, 'Yeah, right, like, when did I do *that*?' "

He laughed and she did too. It felt so good to laugh with her again. It was why he'd gone through all his ordeals, to hear that laugh and know it was her, just her, doing the laughing. Then hers started to get a little wild, and stopped.

"How could he have done that?" she whispered. "I mean, all this year he's been in me? And what, watching? Taking part?" She shuddered. "It's obscene. Disgusting!"

Sobs came again. He knelt beside her, put his arms around her, and, after a moment, she sank into him. They held each other for a long time, while her tears flowed, trickled, ceased. Then they held each other some more.

But it couldn't last. Gently he pulled away.

"What's wrong?" she said.

He'd tried to ignore the feeling that had been building within him. He should really have taken his clothes off; he'd ruined so many in the past year, but he thought Kristin had probably had enough weirdness for the night without a naked cousin flapping about.

But silver light dappled the river mist now, and there was no denying his blood.

He got shakily to his feet.

"Sky?" she said.

He looked down at her. "You may want to look away now."

"What's happening?"

"You remember I told you there were three things I learned in Corsica. . . ." Even as he was speaking the sentence, his voice deepened. And even though she only whispered the word "Yes?" it came to ears already starting to transform to velvet and elongate from his head, like a shout.

294

In the dozen times he'd experienced it as himself— and the once it had happened to him as Tza—it had never hurt. But it wasn't something to grow used to: this sudden electrical surge, shocking each cell in his body; his nose thrusting out, widening, lengthening, nostrils flaring; teeth growing sharper, longer, in a jaw gone huge, around a swelling tongue; arms turned to legs and all four tipping with nails turned to claws.

Some muscles shrank to nothing; others grew huge, thrumming with power. And beyond every other sensation, the worst, the best, the most extraor- dinary was when every single follicle across every mil- limeter of his skin simultaneously exploded hair, instantly weaving and matting into a thick gray pelt.

He was still standing over her, though on all fours now. Her face showed that Kristin's own so-recent horrors were forgotten in the one that stood before her now.

"It's not what you think," he growled.

"Not what I . . . ?" Kristin shouted. "You're a bloody werewolf!"

"That's a little harsh! It's just another form of Fetch."

Her eyes went wide in shock. "What? Your Fetch . . . turns into another Fetch?"

"Every full moon." His huge red tongue came out and poked at his canines. "I tell you, it's a weird world."

She must have heard the laughter in his tone, because she began laughing too. He kept his in his throat because he knew what would happen if he let it go— he'd end up howling at the moon that was just beginning to peep over the trees beyond the river. He could get away with that in the isolation of Corsica. Not here.

She stopped. "But how do you stop . . . running amuck? Slaughtering? As a lynx, I'm driven to hunt, to kill. But as a werewolf . . ."

She broke off to stare. He arched his back, thought of Tza, that time his Fetch had entered hers and he had learned the art of the Mazzeri Salvatore. The Fetch within the Fetch. "Once I learned to control my Fetch," he said, "I always made sure it was my Fetch that turned into the werewolf. Then I could control that too. It, uh, took a bit of time." He shuddered as he remembered certain nights on the mountain, the taste of raw boar. Then he smiled. "But I managed it in the end. So, no slaughter."

They were both silent for a moment. The river mist continued to pool around them, shot through with moonlight. Finally she whispered, "What now?"

He didn't know. He hadn't thought further than this moment. Sigurd was gone. Kristin was back. He was a wolf. And he would remain one till the moon had left the sky.

"Shall we walk?" he said, his snout pointing to the river. "We've got so much to talk—"

He broke off. Kristin's face had changed. The smile had left it. "Oh, no . . . Sky!"

"What is it?"

"My body!" she gasped. "Something's happening to my body."

"You mean someone's interfering with it?"

"I . . . I don't know." She closed her eyes. "I think . . ." They shot open. Terrified. "Where's Sigurd?"

"Sigurd!" Sky stepped up to her. "Quickly! Where is your body?"

"Out there." She jerked her head toward the moonlight. "There's a boatyard, deserted at night. Dirk's guarding me."

"Dirk?" he gasped. "You haven't told him?"

"I had to. Some of it. I mean, he found me . . . walking. And I needed a gatekeeper, remember? Someone to watch over me. Like I did for you?"

Sky bent, snatched up the bloody quartz chisel from the floor in his jaws, thrust it toward Kristin. "Take this," he mumbled. When she had, he gestured to the five runes on the floor. "And those. And there's a lighter in my pocket."

She snatched them all up, grabbed the lighter from the ripped jeans. "Let's go," she said.

She climbed the iron gate, squeezed through the gap at the top. Sky couldn't climb but it was a small leap for a wolf. They ran in the shadows of the college walls, parallel to the river path but not on it. There were people on it.

"Hey," someone shouted, "that's a big dog."

They ran on. "There," she said, pointing.

There was a compound up ahead, boats stacked up, both punts and canoes, surrounded by a head-height metal fence. There was also a hut, and as they got closer, they could hear moans coming from inside of it.

"Oh, no," she cried.

He cleared the fence in one bound. She was beside him in a few seconds.

"Ready," she said, one hand on the handle, one holding the stone.

"Me first," Sky growled. Nodding, she threw open the door.

Some hunting instinct always made Sky take in his surroundings instantly, each feature of landscape, each threat. Here, he stood in the doorway of a small hut.

There was one chair, and on it was the crumpled body of a swan wrapped in a net, its head dangling to the floor, its beautiful white feathers stained with blood. There was a window on the opposite wall, wide open. There was a mattress on the floor. Kristin—Kristin's body—lay on it. Beside her lay Dirk van Straaten, unconscious. And on his chest was another bird. Very much alive. A seagull.

"Sigurd!" Sky howled.

The bird craned its neck around. Its head bobbed in surprise as it took in the beast in the doorway. But their grandfather was never shocked for long. "Hush," he whispered. "We don't want to wake him. Especially as he was so reluctant to go to sleep."

A gasp came from beside Sky. Kristin had stepped in.

The seagull's eyes narrowed, searching her chest for the wound beyond the bloodstain. "How did you . . . ?" He stared at her for a long moment, and then the yellow eyes moved on to Sky. Bird stared at wolf. "My," he said at last, "you did learn a lot in Corsica, didn't you, grandson?"

Sky moved into the room, claws clicking on the wooden floor, trying to keep his voice calm. "What are you doing, Sigurd?"

The bird looked down. There was nothing hesitant in the movement. Yet there was something in Sigurd's voice. "When I first possessed Kristin," he said softly, "it was the hardest thing I'd ever done. It nearly killed both of us. I had to find another way. Listen for another secret in my blood. So I went back, learned from an ancestor . . ." He looked up at Sky. "And do we not both know, grandson, that there is always a price to be paid for such knowledge?" He sighed. "Well . . . this was the greatest I'd ever had to pay."

A shudder ran through the bird's whole body. Then the head swiveled down again. "Still, if you've paid for something, you may as well use it." Talons sank into Dirk's broad chest.

"No!" Kristin screamed, running forward, faster even than Sky was moving, raising his quartz chisel above the vast, spreading white wings. But by the time she brought it plunging down, there was no feather, sinew, or bone to plunge it into. The blade swished through air already empty of substance, barely disturbing the smoke that coalesced into a column and poured straight into the unconscious man's belly.

Van Straaten began to shake violently, contracting around his center. Froth foamed at his mouth and poured down over his chest; his eyes bulged in agony. His mouth opened wide, releasing a long, terrible scream.

A voice came from outside the hut. "I say, what's going on in there?" Footsteps approached, someone running along the river path. They heard the locked gate being rattled. But Sky could not move, even though someone was about to see the wolf for the first time since Filippi Cesare. He could only stand and watch a sobbing Kristin flailing the chisel. Observe

299

for the second time his grandfather Sigurd escape
death by stealing another person's life.

Then the shuddering stopped. Dirk sat up, a hand
rising to wipe away the creamy gunge at his mouth.
The eyes cleared, then focused on the wolf. And even
though the words that came were in a South African
accent, Sky knew it was Sigurd who was speaking
them.

"The Beast of the Backs!" shouted Dirk van
Straaten, leaping off the bed, seizing a canoe paddle,
raising it like a club.

He knew he could fight Dirk. Kill him probably.
But it would be Dirk he was killing, not Sigurd. And,
anyway, where would that leave Kristin? There were
more voices outside now, shouting for help, people
who would rush in, witness the savaging. And Kristin
needed one quiet moment to rejoin her body.

Turning, Sky-Wolf ran out the door.

As he leapt the fence, he heard Dirk shout, "The
Beast! Grab it!"

A couple stood on the path, the man crouching
to reach for him, then leaping up as he saw what he
was reaching for. "Bloody hell," he shouted. The girl
screamed as the wolf careered into her legs.

Sky ran. There were trees in the distance, the other
side of the river. But the narrow bridge he was heading
for was bulging with people, a group of men.

"Look," said one of them, "a damned big fox!"

There were too many to rush through. The river,

Sky thought, even taking a step toward it. But he had no idea if his wolf could swim, had never done so in all his travels in Corsica. He hesitated.

"There! There's the Beast!" came the familiar voice. "Grab it!" The men on the bridge rushed forward. In a moment he was going to be cut off.

Dashing straight forward, he passed the corner of a building. That wall gave way to another, tall, ivy-strung. There was an archway in the middle of it, and a man in a black suit had stepped from it to see what all the shouting was about. "Hey," he shouted, arms spread wide to trap the animal rushing at him. The wolf bared its teeth, and the man jumped back. Then Sky was past him and running into a different courtyard.

There were fewer people here, more space, and a wolf moved fast. His pursuers had just made the one entrance when Sky was through the next one . . . and suddenly claws were scrabbling; he was desperately trying to find purchase on cobbles, sliding along their slickness in an alley.

"Oy!" yelled someone as a tire hit his right shoulder. Sky fell at the same time as the man on the bicycle did. "Stupid dog!" shouted the man, coming up onto his knees.

"Sorry," said Sky, an instant English reaction.

The man's expression told him what he'd forgotten. As did the words. "Cripes," he said, "a talking husky!"

"Wolf," muttered Sky grimly, but to himself as he

scrambled onto four paws. The sounds of pursuit were coming from the yard behind him. Leaving the stunned bicyclist on the ground, Sky dashed on.

It was the wrong way. He came out onto a street, the main one that paralleled the river, ran down the front of all the colleges. It was early evening still, and the street was full.

"What's that?"

"Look!"

"Is it an elkhound?"

Where could he go? He was in the middle of the town!

Behind him, he heard a voice he knew. Dirk had emerged from the courtyard. "Grab that dog!" he shouted.

Sky snarled, snapped at the hand that reached for him. Then, heart pumping, he turned, not caring which way, and ran. People screamed, shouted, lunged. Bicycles swerved. There was a car, the squeal of brakes. As the door opened, Sky could see a man in a peaked cap, hear, after the man's excited shout, a radio voice saying, "Repeat, Smith? Did you say . . . a wolf?"

He'd only gone fifty yards when he heard the door slam, the siren start. The road had widened; there was a church to his left, more ancient gray buildings to his right. Though his fear was telling him to run straight back to the hotel, he knew he mustn't. It was in the crowded heart of the city, with nowhere for a wolf to hide.

He ran toward another college—King's, he thought

it was called. Through it, beyond it, lay the river again, the open fields he'd been trying to reach before, the trees beyond.

The siren had gained on him. He had no choice. Running between the legs of an astonished college porter, he shot onto the college green. It was a short sprint to the edge of the far building. He rounded that as the now familiar cry of "Grab the Beast" came behind him—the rugby player could run; Sigurd had secured himself a fine body. There was another green beyond, willows marking the line of the river at the end of it. Grass gave better purchase for his fleet paws. He halted on the banks of the river just as his pursuers turned the last corner.

"There!" He heard the cry. He looked around. There was a bridge about a hundred yards farther down—but there were people on it as well, and though they hadn't seen him yet, they would if he ran at them. There was the river . . . but *could* he swim? Anyway, there was a parapet on the far bank that would be hard to scramble up for a wolf. He'd be trapped. And then there was . . .

He saw it, a jumble of boats and poles and storage sheds. It was another small boatyard, with punts for the renting. It was his best chance.

He plunged down the bank to the stone wall that ran along the water's edge.

"It's going into the river," came the cry from behind him.

He sprinted into the yard. There were several piles

303

of punts, each flat boat turned upside down and stacked, one on top of another. Pressing himself flat to the ground, Sky squeezed his way into the darkness.

The voices came closer, a jumble of sound until they obviously crested the slope and Sky was able to tell some of them apart.

"Can you see it?"

"It must be in the water."

"Or across already. Faster than a fox, that one." This last was spoken in that familiar accent. It continued, "But it's also twice as cunning. Officer, since you have the flashlight, why don't you and I go into the boatyard here and check around?"

"Thank you, sir. But I think that I know the way of British mammals better than you."

Sky, holding his breath, could tell that the officer was resenting the burly young South African's easy leadership. He prayed he would resent it enough to move on. But he didn't. "Still, no harm in looking. You lot," he called, "spread out along the bank. Check the water; keep an eye on the far side. You want to come with me, sir?"

Far away, getting closer, there came the sound of more sirens. Nearer, feet moved along the boatyard's paths. Sky shrunk deeper into the shadows under the upturned boats.

"I can almost smell him, can't you, Officer?"

"I think you'll find that's turpentine, sir," came the dry reply.

Nearer and nearer the feet came. A flashlight's

beams played along the ground, stopped. "He could have squeezed under one of these piles, couldn't he?"

"Sort of tight, don't you think?"

"Not if he was desperate enough."

The beam moved along the front of his shelter, an inch from his snout.

"I'll take a look," said Sigurd in his new South African accent. His shadow bent toward Sky's lair. Sky bared his teeth. Sigurd might not find his new body so useful without a hand.

"HQ to SO800. We have a sighting."

The radio was loud enough to make them all jump, men and wolf. "Where, HQ?"

"Malting Lane. Think we've got him trapped in a cul-de-sac. We've got the dog patrol out. And armed response."

"They won't . . . shoot him, will they?" Sigurd asked.

"They might have to, sir. Beast of the Backs and all that."

"Where's Malting Lane?"

"Other side of the water here."

"Let's go."

The flashlight flicked away. Footsteps receded. In his lair, Sky's breathing steadily calmed. He'd wait for a while, then move. Whatever they'd seen in this cul-de-sac, they'd be back when they found they were wrong. He had to find a safer place to hide until the dawn.

305

෧෯෧෯෧෯

It's really irritating, Sky thought as he walked through the dawn-lit streets of the town center, how England only has tabloid newspapers these days. The old ones, the broadsheets, now they would give a man some coverage!

He looked down. On his front, the headline proclaimed that a minor celebrity had been caught in some sexual indiscretion. Sky couldn't remember what news covered his rear. When the moon had finally sunk, he'd raided a garbage can, found the newspaper, and had managed to fold the corners of two sheets together, making a sort of kilt with splits up the sides. But one of the corners wouldn't hold, his fingers barely keeping it fast, and the other also now seemed to be slipping.

Fortunately, it was too early for many people to be about. A middle-aged woman had clucked disapprovingly and hurried on. A couple of students, returning late from a night of partying no doubt, had given him the thumbs-up. He remembered how he'd read, on his first afternoon in Cambridge, how a mysterious streaker was lurking about. He'd just provided a second sighting.

Not far now, he thought, and shivered. He couldn't wait to get back to his warm room, his clothes, his body. As a wolf, he'd been fine in the small copse of trees where he'd eventually hidden. But as soon as he changed back to his bodily Fetch . . . it seemed a flaw in the system. Shouldn't Fetches be immune to the weather?

Despite the cold, he was finding it hard not to grin. He had done it! Kristin was free—assuming she'd gotten back into her body. He was sure she would have; him leading Dirk away would have given her the chance.

A car was coming down the street, so Sky stepped into a shop's entrance. As he waited for it to pass, his grin faded. Mission accomplished but . . . now what? Sigurd/Dirk was still out there. Surely his plans were doomed to a madman's failure? But he *had* seized the body of the heir to a telecommunications empire. He was planning something. What would he do next?

As he stepped out from the doorway, Sky wondered if freeing Kristin was only the first stage in a new battle against their grandfather.

Sky rounded the last corner . . . and froze at the flashing light. But it wasn't the police. An ambulance was there, its back doors open. Someone must have taken ill at the hotel.

He moved down the rear alley. At the base of the fire escape he looked up. There were a few lights on in the hotel rooms. Early risers.

It was only when he got two floors below that fear came. One of the lit rooms was his. And he hadn't left any lights on. He took the last flight almost flat to the iron stairs. Slowly he raised his face above the window ledge.

The dagger was still there. He'd been kept safe from the Dead. But not the living. For in the room, two men in uniform were lifting a stretcher from the bed. A third man was bent over it, blocking Sky's view. When the man stood up, Sky saw who was on it. Himself, of course.

A voice came, the speaker hidden from Sky, standing in the doorway. "Will he be all right, Doctor?"

The other man shrugged. "We'll know more later. Your guest appears to be in a coma. Drug induced, probably."

"Kids today, eh? He could have left the bolt off! Look at this door! Ruined."

The doctor was packing up his bag. "How did you know to break it in?"

"Anonymous phone call. Some foreign chap. Probably his dealer. I just don't know . . ."

308 The voices trailed off as the two men left the room. Sky collapsed back onto his haunches.

"How . . . ?" he gasped. "How did Sigurd—"

"How do you think?"

The voice came from close by. Sky jumped, turned. . . .

His grandfather leaned against the railing of the fire escape. Once again he was not the old man Sky had first met in the mountains of Norway, but Sigurd's human Fetch, a man in his prime. And seeing him, Sky remembered something he'd forgotten till then. How, before he'd entered Dirk, Sigurd had transformed into a seagull . . . and how the cries of that same bird had followed Sky to the hotel that first day, after he'd arranged his rendezvous with Kristin.

"It was easy enough, grandson. Describing you to the desk clerk, telling him my fears for your health." Sigurd stretched his neck, a movement almost birdlike. "Now, don't you wish to chase after your body, throw yourself into the ambulance?"

"You know it's not that easy."

"Oh, I do. You need a quiet moment. And the longer you are away, the harder it gets, right? Didn't I always warn you to get someone to watch over your sleeping self?" At Sky's silence, he continued, "A handsome Fetch by the way, your wolf. A little conspicuous in England, but . . ."

Sky wasn't going to tell him the difference of the one summoned by the moon. Besides, there were things he needed to know. Fighting down the panic— he could almost feel his other self being put into an ambulance—he made his tone even. "So you've won, Sigurd."

"Haven't we both? You fulfilled your vow, got me out of Kristin. I said you'd grow powerful, didn't I, my boy? I'm proud of you." He smiled. "And you did me a favor, really. Dirk will be far more suitable for my purposes in the long run. Kristin will tell you how ambitious he is, how he yearns for his father's empire. He's not very bright, though. Not like you. Unlikely to achieve his goals. But perhaps what he needs is a little . . . inner motivation." Sigurd smiled. "It was hard sometimes, being inside a girl, Sky. Have you found that, in your . . . travels? They do things differently than us, don't they?"

There was something so creepy in his tone of voice. Sky swallowed, took a moment to keep the disgust from his voice. "What *are* those purposes, Sigurd? I've never been quite sure."

"It was hard to explain it to the boy you were. But now you are so nearly a man, perhaps . . ." His pale blue eyes glowed with light. "You have experienced so much of the joys of knowing your Fetch, haven't you, Sky? Would you be so selfish as to deny those joys to the whole world?"

Joy? There had been some joy, yes. Ecstasy, even. But there had also been murder, and possession, and terrible suffering. He'd only narrowly survived it all. Carefully, he said, "Do you think everyone could handle it?"

Sigurd laughed, that laugh that shook his whole body. "But of course not straight away, dear boy. They are just children, as you were, waiting to be led." The voice took on a gentler tone, like some kindly teacher. "And like you, we will prepare them slowly. Introduce them to the idea of the Fetch gradually. Dirk will help us there. His father has enormous influence." He let out a sigh. "Though, sadly, he also has a weak heart."

Careful, Sky thought. "And then?"

"Even as that work proceeds, other work continues. You and I are not alone, Sky. There are many in the world who can see, as us, walk free, as us. With powers almost as great. They are just waiting for someone to give those powers"—he smiled—"direction."

"A leader."

"Exactly, grandson. Or leaders." The voice took on an edge of cunning. "Such a hard job to do alone. So much easier with someone at my side. Blood of my blood."

Sky nodded. "It's very tempting, Grandfather. But . . . help me here. I still don't see, with the world prepared and the teachers in place, where it will all lead."

"Oh, Sky, isn't that obvious?" Sigurd had left the railing, stood tall, his eyes gleaming. "I do not seek to possess anyone. I only seek to free the spirit entirely from the body. Then I will not need any . . . body." He said it as two words. "For then I will have attained the goal that mankind has sought from the very beginning of time." He breathed out in a joyous sigh. "Immortality! I will live forever as pure spirit. And I will bring humanity with me."

Sky was finding it harder to keep his temper. "But why would we want that?"

The eyes fastened on him again. "*Why?* You are still so young. You already think you will live forever!"

"No, I don't. I've experienced enough death to know I won't, trust me. But I've also spent a lot of time thinking about life." Sky leaned forward. "And I reckon that the beauty of our life *is* that it will end one day . . . in this form anyway. We both know something lives on. But what gives us our uniqueness is that we are here for such a short time. So we strive to fulfill the potential of whatever this"—he pointed to himself—"this incarnation is. That's what leads to all creation—art, science. Love. Everything. Our mortality, our limited time, drives us to create."

Sigurd gazed at him. "And to destroy, Sky."

"Yeah, destruction too. There's always a price, isn't there?" He lost it. "What would we do in your world of immortals, Sigurd, with nothing left to strive for? Sit around and weave spirit baskets? And who the hell made you the one to decide for us?"

He had hoped to keep probing. Find out more of what his grandfather planned to do so he could make plans to fight him. But his temper had got in the way.

"Well, grandson." The voice was cold now. "It seems I was wrong about you. You've learned some tricks. But no wisdom." Sigurd stepped back to the railing. "Still, you have a little time to reconsider. You know where to find me. I'll be in Dirk's rooms, packing. The time has come for him to . . . what is the modern term? 'Drop out'? I think we've learned enough at college."

"Wait!" Sky remembered what Pascaline had told him in the hut before the first hunt. About what happened to the Fetch cut off from the body. And the body without the Fetch. Both diminishing, wasting away to nothing. A chill shook him, and he said, "Do you know what will happen to me if I can't return to my body?"

"Of course. You will become a ghost." Sigurd gave a cold smile. "So it would seem your ordeals are not quite over, after all, are they?"

Sigurd tumbled backward over the railing, fell toward the ground. Long before he reached it, though, flesh became feather. The gull soared again, sped off, its sharp cries mingling with the jangle of a siren. The ambulance was clearing whatever traffic lay ahead of it so it could rush the boy in the coma to care. And in the sound, Sky realized exactly what Sigurd had done. No doubt if Sky had agreed to join him, his grandfather would have helped him back to his body. But since he hadn't . . .

"You're trying to murder me!" Sky shouted to the empty sky. Then he sank down onto the cold iron and rested his head on his knees.

WITHAIN? he thought. WITHAIN?

Strangely, as both siren and bird calls faded, so did his fear. A different feeling came. His breathing evened, his heartbeat slowed—because he realized he wasn't sitting there alone. He had Bjørn within him. A Viking warrior. And he had Tza. A killer, yes, but also a Mazzeri Salvatore. The blood of hunters and fighters pumping in his veins.

And there was other blood close by as well.

"Kristin," he said. Immediately he rose and hoisted himself up till he was balancing on the railing of the fire escape. He swayed there, looking down the three flights to the ground.

He had not tried to be a hawk since that first time in Shropshire. It would have been wrong somehow, in Corsica, trying to become an English winged hunter.

And he'd had enough going on, as a Mazzeri, learning to free his Fetch at will, mastering the wolf, ending a vendetta. But he had just watched Sigurd's Fetch change to a bird. And if he was going to fight his grandfather, wouldn't he need to be as strong as him?

"No," he said softly. "In the end, I'll have to be stronger."

As he swayed, he could hear the blood roaring in his ears. Ancestors' blood.

"Bjørn! Tza!" he shouted.

Then he stepped off the railing.

It took a moment for fall to become flight, but he wasn't afraid—he was a hawk before he was ten feet from the ground. And as he rose up over the buildings of Cambridge to seek his cousin, one thought came clearly—if the two of them, one with the cunning of a lynx, the other with the vision of a hawk, couldn't get into a hospital and recover a body . . . well, he didn't know who could!

They'd only need one quiet moment, after all.

To Nancy Siscoe

AUTHOR'S NOTE

Long before I thought of writing The Runestone Saga, I read about a book in a catalog, was intrigued, and ordered it. It sat, unread, on my shelf for years. Then, when I first started thinking about the whole idea of the Fetch—this Double we all have inside us—I remembered the book and began reading it. Instantly I recognized a people other than the Norse who also had a tradition of the Double. Except these people called their Fetch . . . Mazzeri.

The book was *The Dream-Hunters of Corsica* by Dorothy Carrington. A professor, she lived on the island for years, got to know its ways, its language, its ancient customs. She was particularly fascinated by the Mazzeri, Fetches that go out at night and hunt real animals, and who, if they make a kill, look into the dying animal's eyes and recognize a person now marked to die. It was so much a part of the Corsica she loved, in a line from a distant, more magical past. Yet even when she lived there, from the 1950s on, the old traditions were fading. The Dream Hunters were dying out.

But as we know . . . nothing dies *entirely*! Something lives on. Someone will continue with the ancient ways. And secrets will still whisper in the blood of Corsica.

Her book is excellent, full of wit and wisdom. It led me to reimagine the whole tradition, as it would apply to Sky, his desires, his desperate need, and I have adapted accordingly. The art of the Mazzeri Salvatore is not much discussed in the book but becomes crucial to Sky. The battle wherein one Mazzeri can kill another is not such a huge part of the main tradition but did exist at one time. Of course, it was irresistible to a writer! I have moved its date, though, from the summer to Jour des Morts. Seemed more appropriate to the story I was telling.

Another tradition of Corsica, one that has, thankfully, died out, is that of vendetta. But the island was one of the last places in Europe where it survived. The last reported case was as recent as 1962. Yet just because it is prohibited doesn't mean there wouldn't be some people longing to revive it. . . .

The Squadra d'Arrozza, to be faced with a knife in the mouth; the *voceru*, sung as both a lament for the Dead and a curse for their killers; the open blades placed to ward the body when the Mazzeri-Fetch hunts—all these and much more form part of the fascinating tradition of the island. I owe Dorothy Carrington a great debt for writing about it so enticingly, as I do to the compilers of the various Web sites that discuss the strange, dark tradition of the Dream Hunters.

As in *The Fetch*, I drew on many influences from my own life and family. My Norwegian grandfather, the one who "walked," also once picked up a blade-shaped rock by a lake in Norway . . . and instantly collapsed, blinded by a vision of this same rock being used, hundreds of years before, for murder. And in a conversation with an old friend, a scientist named Geoffrey Boxer, the subject came up of the newish study of epigenetics—how some of the genes we've inherited could be encoded not only with hair color and mouth shape but with our ancestors' actual experiences . . . and how those genes could be "switched on" in us, their descendants.

Wow! I thought. It's the secrets in our blood. One of the main themes of these books—what we can choose to do with our life, what we have no choice about—because of the switches thrown!

And as for Tza . . . in the eighties, I played the role of Caleb the Zealot in the biblical Roman epic *A.D.—Anno Domini*. In it, I had to attack Roman soldiers with a slingshot. And I was very lucky. Practicing after a dawn run on the beach in Tunisia where we shot the film, I was noticed by the man who ran the local camel concession. He told me how Tunisian boys still hunted birds with the weapons, and then proceeded to give me a two-hour tutorial, by the end of which I could put five stones through a bush at forty paces. On cue. (I still have my slingshot.) Also, in 1583, there *was* a terrible slavers' raid on Sartène. Naturally I threw Tza straight into it.

"WITHAIN?" is my own, much-used expression. Of many examples, one. I was in Java, Indonesia. At four a.m., in pitch blackness, I was dropped off alone

319

on an extinct volcano to climb to its summit to watch the dawn. Except they'd dropped me at the wrong place with a faulty map and a faulty flashlight. As I stumbled through fields of cabbages, as dogs howled in the perfect darkness, and as, near dawn, the call to prayer came from a distant mosque down the valley, I thought, Where-in-the-hell-am-I-now?

Other places. Nevile's Court, Trinity College, Cambridge, is a favorite spot of mine. I spent a lot of time there, in the bitter winter of 1987, privately rehearsing an acting role. The columns in the Cloisters became the other actors in the scene. Ghosts—and graffiti— were there! And Islington Antiques Market, London, 2005. That's where I found Sky's grandfather's lighter— a 1930s Dunhill, with a thumbprint worn in its side by use. Cost me seventy-five pounds. Worth every penny. *Flick. Spark. Flame.*

I have many sources to acknowledge. Aside from Dorothy Carrington and the various Webmasters, *The Rough Guide to Corsica* and *The Blue Guide to Corsica* were both excellent on the island's geography, flora, fauna, food, and folklore. *A Lycanthropy Reader,* edited by Charlotte Otten, gave me wonderful sources for that other ancient tradition of Europe—the werewolf. As in *The Fetch,* many rune books were close to hand, my two favorites being *Using the Runes,* by D. Jason Cooper, and *The Runic Workbook,* by Tony Willis.

And as for the people who helped me . . . Karim and Naomi Jadwat offered their cottage on the river, the Great Ouse, for a writing retreat. Piers Johnson, of OPC Petroleum, let me shelter at his offices in London, where everyone was very kind. I finished the novel in a mad burst in Biot, in southern France—not quite Corsica, but on a clear day I could see it from my window—in an eight-hundred-year-old house owned by my cousin Jan Ridd and his wife, Silvia Reine. Aletha, my wife, was her usual hugely supportive, encouraging self and an insightful early reader. My son Reith learned to talk during the writing of this book and now sits at the computer saying, "I'm working!" I also must thank all at Kidsbooks, Vancouver, for their brilliant sales technique and my first-ever window display for *The Fetch*. The draug is especially . . . fetching?

Professionally, my agent at ICM London, Kate Jones, was as smart in the writing as she was on the business side, as were Karolina Sutton and Margaret Halton. At ICM New York, Richard Abate and Liz Farrell were again excellent in all details.

But the greatest thanks must go to the woman to whom this book is dedicated. Nancy Siscoe is not only wonderfully supportive and enthusiastic, she is smart and funny, with a great eye for details large and small. She shapes the book so subtly and always forces me to do my absolute best. She is, in fact, the Dream Editor.

A final thought. One of the debates Nancy and I sometimes have is over coincidence. She's a little less keen on it than I am. But what most people call coincidence, my wife now simply refers to as "another Humphreys." They happen all the time to me, maybe because my eyes are always open to them.

A recent example. I had just finished the final draft of *Vendetta*. The next day, Aletha, Reith, and I left for a quick holiday. We were to stay in a small B&B in the center of Rome, in a crumbling old palazzo.

At the thick oak door was a row of buzzers for the dozen or so apartments in the house. When we arrived, I reached to press the buzzer with "B&B" on it . . . and froze.

The name on the buzzer above ours was Filippi Cesare.

322

Chris Humphreys
August 2007

THIS IS A BORZOI BOOK PUBLISHED BY ALFRED A. KNOPF

Published in the United States by Alfred A. Knopf, an imprint of Random House Children's Books, a division of Random House, Inc., New York.

KNOPF, BORZOI BOOKS, and the colophon are registered trademarks of Random House, Inc.

www.randomhouse.com/teens

Educators and librarians, for a variety of teaching tools, visit us at www.randomhouse.com/teachers

Library of Congress Cataloging-in-Publication Data
Humphreys, Chris.
Vendetta / Chris Humphreys. — 1st ed.
p.   cm.
Sequel to: The fetch.
SUMMARY: After realizing the enormity of his Norwegian grandfather's betrayal, fifteen-year-old Sky leaves England to follow his visions to Corsica, the homeland of his other ancestors, hoping to find some ways to defeat his grandfather's powers and restore his cousin Kristin's free will.
ISBN 978-0-375-83293-2 (trade) — ISBN 978-0-375-93293-9 (lib. bdg.)
[1. Supernatural—Fiction. 2. Time travel—Fiction. 3. Revenge—Fiction. 4. Cousins—Fiction. 5. Grandfathers—Fiction. 6. Adventure and adventurers—Fiction. 7. Corsica (France)—Fiction.] I. Title.
PZ7.H89737Ven 2007
[Fic]—dc22
2007006898

Printed in the United States of America
August 2007
10 9 8 7 6 5 4 3 2 1
First Edition